KT-116-541

# Something for the Weekend

Pauline McLynn

**HEADLINE**

First published in 2000
by HEADLINE BOOK PUBLISHING

First published in paperback in 2000
by HEADLINE BOOK PUBLISHING

10 9 8 7 6

ISBN 0 7472 6397 3

Typeset by
Letterpart Limited, Reigate, Surrey

Printed and bound in Great Britain by
Clays Ltd, St Ives plc

HEADLINE BOOK PUBLISHING
A division of Hodder Headline
338 Euston Road
LONDON NW1 3BH

www.headline.co.uk
www.hodderheadline.com

For the McLynns
of
Galway and London,

with love, admiration and gratitude.

# ONE

'Barcelona, my hole.' I kicked the car again. Then I began to kick it rhythmically as I shouted 'Dublin-is-a-dump-and-I-am-fed-fucking-up-of-you.'

It didn't help. Now I was soaked to the skin *and* I had a sore foot. Wednesday 26 February, 1997. My thirtieth birthday. I was running late for my first appointment, a ten o'clock with a disgruntled husband. The car had conked out and a dark grey sky was pissing down rain, so I made a deal with myself – whichever comes first, bus or taxi. A trail of vehicles waited at the traffic lights, cross faces leaning over steering wheels urging a change. Still the rain lashed down. I stepped forward to hail a cab and planted my left foot deep into a lurking puddle. The driver cheerily pointed to his backseat passenger and ploughed through another pool, drenching me in a tidal wave. I spluttered and coughed in a fug of exhaust fumes. The occupants of the bus shelter giggled and pretended to look elsewhere. *Bastards*. I retrieved my sodden hoof, but couldn't quite pinpoint my dignity. Fifteen minutes later a bus arrived. Not my preferred option. However, a deal is a deal.

The bus was mouldy with damp humans stepping on one another. I remembered similar days, queueing in employment exchanges, with everyone smelling like wet dogs, and some git telling us to 'move along now girls'. Not the cheeriest thought for a thirtieth birthday, so I shrugged it off and fretted myself into town.

I reached my office building in the heart of the city with a runny nose and steam rising from my clothes. The morning was noisy with rain as it bounced off the road and the pavement with a righteous fury. Inside, the ancient elevator was not to be outdone, of course, as it announced OUT OF ORDER. It reminded me of the nurse in *Romeo and Juliet*, worthy but useless. I kicked the lattice gate on my way past and began my wheeze to the third floor.

Top of the post pile was a letter from the Inland Revenue, which I didn't need to open. I knew off-by-heart the sorry tale of money owed. It did come in handy shortly afterwards, however, when I tipped a mug of yesterday's coffee all over my desk. I had just placed it on the spill when a knock on the door announced the arrival of a Mr Harry Knowles. He heaved his bulk into a chair and gasped like a goldfish out of its bowl.

'Fuckin' lift,' he said. 'Are you trying to kill me or what?'

Harry's problem was straightforward enough. He suspected his wife, Victoria, was being unfaithful and he wanted evidence. They were part of a horsey set that lived in Kildare, so this meant travel for me. 'Someday,' I thought, 'I'm going to have to invest in a reliable car.' In order that I might move about with ease and minimum suspicion, he would organise for me to take a three-day residential cookery course on the estate of the local big-shot, Alex Wood. Mrs Alex Wood ran the cookery course, and her administrative assistant was none other than Mrs Victoria Knowles. Cosy. He would also get me an invitation to the Spring Ball at the Woods' house that Sunday evening, where he felt sure I'd get all the proof he needed. This suited me fine – it was his money, I'm a lousy cook, and I have nothing against parties.

His reaction to me had been text-book. He licked

his lips nervously and muttered 'Um, sorry, I thought you'd be . . .'

'A man,' I said, finishing his sentence. 'Everybody does.'

My name is Leo Street. I'm a private investigator. I live and work in Dublin. My full title is Leonora, whenever my parents are angry with me.

I looked across at Harry Knowles. I knew who this guy was, the whole country did. He had made his fortune in the construction industry in the Seventies and Eighties. Now he was a local political mover and shaker in Kildare, never far from a dodgy deal and a headline. Mid-fifties, heavy-set, with a thick head of wavy hair, his face bore testament to a love of whiskey, and his clothes were expensive. I had seen his wife in the society pages of the glossies. She was a tall, elegant blonde, with fine, aristocratic features, and younger than him by about a decade. It was no surprise that her husband might be neurotic about a possible affair.

'Mr Knowles,' I said. 'I'll do this for you, but I have to be sure that you know what you're letting yourself in for. It's one thing to suspect that your wife is being unfaithful, but *if* she is, and *if* I prove it, you have to be sure that you can handle it.'

This was all standard stuff. Sometimes people think they want to know the worst, and they really

*really* don't. I watched as he weighed up his answer. Small beads of sweat stood out on his forehead. I doubted he wanted the alleged affair to be made public, he was under enough scrutiny without that. He probably just wanted to keep his wife under his pudgy thumb.

He looked at me disgustedly. 'I'm paying you to shovel some shit on the bitch I'm married to, not sit around holding my hand and counselling me. If you don't want the job, just say so and I'll fuck off somewhere else.'

This was a bit of a bluff and we both knew it. It would be very short notice to find someone else willing and able to travel the following day. And I think he'd begun to realise that a woman suited his purposes much better than a man. A quick scan of the Yellow Pages would confirm that female private investigators aren't all that numerous, and he wasn't stupid. Oh no, stupid was one of the last things you could accuse Harry Knowles of being. I left a pause to allow him to calm down. After a short time he spoke again.

'That bitch has bled me dry for the last fifteen years,' he wheezed, 'and I get nothing in return. Not unless she wants even more. Well now it's my turn. Just who does she think she's fuckin' with here, hah? The wrong fuckin' person, that's who.

*Definitely* the wrong fuckin' person if it's not me.'

By now my desk was sprayed with spit. I really could not imagine anyone wanting to bed Harry Knowles. Still can't actually. And it didn't help that I found him extremely challenged in the personality department. But a little voice told me to think of the money. Never get personal, business is business. 'If you wanted nice,' said the little voice, 'you should have become a florist.'

People often speak in harsh terms when they come to see me – they're angry at a betrayal – so I wasn't too surprised at his colourful language. But I did get the distinct impression that Harry was like this all of the time. He smacked of the bullyboy. The newspapers usually referred to him as 'plain-spoken', surely a euphemism for downright thick and ignorant. I really didn't want to spend any more time than was necessary in his company, so I settled a few details and he left. It was 10:45 a.m.

I felt like washing the Knowles grease off, but lacking an en-suite, or even an off-suite, I settled for blow-drying my tax demand and filing the coffee-coloured document under Maybe. At least *it* smelled better now.

This feast of paperwork led me to the monthly statements. Well, I *was* thirty today, and that's sup-posed to be some sort of life crisis, so it seemed like the perfect time for accounts. I glanced around the office for a diversion of any sort, but the tiled floor, the sturdy old desk and the battered leather chairs offered nothing. Reluctantly, I tapped in my password and began. All the old, familiar names appeared on the computer screen. And all the old, familiar jobs not yet paid for.

One of my regular employers, an insurance company, has a man called Tony in accounts. Although I have never actually met Tony, I have spent more time on him than on most of my friends. You see, Tony finds it a personal affront to be asked for money. I often wonder if he's on some sort of commission for keeping funds hostage. I have long since stopped phoning to wheedle a cheque out of him – it always ends up in innuendo, and with me feeling dirty. Now I was trying the tack of pathetic notes. 'Me again, the pest. Any chance of a cheque? (Here I would add that it was my birthday, or Christmas or tax return time, hip replacement, or whatever.) Hope you're well, talk to you soon. (Not if I can help it, you sad bastard.)'

Most of my work is mundane – insurance claims, infidelities, fraud and sometimes a missing person. Jealousy, spite, greed and despair, that's my currency, so I don't usually meet people at their best, even if they have one. The cops deal with the glamorous side – murder, drug-dealing, terrorism, and sometimes they wear a uniform. I take up whatever they don't, won't or can't do. But at least *I* get to choose my own hours and jobs, or so the theory goes.

I had wanted to be a policewoman, but at five foot four inches I wasn't tall enough. Michael Nolan, family friend and ex-Garda, suggested joining his private detective agency and security firm. I was his apprentice for five years, and when he died of a massive coronary on a golf course (he was losing) I found a note in his desk which read:

Street,

You should have left a year ago. I can't nurse you all my life, especially if you're reading this now. Make me proud or I'll haunt you,

Mick.

P.S. Don't bother with golf, it's a bloodsport.

He left me his cameras and a thousand pounds, and I was on my own.

I felt a bit lethargic after the accounts stint. It's an activity that always puts far too much perspective on my life, and that was probably the last thing I needed on a birthday. I decided to make a cup of coffee. Surely caffeine would lift my spirits.

As the kettle boiled, I looked out over the city roofs. Four cranes were moving slowly and silently, in the distance. They were giant sculptures in the sky, but sculptures with a purpose. They were building the Dublin of tomorrow, each chasing a deadline, then moving on to another part of town and chasing again. Everyone wants to beat the Millennium. It occurred to me that I'd never seen one being put together, or being transported from one place to another, only ever the finished crane. Who spirits these gentle giants from place to place? And where do they go to when they're not needed any more?

My favourite bit of the office is the window; it is the reason I chose it as my base. Well, that and the rent. It's a classic detective's semicircle, straight out of Chandler. I haven't yet succumbed to the Bogart mac, though. I spend a lot of my time daydreaming into the view. The moving sky and the immobile buildings are reassuring, unchallenging, like a hearth-fire. Or bingo. Normally they're beautiful to me, mesmerising. Today I just shivered and felt a bit sour. I was still soaked through.

There has been a lot of talk about Dublin being the new Barcelona, complete with café culture. Well I'm sorry, but no. On days like this, Dublin is the shite Barcelona. And no one wants to sit outdoors in the pouring rain drinking damp cappuccino. My caffeine hit was not working.

Sammy the Sandwich arrived with the luncheon goodies, or what was left of them, in his wicker basket.

'Sorry Leo, I had to start at the bottom today and work my way up the building because of the lift.'

'Don't worry Sammy, I'm having one of those days, so that fits in just perfectly. On top of everything else, I'm thirty today. I thought it wouldn't make any difference to me but I'm a bit grumpy, and I suppose that could be why. I don't feel any different though. Ah, it's a nightmare.' I rooted in the basket and selected a smoked chicken with coleslaw on rye. 'Maybe things are looking up, I'd probably have chosen this anyway.'

'Don't you dare put your hand in your pocket,' he warned. 'It's on the house. And I'll tell you what you should do – buy yourself a nice bunch of flowers on the way home. That'll cheer you up. It always works for me.'

My first birthday present, a sandwich, and damn nice it was too. After years of being shackled to the plain 'hang sangwich', we've gone global, with different breads and rolls and fillings. I suppose we should have seen it coming years ago when mayonnaise started to replace salad cream.

The phone rang and Harry Knowles barked an order: 'Don't forget to bring something decent to wear to the Spring Ball. I don't want you sticking out like a sore thumb.'

'Oh, don't worry,' I reassured him, 'I'll root out something nice and frilly for the occasion.'

When I heard the dial tone, I realised that our exchange had ended. 'Stylish and charming,' I thought, fingering his money.

Mrs Mack stuck her beaky head around the door. As always she was a symphony in beige and brown.

'Oh, you're busy,' she twinkled, 'I won't disturb you.' This meant no cleaning for today.

In a rigorously controlled experiment, I had worked out that all she ever actually did was stand in the doorway and wipe with the mop from there. This meant that a semicircular area, of approximately three feet in radius, got a lick every so often. Unless you were foolish enough to be in your office when she arrived. Then you could not be disturbed. Similarly, she would never approach the desk or filing cabinets.

'Miss Street, I'd *never* be able to forgive myself if I destroyed evidence and lost you a big case.'

Today's skirmish went to her. But the week wasn't over yet.

Mrs Mack takes a fortnight's holiday every year at

the beginning of August. Religiously. In the final days of July, and indeed coming up to Christmas, she lays siege to the building. It is appropriate, at these times, to press a bonus upon her. August, then, is nirvana – her deputy cleans and shines, and leaves the offices ready for another fifty weeks of neglect.

I sat at my desk and faced what I'd been avoiding for days. Before me, in identical envelopes, were two rather different reports of one particular job. They were both addressed to Mrs Annette O'Neill, and both would break her heart, one more than the other. This, too, had been an infidelity case, but Annette O'Neill couldn't afford to throw money at her problem the way Harry Knowles could. She was married with three kids under ten, and very, very vulnerable. I had been reluctant to take this assignment from the beginning. Annette was a friend of my sister-in-law, and that's how she met me. It was almost like raking over family dirt, and I don't like to mix my professional and personal lives. But Annette was desperate, and, uneasy as I was, I agreed to take the job. It was made worse by the fact that my sister-in-law did not know any of this, and would have been horrified if she had. Events were getting muckier by the day, and I was eager to be shot of the case. Which report to send? How much did she need to know if her life was going to fall apart either way? I ducked the decision, and put both envelopes in my bag.

I share a birthday with my mother, Geraldine, which has made for some maudlin moments over the years. I phoned to wish her a happy sixtieth and she was in philosophical mood – only three years to a new century, maybe she should look after herself and get to the year 2000.

'It does seem like a waste to feck it up now,' I agreed, 'having made it this far.' General opinion is that only a silver bullet will stop her.

I made travel arrangements with my brother for the family gathering that evening, and took some slagging off about my car. Then I rang my mechanic and took some more slagging off about my car. But at least he promised to try his best to salvage it, for money.

The excitement was entirely bearable, so I leafed through the rest of my post. It was the usual assortment of junk-mail and bills, and the yearly Mass card from my granny. This one had a fiver inside, and a message to buy myself something nice. With my soul saved, I locked up and gave myself the afternoon off. I am the boss, after all.

As I stepped on to the street, I remembered Sammy's advice and bought myself a bunch of mad, exotic flowers. He was right, I did feel better. Armed with public proof of my birthday, I walked along Dame Street towards Trinity College. Even in the gloom of bad weather it looked thoughtful. I think it was Brendan Behan who once said that the cream of Ireland's youth could be found there, rich and thick. It was also remarkably dirty compared with the newly cleaned bank across the road. I guess the bank has the money, the college has the intellectual edge. I could hear a cynical Mick Nolan scoffing, 'Money talks and bullshit walks.'

I tapped my number into a cash machine, and it kindly produced some. A small boy was watching, fascinated. 'How much did you win?' he asked. Just as an advice note appeared to remind me how perilous my finances were, I remembered Harry's cash payment, snug in an envelope in my bag. Even if this *was* a landmark birthday, surely I wasn't old enough to lose all powers of memory. I speedily lodged the money and continued on my way, along Westmoreland Street and across O'Connell Bridge. Apparently there is a plan to put a digital clock in the river here. It will count down to the Millennium. Good luck to anyone trying to see it is all I can say; the water is always so murky I don't believe that will be possible.

I began to feel mean about my negative thoughts.

Dublin is a great place to be. I've lived here all my life and I love it. It's vibrant and friendly, and the city centre is so compact you never have to go far to meet someone you know. Of course, the flip side is that it can be equally hard to avoid someone and in my line of work that could grow to be a problem. Those negative vibes were seeping back in. But like the people that I know well, I can see the city for what it is, warts and all. Tough love.

I rarely go very far along O'Connell Street if I can help it. It is a huge, wide street, with an attractive middle walkway along its spine, but it has become an injun territory of fast food joints, neon signs, pound stores, fun emporiums, and some quite odd municipal sculptures. Instead, I turned to the right and squished my way to Lower Abbey Street to get a bus back home to the Northside. A weak sun was trying its best to get some recognition in the sky. Pedestrians jostled and bumped, wielding closed umbrellas like weapons.

Incredibly, the bus stop was offering a double-decker on my route, so I paid my fare to a disinterested driver and went upstairs. The front seats were occupied by two schoolboys, who'd scratched gunsights into the condensation on the windows and were busy fighting other airplanes. All the way home they waged battle against the baddies, rat-tat-tat-tat-tat, rat-tat-tat-tat-tat.

On Saturday mornings when we were young, my two brothers would spend an hour carefully placing Airfix soldiers throughout the living room fortifications, then bomb it all to hell in twelve minutes flat. I don't think anyone ever won those battles, it was all about the taking part. The bombing and crashing and shooting mouth-noises were interspersed with immortal dialogue like, 'Aagh, Johnny, he got me – Johnny, I'm hit, I'll have to walk all the way home with this bullet in my leg – look out Johnny – take that pigdog.' All the good guys were called Johnny.

The bus ambled in a north-easterly direction towards Clontarf. We passed the choppy sea on the coast, which is exactly where you'd expect to find it really. I spotted some hardy types walking themselves and their dogs. I have a nodding acquaintance with most of them. We recognise one another from the local shops and cafés. It's like living in a little village, but with all of the benefits of being close to town. We're a community. We have yuppies and peasants, professionals and loafers, big houses, small houses, public houses. We have apartments and flats. We have public housing, private housing, dodgy housing, homeless. We wear our Northsider status like a badge of honour, and we trash the Southside for being overpriced and pompous on every available occasion.

I got off at my stop, along with the two boys. Now they were on horseback, leading a cavalry attack, or 'calvary attack' as one of them put it. They raced around a corner after the enemy. The sky began to spit on me again. This was reaching the point of rudeness as far as I was concerned, particularly as I had neither an umbrella nor a hat.

I made for a little estate of triangular houses. It is known locally as The Toblerone, and is set behind a complex of expensive new apartments. One of these was 'To Let' but some wag had added an 'i' between the two words on the sign, and now it advertised something completely different, and presumably cheaper to rent. I lived at number 11, The Villas. A lot of people think this is a splendid irony, given that I'm named after most of the city.

The Villas was built as an estate for the working classes in the Fifties. The houses are two-or three-bedroomed, with a garden front and back. They are made of pure concrete, which means that damp is rarely a problem. It also reduces grown men from the gas company to tears if they have to drill an air-vent, because the walls are tougher than solid rock. It is also a major event to get a nail into one of them to hang a picture, or, bless the notion, a curtain rail. Barry, who lives with me, has long since abdicated any responsibility for DIY projects as a result. He also reasons that, as an artist, he's above that sort of menial activity, and he's also got to have all moving parts in working order. He can be a right lazy git.

Property prices have gone bananas in Dublin, and even the most basic of houses can go for an unreal price, if it's close to the city centre. The Villas is. As the houses on the estate change hands, we're acquiring a colourful and disparate community. There are still some older couples, visited by their children and grandchildren on Sundays, birthdays and Christmas. There are young couples with children, gay couples with dogs, and one young blood with a Porsche moved in three doors up recently. Barry hates him. He seems fine to me, and I just love the car.

A curtain twitched in the first house on my row. I couldn't see past the vase of plastic flowers and through the patterned net, but I knew who was there. Marion Maloney, local busybody. She would probably prefer the term 'historian'. She records all of our comings and goings, and I'm sure she would make an excellent detective. I couldn't resist waving at her. She stayed hidden, no doubt furious that she'd been spotted. We had managed to get on speaking terms with her one day when Barry said, 'Howaya,' as we struggled up the street with the supermarket shopping. She was washing her windows – a clear pane of glass is essential for her hobby. She turned around and said, 'Don't call me "howaya", my name is Marion.'

The whole place was an obstacle course. It looked like Dublin Corporation might be digging up the road. Then again, it could be the gas company or the cable television lot. I bet Marion knew. A chunky man was threading strips of coloured, striped plastic around the various hazards, while a small group huddled around a stove drinking tea and exposing several kinds of arse-crack to the world. I hoped it was the Corpo doing something about the water pressure; I was sick and tired of spending half an hour filling the bath, only to have it tepid when I got in. I asked a man in one of the holes.

'Ramps, love.'

'Ramps?'

'Yeah, to stop people speedin', yeh know. Or joyriders.'

Great, it would probably take weeks of noisy drilling and digging.

'How long will ye be here, do you think?'

'Hard to say, love. It's a big job, yeh know. And we can't be rushin' it. It'll be the three weeks anyway.'

'And then some,' I thought. It had taken them twice as long to do what we all assumed was a major new one-way system on one of the busier roads in the area. It turned out to be a flowerbed.

# TWO

Maeve Kelly was standing on my doorstep. 'You're late,' she said.

'Yeah, the car's in a coma, I'm thirty years old, it's all downhill from here.'

'Get used to it,' she laughed. 'It's just a race against time now.'

I went through my pockets looking for the key.

'Soon,' she continued, 'thirty will be a distant memory and you'll be worrying about forty, and all along you'll only be nineteen or twenty *inside*. Take my advice, stay in your thirties for a very, *very* long time. I know that's what *I* intend to do.'

'Well, another thing,' I said, putting the key into

the lock. 'My mother told me that once you're over twenty-one you're supposed to stop getting spots. Rubbish talk. I woke up this morning with the king of all shiners on my chin. Where's the justice in that?'

'Lovely flowers. Who are they from?'

'Myself. Charity begins at home.'

'Yep, help the aged.'

Inside, it was clear that Noel had had a field-day with the new rug. It was piled in a pyramid in the kitchen, although I had earlier placed it neatly in front of the fireplace. Butter wouldn't melt in his feline mouth. Bridie was missing, and Snubby was curled up in pole position on top of the armchair by the window. A fine tumbleweed of cat hair rolled by, daring me to do some hoovering. I detest housework.

Maeve waved a bag in my face and announced, 'Two bottles of finest New World Chardonnay, straight from the off-licence fridge.' Then she shed her simple-but-beautifully-cut navy linen coat, to reveal a slimline trouser-suit of effortless elegance.

'That's a bit gorgeous,' I said.

'Yeah, but if I put on any *more* weight, I won't be able to wear it.'

'Maeve, I'm not even going to dignify that remark with an answer. We've been through this before.

You're *not* putting on weight.'

'That wasn't an answer?' she asked.

'Fuck off, smart cow.'

'Again, a dignified response. I can only hope that you're not going to your *mother's* in your uniform,' she continued. 'You *know* what mammies are like, they like their daughters dressed as girls.'

My mother hates my habitual black jeans and jumper. So I keep an emergency frock handy for family occasions. Actually, I have a few, but I would never admit that to her.

'I've given up explaining that a detective can't go around dressed like a young Edna O'Brien all day, but she refuses to believe me,' I said. 'Impossible woman. You busy today?'

'Yep. A sexy ad for sanitary towels.'

Maeve is an actress who I met through my partner Barry about three years ago. Now she's a better friend of mine than his. (I hate that word, partner, unless it's a business term, but sometimes it covers a lot of ground.) She makes most of her money from radio and television voice-overs. It feeds her theatre habit, she says.

'Deep tones, sultry saxophone, dry-weave top-sheet. It's no job for an adult. And you should see the *state* of the fella I did it for. He's got this *unfeasibly* long beard. Hopefully he's growing it for charity, otherwise it's a *tragic* fashion decision. His wife mustn't know whether to shag him or shave him.'

I poured two generous glasses of wine, and admired the buttery liquid. Then we knocked them back.

'Yummy,' I said. 'The Australians may be the natural enemy of the friendly person, but they sure know how to put a wine together.'

'Agreed,' purred the contented Maeve Kelly.

I'm not the easiest person to stay friends with. I don't have a routine life. If I'm on surveillance I could be out on duty at any time of the day or night, so it's hard to plan a social life very far ahead. As a result, I've lost touch with many of my school friends. Most of those who are still local are married and having families now, so they have preoccupations of their own. I also have a problem with telling people what I do; I don't like to draw attention to it. And in general, a private detective does not attract people's attention unless they have a grievance. Then they come looking for you.

If I make a new friend, I find it difficult to put in the groundwork and to keep in touch. Maeve understands this, and oddly enough her life is not unlike mine. She only really gets to see the people she's working with. As a result, ours is a very relaxed arrangement, and we pick up where we left off whenever we get together. There are never any recriminations about unreturned lunches or calls.

'How is The Magnificent Michael?'

Her sometimes boyfriend was a magician who rejoiced in the professional title 'The Amazing Armand'.

She shook her dark brown bob and sighed.

'He *hates* doing kids' birthday parties. Well, actually, he hates kids full stop. *And* the local cat got all of his doves during the week, so he's in even more of a foul temper than usual over that.'

'I'd better make my three mogs scarce when he comes round next.'

We agreed that this would be wise.

'The last kid's birthday I remember being at was when I was eight. Mary Boyd from up the road hid a load of buns in her knickers when she was leaving. I could never understand why – she was allowed to have them, so why steal them?'

'Women,' exclaimed Maeve, reaching for the wine. 'And how was your day at the office, dear?'

'Well, I'm off on a paid weekend away to Kildare. Husband-and-wife jobby. She's supposedly doing the dirty. It'll be a nasty piece of work, I just know it. And I didn't like him at all.'

'He paid up front then.'

'Oh yes.'

Bridie sauntered into view. She stopped in front of Maeve and stared up at her.

'Cat, you are *not* to jump up on me.'

'You're probably wasting your breath,' I told her.

'Why is it that they only ever leave white hairs on my dark clothes, and dark hairs on my light ones.'

'It's one of those ancient cat rules that you just have to roll with,' I explained.

She handed me a parcel. 'A small, votive offering.'

Inside was a red silk scarf. 'Oh Maeve, it's beautiful.'

'I *know*, it *kills* me to part with it. I wouldn't mind one myself, but I don't suppose even the *heaviest* of hints to Magic Mickey will have any success. Has *your* hero coughed anything up yet?'

'No, not yet. He's gone to an audition for some new Irish play this afternoon, so he's a bit preoccupied.'

There was a pause.

'That sounded awfully like an excuse, didn't it,' I said.

Another pause.

'Is he even paying you rent on this place yet?'

I began to burble. 'Well, it is my house, Maeve, I mean I'd be paying the mortgage anyway. And he's not working at the moment. If I took some of his dole, he wouldn't even be able to go out for a few pints.'

'Look Leo, I've known Barry a long time, and I really like the guy. He's great fun, he means well, but he's careless with people. And most importantly, he's lazy as sin. He's never going to get up off his arse and do something if you don't insist on it. In the end of all, you're doing him no favours carrying on like this.'

Where are her camp emphases when you need them?

'I know you're right,' I said, 'but I'm not even half drunk enough to think about it now. I just want to toast being over the hill.'

She raised her glass. 'Cheers, old crone. And don't mind me, my *own* love life is a bit of a joke – *without* a punchline.'

'But with a cast of thousands,' I reminded her.

'I suppose you could say that Barry is proof that there's no such thing as free love any more. Men,' she laughed, 'fuck them.'

I raised my glass. 'If only.'

Maeve began to fumble in her bag again.

'Is it my imagination, or is that thing getting bigger all the time?' I asked.

'As the actress said to the bishop. I can bloody well find *nothing* in it, even though everything I *own* is probably in here.'

'It's more of a tardis than a bag,' I pointed out.

'Yeah. And Freud would have a *field-day* with some sort of anal retention theory, wouldn't he?' By

27

now she had all but disappeared into the thing. 'Where the *hell* is that yoke? Aha! Have a hairdo on me,' she said, handing me a gift voucher.

'Oh God,' I groaned, 'you're turning into my mother. She's forever at me about my hair. I wouldn't mind, but it's her fault I have this kink in it in the first place. If she'd married a man with straight hair I might have been spared.'

'No, no, you only *think* you want straight hair. Look at mine. Every time I go to a hairdresser they lift up a section of it, with real pity, and say, "It's very *fine*, isn't it", and I just want to scream, "Yeah well, that's all I have, so just *do* something with it".'

'At least you have a choice – straight or curly, I just have kink.'

'Leo, if you could just have *seen* some of the awful perms I've had over the years. I've had shaggy, frizzy, tight, screwball and *shite*. Not to mention the time I decided to go blonde as well, and my hair started to fall out. It was a *nightmare*. Not even your mother could have approved of it. So it was back to my own little offering of *thin*. If anyone wants anything else, they can get me a wig.'

'The trials of being a woman. More fine wine my dear?'

Maeve is all about the art of the possible. So when she stuck in a tape of music she'd found in her bag, it was only natural that we would start singing and dancing along. My neighbours are regularly treated to my lit-up front room bedecked with bouncing, laughing women, and a soundtrack of the latest hits. It's the magic of Maeve. She's encouraging and open and generous and unafraid. She embraces life.

She's also good at knowing what will pass muster with a mammy. So while I sluiced down in the shower, she ransacked my wardrobe for suitable birthday clothes. A lot of the trendy stuff that I'd bought recently had been while on shopping trips with Maeve. She's a pro when it comes to retail therapy. Trousers and jeans are the only sensible option for me on a working day, and consequently Maeve has forbidden the buying of pants on our excursions, unless they are from a lingerie department. Now I have lots of skirts and occasion-wear. All that's missing, usually, is an occasion.

She'd laid out various combinations on the bed for us to argue over.

'I don't know *why* I'm pretending to give you a choice at all,' she said, 'because tonight you're going to show off those *gorgeous* legs of yours, so that means the little jersey dress.'

A short, civilised spat later, she was admiring me in the full-length mirror. I started to laugh.

'Barry is usually the one to admire himself in this.'

'Now why does that not surprise me,' she grinned. 'Oh, I shouldn't slag him off, really, *all* actors are vain, in their own peculiar way. And at least he keeps himself in shape. You look *fantastic*, birthday girl.'

Actually, the result wasn't bad at all. The plain, long-sleeved dress came to just above the knee, and Maeve had inveigled me into a pair of high-heeled slingback sandals. I looked almost willowy, or tottering drunk, depending on your point of view. She made me scrape my hair back into a sort of low Spanish bun, and we matched this with some make-up.

'If that doesn't take the eye out of Barry Agnew's head, then he's certifiably dead,' said Maeve.

I draped her beautiful present around my shoulders. 'Thank you Maeve, you've worked a miracle.'

She looked at me quizzically. 'Don't be ridiculous, Leo,' she said. 'Jesus, you need to get out more. If we don't get you over this shy, modesty thing, it'll just become plain *annoying*, rather than charming. We need to get you some self-confidence, woman. *You* need to get yourself some.'

'I'm sorry. I find it nearly impossible to take a compliment, Maeve, that's all. I'm not being ungrateful, and I'm thrilled with all of this. It's just that I'm not used to taking that much interest in my appearance. I mean, the last thing you'd want to do in my line of work is draw attention to yourself.'

'Point taken,' she said. 'Right, now that I've done my bit for the rehabilitation of the elderly, I really must go. So, one for the door, and then I'm off.'

We also had one for the road.

By the time Barry got home, Maeve had left and I was feeling nicely sozzled. Precisely the right state of mind for facing the Street mob with a boyfriend they didn't approve of. They liked him well enough. Just didn't approve of him – an apparently, and actually, out-of-work actor, living off their only daughter's meagre earnings. But, as Maeve often pointed out, an actor is for life, not just for Christmas. I didn't mind. If it had been the other way around they wouldn't have batted an eyelid. Or so I reasoned. Not much of an argument, but it was the best I could muster at the time.

A human whirlwind banged through the door. He shook some raindrops from his dark curls and swore.

I posed by the fireplace so that he could admire my finery. 'How did the audition go?' I asked.

'Ah Jesus, don't talk to me. I've just spent an hour of my life wanking in front of a dozen strangers. With all my clothes on. We "improvised", yaw?' He had the rabbit's ears fingers out on both hands and wiggled them. 'I was a squashed grape-fruit, a remould tyre, and a right prick if you ask me. It proved we have no inhibitions, yaw? I hope to fuck I don't get that fucking job. C'mere till I give you a kiss.'

I smiled and began to walk towards him. He reached out, grabbed Snubby, and planted a big one on her furry black head.

# THREE

Peter Street was in something of a catch 22 situation.

My brother was a taxi-man, and our dad's latest gambit was to call him when he was ready to leave the pub and have Peter take him home. For this he would pay a nominal £3. But when Peter charged him he was a bollocks for charging his own father who'd reared him, and if he didn't charge he was a bollocks because he has himself and a wife and child to support and can't afford to be giving fares away.

'He doesn't even ask for me by name or taxi number any more,' my brother explained. 'He just phones the office and tells them to send the bollocks around.'

'It's even more worrying that the office know exactly who he means,' I pointed out.

'Isn't it,' he laughed.

Take the money as well as the abuse was the general consensus.

'Happy Birthday, Mammy,' I said, presenting a hefty tome on Cézanne which I knew she'd been visiting in the National Gallery Bookshop for weeks now. My mother paints. My brothers found this an embarrassment when they were younger, because the walls of the house were festooned with nudes from her life-drawing class. It was a short-lived embarrassment, and in time they became positively interested in those naked women, as did their teen-age friends. These days she was wrestling with landscape.

'Arra Leo,' she said, 'this is far too much.' She kissed me on the cheek. 'Aren't you just gorgeous when you get out of those awful trousers you're always in. Isn't she, Barry?'

'Oh yes,' he said, over his shoulder, as he hung up the coats.

'I clean up good,' I said.

'Leo, Barry,' acknowledged my father. 'I see ye got a lift in the Special Branch car.' Peter's new taxi was indeed an ex-Branch motor. 'Did the bollocks charge ye?'

'No Dad, birthday present.'

'It'll be grand when he gets the bloodstains out of the back seat, I suppose.'

'Daddy, there are no bloodstains on the seats, nor are there any used hypodermic needles waiting to prick your sorry old arse,' I explained.

'Lovely. Lovely talk from a girl. I don't know what the world is coming to. I suppose you'll be drinking pints next.'

'And voting,' I said.

'Where did we go wrong?'

'Well, I don't know, Dad, but personally I blame the parents.'

'Howaya Leo, Barry.' My sister-in-law, Anne, stood in the kitchen doorway. 'You're looking great, Leo, you've lovely legs, do you know that? The rest of the gang are in the dining room, so grab wine and in you go. I'd let you stir the gravy, but we're trying to avoid that kind of disaster this evening.'

'Anne,' I explained, 'it's all part of my devilish and cunning plan to distance myself from the shackles of domestication, and thereby further the twin causes of feminism and equality, after centuries of oppression.'

I gasped for breath.

'Yeah, yeah, and the Pope is a Protestant,' she said.

I caught sight of a large, white, hairy thing, with a bushy tail held high in the air. 'Hiya Smokey Joe,' I called. He didn't even deign to pause. I didn't take offence. I was used to being humiliated by him in front of people, we all were; it was a regular occurrence and he showed no mercy. Smokey Joe Street is the coolest cat alive. We have a fantasy that he spends his nights sitting cross-legged on the garden wall, drinking vodka-martinis and smoking whatever is on the go. He rules.

Stephen Street was covered with his two children in the next room. As they bounced up and down on their father, Mary announced, 'We are getting a new baby.'

'Yes,' agreed her brother, Dominick, 'and he will be called Gordon or Toby or Edward or Percy.'

Their pregnant mother, Angela, threw her eyes to heaven and explained, 'They're all train engines, friends of Thomas.'

'Or Baby Bottom,' said Mary. Not, as far as I'm aware, a friend of the famous tank-engine.

'That's a fantastic outfit, Leo, really suits you,' said Angela. 'God, what must it be like to be able to see most of your legs, and to fit into something that doesn't have to have expanding elastic panels.'

'Not too long to go now, Angela, and all that'll come back to you, like riding a bicycle.'

'Actually, riding a bicycle is one of the last things I'll be contemplating,' she said. 'Sitting on a cushion will be more the order of the day, if memory serves.'

'Dominick,' said Stephen, 'tell Aunty Leo what Daddy is.'

'Daddy is the boss,' said the four-year-old.

'And what is Mummy?'

'Mummy is a dictayto,' came the reply.

'Little traitor,' said his mother. 'Last week he told a neighbour that Daddy buys *newspapers* with Daddy's money, and Mummy buys *magazines* with Daddy's money. He'll learn the word B.I.M.B.O. next and just cut straight to the chase.'

'Where's Granny?' I asked.

'El Dorado can't make it because she's got a bad chest,' said my dad. He was referring to his mother-in-law, Mary Ellen Doyle.

'I suppose you got the Mass card,' he continued.

'Yeah, and a fiver.'

'Well, that's five pounds more than your mother got.'

'Don't be jealous now Leo, but I did get three pairs of tights,' Mammy said. 'They're Tawny Tan though, and that's not really your colour.'

'At least she's not getting us the big knickers any more,' I pointed out. 'Mind you, they were damn comfortable.'

'Ah Jaysus, we're not on to toilet talk already, are we?' asked my father.

'You're looking glorious, Mrs S.,' said Barry. And she was.

'I've been spoiled all day. Anne brought me to the hairdresser this morning, because my hair was like a whin bush, the state it was in. And then we had a lovely posh lunch with Angela in town. And in the afternoon my husband bought me this lovely outfit.'

'Did he go with you?' I asked, incredulously.

'Ah now, don't be stupid, Leo,' she said. 'Isn't it hard enough to get him into a shop when we're trying to get clothes for him?'

'Correct,' said my dad, smugly.

'And myself and Angela got her the new glasses,' said Stephen, 'because we couldn't *bear* the old ones held together with masking-tape a minute longer.'

'I dunno,' said Barry, 'I thought they had a certain something. Stylish in an unconventional way, what say you, Mrs S.?'

'Quite right, Barry,' she agreed. 'Oh, and thank you for your lovely card.'

So he'd sent her a card, sucky bastard.

'And here's one that came for you, Leo,' she said.

It had an illustration of a teddy-bear on the front, with a badge stuck on to it which said: 'I am 3'. A zero had been tippexed in beside the 3. Inside, the verse read:

> 'Today you are three
> I hope it will be
> A special birthday
> In every way'

Underneath was written 'all my love, B'.

I put the badge on and said, 'Barry, it's what I've always wanted, how did you know?'

'A brilliant guess.'

'Did anything else fall out while I was opening it?'

'Now, now, Leo, patience, patience.'

Anne staggered in under a mountain of food.

'Everyone to the table, and I want no kicking-up from anyone.' She darted a warning glance at her father-in-law.

He obliged, by wheedling, 'Spuds, Annie, spuds, where are the poppy-woppies?'

'Calm down you, they're on the way.'

My dad gets cranky without his daily dose of potatoes. It's a carbohydrate thing, nothing national-istic or cultural, and he's specific about what kind of carbohydrate passes muster at a dinner table. Show him a ring of rice and he goes into a decline. His ability to eat the humble spud, with anything, is surpassed only by his ability to insult anyone to their face, and get away with it. They think he's hilarious. And though he often is, it's not something to be encouraged.

I could hear Peter in the hallway calling their daughter down to dinner. Lucy Street is fifteen years old, and now occupies my old room in the house. It's known as 'the fridge', because it's nearly impossible to warm up. And it's a wonder to me that it's not full of poltergeists from all the youngsters who've been so busy being teenagers in it over the years. She lurched into the dining room a few minutes later and muttered something to me that sounded vaguely like Happy Birthday. Then she planted herself beside Barry and enveloped herself in his every word.

'Lucy-fer,' he said, 'good to see you. You look great and you smell even better. I might have to take a wee bite out of you later, if that's all right with you.'

An ecstatic, crimson blush burned on her cheeks. She was in heaven. I would have been there myself if only he'd said half as much to me.

There was no doubt in my mind that my niece was going to be a beauty; she was already an occasion of sin. Lucy had kohled her eyes with a smudgy black pencil, and her long hair hung loosely around her shoulders. She was wearing a tight Lycra T-shirt over combat trousers, and trainers that probably cost more than my car was now worth. I guessed that she had spent hours changing outfits before settling on this one; I know I did in that same room in my day. I gave a sigh of ancientness. I felt *old*.

Peter, Anne and Lucy moved in with my parents five years ago, and the three generations living together gave the house a splendidly Continental feel. I think it has probably also added an extra ten years to my parents' lives. We kept teasing Peter and Anne that this was a miscalculation.

Tonight was a bit like Christmas. We were eating turkey, and listening to my dad explain how he'd saved the day by insisting that Anne make bread (and potato) stuffing and 'none of your old sausage-meat nonsense.' The good crystal glasses were out, and everyone was on their best behaviour.

Instead of party-pieces, we talked rubbish and told old, familiar stories. My mother likes to reminisce about my father's torture of a young country cousin, Dixie Delaney, who stayed with them while attending college. And my dad loves to hear the heroic retelling of his great villainy.

Dixie had a devotion to the Kennedy family, and was devastated when J.F.K. was assassinated. To tease him, my father turned the front room into a place of mourning. He draped black material around a portrait of the dead American president, and insisted that everyone visit it each evening for a week, and sign a book of condolences. When Bobby was shot, he drove Dixie completely crazy by staging a pageant. Daddy was *always* Bobby, my mother was the crowd, and Dixie *had* to be the assassin. As 'Bobby' lay dying, he would ask for rosary beads. My mother would give these to him and he would ask 'But is it an *Irish* rosary?' and expire.

The house was full of human strays like Dixie when we were growing up, and it felt as if we were on a ley-line of bohemian chaos. It caused quite a stir when Mrs Leonard from two doors up found out that we had our main meal in the evening. 'They have their dinner at night,' she pronounced, 'just like the aristocrats.' Naturally, all the other kids on the street wanted to move in. I would have myself if I hadn't already been an inmate.

My dad was a rep for a big battery manufacturer, and he had a van full of them in all shapes and sizes outside the door. Christmas Day was his biggest on the domestic front. Frantic parents would offer any amount of money to replace the batteries they'd worn out while playing with their children's presents from Santa Claus the night before. We went everywhere in the van, though as we got older and bigger, some of us would be banished to the back when the cab got too crowded. This was referred to as 'the cage', and no one ever willingly volunteered for it – the view was no good from back there. But our biggest disappointment was during the late Seventies when we got a swanky new car. Although it was more comfortable, it was totally useless for seeing over hedgerows and walls. Mushroom-picking went on hold for the best part of a year until my father finally gave in and went back to the van again for family outings.

When the cake arrived, the kids sang a loud, tuneless version of Happy Birthday, and blew out the nine candles.

'There wasn't room for ninety of them,' explained Anne.

'Thank God for that,' said my mother.

'A toast, but hopefully no speeches,' said my father, raising his glass, 'to The War Department.'

'The War Department,' we echoed.

My mother smiled and sipped her drink.

'And to Bertha,' he continued.

I was very clumsy as a child, and earned the nickname Big Bertha. My dad shortened this on big occasions, to be subtle. My brothers preferred Hook Nose.

43

'Leo, are you not wondering where your present is?' asked Peter.

Stephen laughed. 'Oh, the holiday'll be over if she doesn't get it soon,' he said.

My brothers have a theory that I can't last long back in the family home without rearing up on someone, and telling a few home truths (as *I* see them). I deny this. But just *maybe* they've got a point. Hence, the safe period, or 'holiday'. They maintain it gets shorter as I get older.

'Wrong,' I announced. 'I am perfectly happy with an evening in the bosom of my family. But if, on some *extraordinary* off-chance, you've broken the family taboo and actually got me something, I'll be delighted to accept it.'

A round of applause and some cheering celebrated my graciousness.

'We have two presents,' said my dad. 'One is big, and the other bigger.'

Dominick and Mary giggled helplessly as they dragged over a large brown-wrapped parcel with a big yellow ribbon. A rectangular envelope was taped to it, addressed to Miss Leo Street.

'That looks like it's for me,' I said to them. 'Which one should I open first?'

They had another fit of giggles.

'I think I'll open this envelope first.'

It was a £500 voucher for the spy shop beside Dublin Castle. I was overcome.

'It's way too much,' I stuttered.

The card was signed by all of the family. And Barry. I pushed a meanish thought to the back of my mind – why hadn't he got me something personal, individual, why be part of a communal present?

'Thank you all *so* much. I was just about to get a new video camera, but the one I want is so expensive I never thought I'd be able to afford it. And now I can. I'll hug you all in a minute.'

There were groans all round.

'But first, I wonder what could be in here? I think I might need some help getting the wrapping off this one.'

The gigglers obliged, and a moment later I was looking at a year's supply of lurid pink toilet-paper. We all began to laugh.

Angela stood stroking her belly, saying, 'I believe that's next year's black, Leo. Very fashionable.'

'It'll certainly wake me up in the mornings,' I admitted.

'I bet it's luminous,' said Barry. 'We could use it like the emergency strip-lighting on a plane, to guide us to the loo.'

Lucy thought this was the funniest thing she'd ever heard.

Soon it was time for Stephen, Angela and the kids to go home. Mary had put on a straw hat and a kimono, and was bowing to everyone while singing 'Goodnight, goodnight, goodnight.' Dominick was smiling his elfin smile and chuckling. They were both wearing swimming goggles.

'I swear to God those children are getting more eccentric by the day,' smiled their mother.

'This is another brilliant thing about the wife being pregnant,' said Stephen. 'I can have a few jars, and Angela does the driving.'

'Consider it the last time we'll have this arrangement,' warned his wife. 'For one thing, I am not having another dry Christmas. So never again.'

'Never is a very long time,' said Stephen. 'Besides, you know you can't take your hands off me.'

'Smug bastard,' she laughed.

'Now, now, Angela, language in front of the children.'

She beat him out to the car.

As we watched them go, my father announced, 'That wine goes through me like shit through a goose. I could murder a pint.'

This was where things could get messy. We were all well oiled, and it wouldn't be long now till the crying stage of the evening. This could take one of two diametrically opposed forms – a person could be the best person in the whole world, *or* need to be put straight, in no uncertain terms, about where they were going wrong in life.

'Have we all not had enough to drink?' I tried.

'Sure, what harm would a wee pint be?' asked my father.

Lucy stomped loudly up the stairs, knowing full well what would unfold. She was too young to accompany her hero, Barry, on the next leg of his quest. Unfortunately, the rest of us were not, and a quarter of an hour later we were sitting in the snug of Kilbride's Bar and Lounge.

Toss O'Driscoll was the first to greet us when we walked in the door. A notorious drunk, he'd been barred from all the other pubs in the area. He's holding on in Kilbride's for dear life, so he's an angel to anyone who drinks there. I've heard many legends as to how Toss came about his moniker. They range from the ridiculous to the downright unsavoury, but all seem to oscillate around his ability to reach great distances in a peculiarly male pursuit. He lives in a tidy little house, known as The Toss Pot to all. He calls it 'Tivoli'. And his own real name is Walter.

Toss would never be seen in public without a shirt and tie, and he is never disrespectful to 'the ladies'. According to my mother he was a real looker in his day, and, in fairness, he still makes an effort, slicking his hair into an Elvis quiff every day. Standards are important to Toss – you start to let them slide, who knows where you'll end up. He also plants himself in a spot in Kilbride's where it's impossible to pass by without having a chat and buying him a pint. There are no flies on Toss.

'Jaysus Leo, but you're lookin' mighty tonight,' he said.

'Thanks, Toss, it's my birthday.'

'Well, I won't ask a lady her age. Many happy returns to you.'

Barry put a proprietorial arm around me and ushered me to a seat. Maybe he wasn't made of stone after all.

Anne was laughing at my mother's long face.

'What's up?' I asked.

'She's uppity because Toss didn't remember it was her birthday too.'

'There was a time when he would have,' she sniffed.

'Don't tell me you're jealous.'

'Oh, don't be ridiculous,' she said. 'He's like something out of The Simpsons.'

'God, someone change the subject,' Anne said. 'The thought of Toss O'Driscoll being yer father is too much for any human to take after a big meal.'

'So, Barry, what are you up to at the moment?' asked my dad.

'I've been to a few auditions over the last while, so I'm waiting to hear about those.'

'I thought you said this place had been done up,' I said to Peter, to divert attention elsewhere.

'It has been,' he replied. 'They took down all of the old red flock wallpaper, and the walls were bare for weeks. Then one day when they opened up, it was all back up again. Apparently, it costs a fortune, and has to be ordered in from England. And they just thought "why change the look of the place when it's done so well for so long?" '

'Don't fix it if it's not broken,' nodded my father sagely.

'Didn't we have a green version of that on the walls of the hallway sometime back in the Seventies?' I asked my mother.

'Oh yes, and it was a bitch to put up. We thought we'd got a bargain, but it all turned out to be seconds and none of it matched like it should have. I thought I'd eat the stuff by the time we were finished.'

'And it was useless for covering our school copy-books,' I recalled. 'Far too humpy and bulky.'

'Yeah,' agreed Peter, 'a bit of a disaster all round really.'

'I bet the nuns were dead curious to see what kind of wallpaper everyone came in with. It must have been like visiting people's houses for them,' said Anne.

'Ah, not only that,' added my mother, 'I know of people who went out and bought just the one roll of good wallpaper to cover those same copybooks, so that everyone would think they lived in a really swish place.'

'Who?' we all asked in unison.

'Now, I'll not name names. All I'll say is that some of them don't live a million miles away still.'

No amount of begging could wheedle those names from her. She was delighted with herself. She had one up on us. Information was power.

We ordered a round from a lounge boy, and my dad sank back into the vinyl banquette. 'This is the life, eh?'

Kilbride's is a huge community centre for drinking. The floor is a nondescript linoleum, the stools are plain and uncomfortable, and the rickety tables are brown Formica. It's wonderful.

My eyes were drawn to a familiar sight at the bar. An old codger called Lar Brogan was planted in his usual spot. Lar has been drinking in Kilbride's for longer than I've been alive. He has a luxuriant handlebar moustache, now grey, and his favourite tipple, unsurprisingly, is a pint of stout. Lar's drinking of the pint, however, is unique. He sucks back a good half without pausing for breath. Then, to clear the moustache of froth, he uses the rim of the glass to scrape it all back in on top of the pint. He was doing that now. All subsequent pints would be treated in the same manner. 'I fucking hate that habit of his,' said my father. I couldn't disagree.

Barry was entertaining the others with his latest awful jokes, and my dad got to asking me how business was. As I got older, I realised that he liked hearing my news from me personally, rather than via my mother. We have no real facility for discussion or dialogue or whatever the buzzwords are. I've never heard him speak about his feelings, and I don't suppose I ever will. He keeps all that in, like most Irishmen of his generation, and our talks remain on a chatting level. I know he's really trying hard though, and I'm touched by that.

'The old bird is looking well,' my father said.

'If you're referring to my mother, and your lovely wife, then yes, she is,' I agreed.

'Here's a bit of advice though. Don't let her get talking about her new passport. She has to renew it, and she loves nothing more than to cry into a glass of whiskey about how it'll be her last. She's like a feckin' cracked record when she gets going.'

'Enough said. Thanks for the warning.'

By now, the whole pub was looking a bit bendy, and another table of revellers had started singing Nat King Cole songs.

'Time to go, I think,' I said to Barry.

'Is that bollocks ever going to buy a round?' asked my father.

I had subbed Barry twenty pounds earlier so that he would have the technology to do this.

'He got the last one,' I pointed out.

'Oh.' I could practically *hear* my father's thoughts regrouping. 'Time for the fucker,' he announced. Standard pub fare, this.

The Mammy wanted to talk 'art'. She was 'confronting her image' she said. Uh-oh. Once upon a time, her favourite subject when drunk had been nuclear war. Then there was a middle-period of religion. But now this, the most serious of all. If you got involved, your brain would be scrambled for days.

'Barry,' I said, 'I really think we should head.'

'Ah no, sure, ye'll stay the night.'

This wasn't a great idea for me. I nurtured the vague hope of having sex with my boyfriend, though this was something of a distant memory. Birthdays, Christmas and the odd shag on holiday didn't seem too much to ask for. Yet even though we

were openly living together, with splendid and per-
verse Irish family logic, staying at my parents' would
mean separate beds in separate rooms.

'Can't Mammy,' I said, 'we didn't leave any food
out for the cats.'

'But sure those yokes could live on their fat for a
week.'

'No, Mammy, really. And besides, I've got an early
start in the morning.'

'Well, we'll have one for the road so,' declared my
dad.

'It would be wrong not to,' agreed Barry.

'Motion passed unanimously.'

Anne smiled sympathetically at me. 'Nice try, Leo.'

My hopes of that special treat were fading fast.
Barry didn't have the age-old problem of brewer's
droop, he'd be unconscious long before that. I
heaved a sigh and waded in, 'White wine. Make it a
large one.'

An hour later, we fell in through our doorway and
Barry disappeared to the couch, his natural habitat. I
washed my teeth, left my make-up on, and made a
pathetic attempt to drink a pint of water. By the
time I returned he'd fallen asleep. I tried to rouse
him but, no go. So I climbed the stairs and got into
bed, alone.

Happy Birthday, Leo.

# FOUR

By 9 a.m. the next morning my mascara had welded my eyelashes together, my mouth was entertaining a bale of cotton wool and my brain was fuzzy at the edges. The air was so dry that I was convinced my head had shrivelled to the size of a prune. My hair smelled like an ashtray from the smoky pub and my fingernails were encrusted with dirt. It never ceased to amaze me just how dirty my hands can get from a night on the tiles. Something evil was happening in the whole below-the-waist area, and a nasty burp suggested that this could go both ways.

Barry was snoring loudly beside me, so I thumped him and tried to turn him on his side. No use. I shook him, but he remained as lifeless as a sack of potatoes. His mouth had fallen open and his chin was buried in his chest; it was not a pretty sight. The droning continued, so I shook him again. This time I knew I had impinged on his subconscious, because he shrugged me off and turned away. After a few moments he started up again, so I gave a series of almighty heaves, until he burst out with, 'Are you satisfied? Now we're *both* awake. What's the point of that?'

'I can't get back to sleep if you don't shut up snoring,' I yelled.

He turned back on to his side, muttering, and promptly started to snuffle again. I got out of bed and put on my dressing gown. In case this looked like he'd won, I reached back, shook him a bit more, and called him a selfish bastard a few times, for good measure. Then I made my way to the kitchen to make a slow, weak cup of tea. I had a number of things to do before I set off for Kildare that evening. I started with a not-very-bracing shower, and decided to tackle the car problem.

There was no point ringing Mullaney Motors. Ever. Company policy forbade telephone-answering. My seedy hangover reasoned that the walk would do me good, and twenty minutes later, amidst the smell of oil, fan belts and Swarfega, I got the lecture.

'The main problem is the clutch, Leo,' said the heavy Dublin accent. 'Yiv rid the arse out of it. Didya not hear it scrapin'?'

I squirmed guiltily. 'I thought you told me these things were like hairdryers, they go forever.'

'*And* yiv not been lookin' to the oil neither,' he continued, ignoring my bleats.

This could go on for some time.

'Mull,' I whined, 'I *need* it. I have a really urgent job in Kildare and I can't get there any other way. *Please* Mull. I'm practically a shareholder in this business for Christsakes.'

He scratched his balls contemplatively. 'I'll see what I can do. Come back at half three, but I'm not makin' any promises.'

'I love you, Mull,' I said, kissing him on the cheek. 'Your reward will come.'

'It better,' he growled, blushing. 'Now get outta me sight till I get some work done.'

I blew him another kiss and hightailed it.

Things were looking up, so I nipped by the office. I got to the second floor and was greeted by a snacking Mrs Mack. She was holding court in her tearoom. As I turned to tackle the final flight of stairs, I noticed that the lift was wedged open by a large vacuum cleaner, on which someone had written UFO in black marker. I returned to present myself at court.

'Mrs Mack,' I said, in as even a tone as I could muster, 'is the lift stuck on this floor because of your cleaning equipment?'

'Oh that,' she said. 'My heart is scalded, Miss Street, by little gurriers calling that yoke down to the ground floor for no reason. Other times they joyride up and down in it till I threaten to call the Guards on them.'

'So it's not broken at all then.' The tone had risen a note or two.

'Not at the moment, no,' she reassured me, 'but sometimes it is. Best to keep it out of harm's way.'

'Just one of those things so.' The tone was positively tight now.

'Oh yes, just one of those things,' she agreed, nodding her permed little head. 'Anyway, I know you like to keep fit, in your line of work and all, so it works out well for all of us.' She smiled triumphantly and slurped back to her tea. I bit down hard on the inside of my cheek in an effort to save her life, and left the scene of the potential murder.

'The only way is up,' I thought, and climbed the remaining steps.

The office was quiet and still, and had not been disturbed by modern cleaning chemicals. Obviously, Mrs M. was afraid to bung up my sense of smell, so useful for all that tracking on those long chases cross-country, when I had to be a superfit human beagle to 'get my man'. A red light blinked on the desk, and my answering machine told me I had one message, left at 10:02 a.m. I pressed 'play' and Annette O'Neill's voice filled the room.

'Ah, hello Miss Street . . . ah . . . Leo. Em . . . God I hate talking to these things. Ah . . . I know you said it might be a while before you had any news for me, and, eh, I'm not trying to rush you or anything. Em . . . I suppose I just wanted to talk to someone really. Gillian, don't draw on the couch, draw on the paper I gave you. Ah, sorry about that. So! Just to say that, eh, he's not home much at the moment, so I thought you'd like to know that. Well you prob- ably know that already. So, eh, I look forward to hearing from you soon . . . Oh God, it's Annette, by the way, Annette O'Neill . . . Em, goodbye.'

Which report to send – the truth, or the whole truth? I decided to think about it for a few more hours, but resolved to post one of the brown envelopes to her that evening.

I grabbed my old video camera and headed for the spy shop, where I presented it, with my birthday voucher, as barter for a new, swish model. After much haggling, I left with a tiny beauty that wouldn't make even the slightest bulge in a clutch bag. The world is becoming miniaturised by the day;

I have cameras in pens and plugs, listening devices so small I'm terrified of swallowing them with my tea. Personally, I prefer the larger items, simply because of the ease of handling.

I had made a set of decisions about procedure on the Knowles case. Infidelity is as old as the hills, so this was as traditional a job as you could get in my game. I decided to go back to basics. I had asked Harry to describe Victoria's office to me, and based on that it seemed to me that she would notice any intrusion, even down to a strange pen. Therefore, I was going with my new, yet quite standard, video camera. I didn't want to put anything into a plug hole either, not least because I wasn't sure that the view of the room would be any good from there. I was going on tour to a strange place, flying blind, so there was no time for flashy showing off. And time was tight. I felt like a Le Carré pro.

However, even super-spies have to eat, so I stopped by the bakery on the way home and bought three kinds of bread, one of which was vaguely healthy. And a cream puff to lure Sleeping Beauty out of bed.

The new Barcelona was looking altogether better today. It was still not warm enough to sit outside with a mint tea, but at least everyone was in higher spirits. Of course, every up has its down; I had to wait for a bus for twenty minutes. 'There's always a price to pay,' I could hear my Gran intone. 'Why?' I've often wanted to ask. 'Why does there have to be a price tag on everything? Why do we have this reward and punishment system, and is it real or perceived?'

I walked by the sea wall and enjoyed the invigorating breeze. I was being gently cleansed and refreshed by the elements. This morning, the white crests of the waves contrasted with a blue sea, reflecting a cheerier sky than yesterday's morbid grey. It was, however, very cold, to which my purple hands bore witness. I stepped up the pace and headed for The Villas.

The workmen were back at their station on the road, going full tilt at another tea-break. During the night some of the red and white plastic had escaped, and it was draped in the branches of a tree, waving gaily to all. The huddle greeted me as I went past. At this rate we would be bosom buddies by the end of their three, or more, weeks in situ.

I didn't even get a politically incorrect whistle or comment. I wondered about this briefly. I had gone, overnight, from being a young woman in her twenties, to a woman in her thirties, without an adjective. Did it mean that I was now too old to elicit workmen's attention, or that I was never worth it in the first place? My sister-in-law, Angela, says that it's even worse when you've got kids, because then people don't even notice you, they just see the buggy.

To my dismay, I saw that today had been recycling day and I had missed the pick-up. The Corporation had given each house a green, plastic recycling box, and we were to fill these and leave them out for collection on Thursday mornings. I had been so dopey and preoccupied when I'd left I hadn't seen them; even at that stage it was probably too late, as the Corpo liked to swoop very early. I was a familiar sight, flapping after the noisy dumper each week in my dressing gown. Someone had snaffled my green box, and I was now having to use a pink laundry basket. There was intense competition on the presentation of boxes. Following Marion The Howaya's example, each cardboard cereal packet was folded, bottles washed, and plastic neatly crushed into an acceptable and pleasing shape. I had often seen her out checking other people's rubbish late on Wednesday nights; there were standards involved.

I looked in at my little house from the kerb. It was painted a plain magnolia, with a red door, but the walls and wood were a bit chipped and showing their age. 'Like their owner,' I thought. Then I sighed to think that I wouldn't in fact *own* the house until I was forty-nine; the bank just allowed me to say it was mine while I paid off the mortgage. If push came to shove, it was theirs. Oh yes, you're in the system now, Street, you've bought into the package.

Inside, the heating was on full blast, along with the fake coal fire. My hands began to thaw immediately. All three cats were flaked out on various soft furnishings. Bridie, in particular, looked very comfortable indeed, embedded in a pile of clean washing. The clothes were now matted with cat hair, so she could be justifiably pleased with her morning's work.

Barry was sitting on the couch, smoking and watching a daytime cookery show.

'I didn't expect you to surface until later in the afternoon,' I said.

'I had to give in and get up, those feckers haven't stopped with their jackhammers all morning.'

'They're just making the world a safer place to be, Barry. And get used to it, they'll be with us for a long time yet.'

'There's no cat food,' he announced.

'I don't suppose it occurred to you to get off your skinny arse and go and get some?'

'Ah, gimme a break, Leo, I'm only out of bed.'

'Barry,' I sighed, 'someday I'll be dug out of you,

and no jury in the land will convict me for what I'll
be driven to.'

I rummaged through the kitchen presses and
found a large tin of salmon, which was gratefully
devoured by the moggies.

'Any chance of a cup of coffee while you're out
there?' shouted Barry.

'Make it yourself, you lazy bastard.'

'*Jesus*, I only asked. What's up with you today?
Definitely out the wrong side of the bed.'

'Barry, I'm warning you now, don't try my
patience.' I should have stopped there, I knew that,
but escalation was the order of the day, so I added,
'I'm sick and tired of waiting on you hand and foot,
and I get fuck all in return.'

We were off.

'Oh great, back to the two basics again, money
and sex.'

'Well you have to admit that I see little enough of
either of those from you,' I spat.

The kettle boiled and clicked off. I turned back and
looked at it in silence. Barry came out and put his
arms around me.

'I'm sorry,' he said. 'You're right, I am being a
selfish bastard. I'm a bit cranky and hungover, and
I'm sorry. And I'm mad with myself that I didn't tell
you how gorgeous you looked last night and that I

love you.' He kissed me lightly on the neck. 'Sit down and I'll make us both a cup of coffee.'

I did my impression of a lump of putty. 'To be honest, I'm a bit off myself,' I admitted. I produced the peace offering. 'Here's a little treat from the bakery.'

We retired to the couch to watch The Urban Peasant make a lentil lasagne from his cupboard – 'use what you've got.' Snubby insinuated herself on to my knee. I tried to discourage her, but it was no use, her mind was made up and resistance was futile. She was in a frenzy of purring and love as she settled down.

The Snub was rescued from the Southside and originally named Pat O'Hara after my local vet. That didn't last long. On her first visit to him, he drew himself up to his full six feet two inches and said, 'It's a little lady.' A tom cat had done in one of her eyes when she was a kitten and she'd recently had all but two teeth out, so she was now a toothless old hag, with lots of personality and a very smelly bottom. She looked at us humans with pity some-times. I'm sure that we looked diseased to her; we've only got patches of hair here and there, whereas cats are covered in luxuriant fur all over, barring their actual apertures.

After The Urban Peasant had rustled up a soup

from thin air, we hoisted ourselves into action. Barry went for cat food and I made a phone call.

Andy Raynor was a friend of the family; his parents still lived near mine. He was a part-time journalist, full-time political lobbyist, and a very handy source of information. He was also, strictly speaking, my first boyfriend. Actually, we'd grown up together, and dated for a while when we were teenagers. He'd always been a firm favourite in the Street household. Way back when, he'd been sporty, playing rugby and soccer particularly well. Such hero activity made him much sought after by my girlfriends, and in time he worked his way through all of them. He was equally popular with their brothers. For different reasons, as far as I know.

In those days he kept his hair long, so that it flowed behind him as he ran down the wing. A lifelong Liverpool supporter (another plus with the Streets) he, mercifully, had never opted for a Keegan perm. The romance dwindled when he boasted that he'd taken a bite out of someone's backside during a rugby scrum; amateur bottom-biters always make me nervous. Besides, Andy is a lounge lizard name.

I'd caught him between meetings and he was in a hurry.

'I'll forego the mandatory flirting today, Leo, you can owe me. Right, what do you want?'

I had to admit to myself that he'd got a very sexy voice. I didn't remember that from our teenage trysts. I'd been too busy trying to keep his hands out of my knickers. And then hoping that he'd never take them out.

'Anything dodgy about Harry Knowles that I won't have read about in the papers?' I asked.

'Ah God Leo, you're not going after Knowles, are you? He'll eat you for breakfast.'

'No, it's not him exactly, it's a parallel matter.'

'As half lies go, Leo, that'll do. I really don't want to know any more.'

'What I mean is, has he ever been offside, maritally or whatever?'

'I'll leave "whatever" alone if you don't mind, I don't even want to begin to picture that,' he said. I knew what he meant. 'All I'll say is that he's *very* discreet at home, and he goes on a lot of foreign holidays and trade trips, alone.'

'Straight?' I asked.

'As far as I know, never a whiff of anything else.' He paused a moment, then added, 'Leo, I can't tell you exactly why, but I'd prefer it if you spent as little time as possible on whatever it is you're up to with Knowles. You might get in the way of something else, something bigger.'

'Intriguing,' I said. 'Now I'm hooked.'

He swore a bit on the other end of the line.

'Don't worry, Andy, I'm just doing a very basic job for Harry. I won't be in anyone's way, believe me. I just need to know about his sexual proclivities, that's all.'

'Well, while we're at it,' he said, '*I'm* wondering when you're going to dump that useless piece of shit you're living with and let me show you a good time?'

'How do you know I haven't?'

'Your mother, of course.'

'I should've guessed. Well at least you'll be the first to know when I turn up on her doorstep a snivelling wreck.'

'*Spinster* is the word you're searching for,' he said, teasingly. 'Don't leave it too late or I may have to run off with another lovely girl.'

'What? And break my poor mother's heart? Never.'

'Gotta dash. And remember, you owe me. I'll let you know what reward I've settled on in due course.'

Before I could argue he was gone, and I realised that I was grinning from ear to ear. 'Cop on to yourself,' I thought, 'it's *Andy*.' We go back far too far for any of that nonsense.

I hunted out my one formal dress. It was a long,

black classic that I'd snapped up at a sale, and it looked every penny of the £250 it hadn't cost me. My high-heeled shoes were a bit dingy though. Still, they only had to do for one night, so a lick of some-or-other black unction on the bald bits would do the trick. Hopefully, no one would be so bored, or so fascinated, with me that they'd be staring at my feet.

Feet are very personal things. I'm not a fan. Yes, they're incredibly useful. But nine times out of ten, they're also incredibly ugly. I worked as a reception-ist for a chiropodist once, during a school summer holiday, so I know a thing or two about feet. And I haven't met a pair yet that didn't have something wrong with them. Keep feet under wraps, that's my advice.

My stint with the chiropodist was memorable for a number of reasons. I took a morbid delight and fascination in the Verruca Pedis. This was, in part, because I had two myself. The treatment was painful and spectacular. The chiropodist was Miss Agnes Doyle, an ancient spinster of this parish; upsettingly on the same unmarried singles' shelf as myself, strictly speaking. From my work, I know that there is also a 'married' singles shelf, and this causes even more trouble than the one I'm on. Agnes would apply some acidic crystals to the infected area, cover it with ointment and a bandage, and wait for a few days while a breakdown occurred. 'Meltdown' might have been a better word for the process. When the bandage was removed, a green and yellow fungus covered the infected area. She then scraped this off with a scalpel so that you could see your own dermis. Basically, you were seeing the inside of yourself.

While my own meltdown was happening I went to the local youth disco at the parish hall. It was very handy to be able to ward off creeps during the smoochy, slow set with the words, 'I've got a verruca.' But then Andy Raynor took me aside to show me that there were other ways of enjoying yourself at a dance besides dancing. He was right. That's when his hands became a nuisance to my underwear. He nearly blew my head off with pleasure.

'It's even better when I do that with my tongue,' he said.

I was gasping with horror at the whole notion of what he was suggesting when he kissed me long and hard on the mouth, then walked off, leaving me for dead. If he could use his tongue that well for activities other than mouth-kissing, maybe he was on to something. He was. And six weeks later he showed me.

My reverie was broken by a familiar roar, and I

realised that my car had pulled up outside the house. By the time I got downstairs, Mull was at the door.

'Wow,' I said, 'an hour and a half early *and* delivered in person, an honour indeed. Sorry to be a bit mean, but is this going to cost me any extra?'

'You're a terrible woman, d'ya know that?' he said, shuffling from foot to foot. 'I just thought a breath of fresh air would do me good, that's all.'

'Come in and I'll get you a cup of coffee and a cheque,' I said.

'Ah no no, sure you can fix up with me again.' He was still shuffling. Then he spotted Barry coming down the road and his eyes lit up. 'The very man. I'll see you soon, Leo, take care.'

My heart sank. I stood in the doorway and watched the two of them have a laugh, then reach into their pockets and exchange the contents. I walked back into the house. By the time Barry arrived, I could barely keep my anger in check.

'You sold him some dope, didn't you? *Didn't* you, Barry?'

'It's nothing, Leo,' he said, 'I just gave him half of what I had. Don't look at me like that. Jesus, anyone would think I was *dealing* the way you're going on.'

'What exactly is the difference, Barry? I saw money change hands.'

'Well I'm hardly going to give it to him for free when I had to pay for it in the first place, am I? I mean, what kind of eejit would I be if I did that?' He gave a shrug of the shoulders and a half laugh. Another time, this would have melted me and dispersed the tension. Another time, I would have told myself to loosen up and not make a mountain out of the proverbial mole hill.

Another time.

I started to tremble. 'How would it look for me if you got busted for selling dope? It's against the law for a start, in case you hadn't noticed.'

'Oh, and you're always on the right side of that, are you?'

I ignored the taunt.

'Do you really think anyone would say, "Ah sure, it doesn't matter, he wasn't charging extra, he wasn't making any money on it, so that's not really dealing", *do you*? I don't mind you smoking some now and again, but I'm not having anything else. Do you hear me? Do you, Barry?'

He gave me a withering look. 'So you don't mind me breaking the law smoking the stuff, just don't pass on any to my friends, is that it?' Then, after a dramatic pause, he added, 'You know, you can be one stuck-up cow when you want to be, Leo. Do you know that?'

I could feel tears beginning to sting my eyes. Everything was falling apart. How had we come to the point where we couldn't even have a civilised row? We just had to hurt each other, chalk up scores. Over and over again the horrible realisation hit me that I didn't trust Barry any more. So how, then, could I say that I loved him? But like every other time that this had happened, I sidestepped.

'Not now,' I thought. 'There's no time for this now, I've got to go do a job.' I steadied my breathing. 'We'll settle this when I get back,' I said, and went upstairs to finish packing.

Fifteen minutes later, and three hours ahead of schedule, I sped towards the motorway. I couldn't wait to get out of Dublin, away from my home. And I didn't relish the thought of returning to face the mess that I'd left behind. And it would be the same mess, still there, still waiting for me.

But life is full of multiples. It's never just one problem, one mess. Half a mile from my house, I passed the flat in which Tom O'Neill lived his other life, with a young woman soon to have his fourth child. Her name was Mary Ryan, and by all accounts she was a nice, hardworking type, with an unfortunate penchant for older, attached men. The same could have been said of Tom's wife, Annette. Well, there was something simple I could do about this one. I stopped the car by a postbox and put in the slimmer of the two envelopes. This was as much information as Annette O'Neill needed to confirm her suspicions, just. Everything else would come out in the mix eventually, but for now this was all she really needed to know. By the time any further revelations happened, I would be back in town and on hand. And if Annette's marriage was as full of arguments as my own stormy home life, maybe she was better off shot of it. I watched the envelope disappear into the green box. One problem half solved, the other still looming large. Barry.

So I did what I always do when faced with a situation that I just don't want to, or cannot, deal with – I stuck my head firmly in the sand. The knot in my stomach told me that I wouldn't get away with it this time. This one would just rest awhile on the back-burner, biding time till ambush. But it's always worth a shot.

'First things first,' I said aloud. As always, the convenience of first things first.

# FIVE

I made a mess of it. I didn't drive straight through town and out the other side to Kildare. I was feeling sorry for myself and so I allowed an invisible tracking beam to lure me to the family home. I suppose I wanted to feel safe. This was a ridiculous notion if family, and particularly parents, were to be involved. They're bloodhounds. And mothers, above all, can smell trouble and intrigue at a thousand paces. It was a risk I was willing to take. At least I'd get a cup of tea. Sympathy would be optional.

When was I going to stop this, I wondered, running home to Mammy any time anyone looked crooked at me or said 'Boo'? Maybe I would never stop, maybe we never do until our parents are no longer there and we've taken over that mantle with our own children. I had to stop this line of thinking. Next I'd be suggesting babies to Barry, as the ultimate commitment and adhesive. And I've seen enough in my profession to know that this doesn't work. Anyhow, I thought bitterly, you have to actually have sexual intercourse to get pregnant. Or at least most of the time that's true.

The driveway was empty, which probably meant that the Street men and Anne were out. My mother drives as little as possible, by request of the rest of humanity. Her motoring skills, if they could be termed such, are at best skittish, at worst highly dangerous. She's usually at her worst. The only driving that she's good at is the kind that leaves her family around the bend; here, when she's on form, she excels. I would take my chances.

I rattled through my enormous bunch of keys until I located the appropriate one for my childhood home. I made the usual mental note to check each of these soon – I couldn't believe that they all still filled a function. Nobody could need that many keys, it stood for too many locks in a life. Lately, I had detached my own house key so that I would only annoy myself once a day with the enormous bunch, when I was unlocking the office. Psychologically, it was probably a wrong move, in that it associated the annoyance with work.

I pushed the heavy door and called, 'It's me. Anybody home?' in the singsong voice we all keep for these moments. A lonely silence answered. With a sigh, I loped into the dining room where we'd laughed last night. The only traces of a party were my mother's birthday cards on the mantelpiece. I flicked through them – Barry, Gran, the lads and their wives, Lucy and a special handmade one from Dominick and Mary (the 'r' in Mary was back to front). Last, but by absolutely no means least, was a beautiful card from Andy bloody Raynor.

This was life imitating life. When my mother was a teenager and had tried to date other boys, my dad would still knock about the house, taking my grandmother out to the pictures, or sitting giggling in a corner with her, reading the dirty bits from *Lady Chatterley's Lover*, a banned book at the time. My mother was doomed, and was bound to end up with him. Mind you, that was quite different, because my dad was obviously a far better man, and catch, than bloody Andy.

And if he could remember my mother's birthday, he definitely knew it was mine too. So where was my card? I knew that I was being unreasonable. After all, why should he remember my birthday, I never sent him a card on his – 14 August, as it happens. But I was really agitated. And because I was alone, I felt that I couldn't make any actual noise about it. I wanted to swear out loud, but was somehow embarrassed. Eventually I settled for lightly kicking the sofa and throwing a few cushions around. Then, feeling utterly childish, I headed for the kitchen.

'Jesus, Mary and Joseph, Leo, you frightened the life out of me.' My mother stood holding her hand to her heart. 'I didn't hear you come in. I was out in the back garden checking the slug and snail damage. You'd think they'd have the decency to wait the winter out. But no, bloody global warming has them gone rampant. I'm close to admitting defeat.'

'I thought you were doing the beer trap thing.'

'Yeah, they love that, and at least they drown happy. Unfortunately, your father has found my stash, and if he doesn't stop he'll be the biggest slug to die.'

'Oh God, I've just had a vision of his big, cheery, beery body lying in a huge saucer in the middle of the lawn. No daughter should have to go through that.'

'No, that's true. Sit down and I'll make us a nice cup of tea.'

Without looking, I pulled one of the chairs away from the kitchen table and was halfway to a seated position when something very sharp stuck into my thigh. I had disturbed Smokey Joe Street in the middle of his afternoon nap and he was having none of it. I stood, captured in his grip as he let off a huge yawn and flexed his claws once more, all the while keeping the one in my thigh in position.

'Get off me,' I said, swiping at him. He was unmovable.

'Can't you leave the cat alone and not be annoying him, Leo. There are plenty of other chairs in the kitchen.'

I gingerly removed his weaponry from my leg and limped off to the opposite side of the table.

'Trust you to take his side,' I muttered.

'Now, now, who's in bad form,' she cooed, delighted with herself. The bloodhound had captured the scent. I changed the subject.

'I see you got some lovely birthday cards. Even one from Andy Raynor. I didn't know you two were so pally.'

'Oh yes, he keeps in touch. He's a great lad isn't he, and a credit to his family. I was always sorry that yourself and himself never made a proper go of it. And he's doing very well now, you know.'

'Yeah, I'm sure that according to him he is. Anyway, if he was that keen, he would have sent me a card too.'

'Didn't he?' she asked, genuinely puzzled. 'I thought he had.'

'Well he didn't.'

It would be good to get off this subject as well I thought, but I had nowhere to go. Worst of all, I could feel the beginnings of tears in my eyes.

'Any sign of that tea?' I asked lightly. Actually, I really wanted the tea now, and the cup would be useful to play with.

My mother casually placed a plate of digestives on the table, along with a jug of milk and a bowl of sugar, even though neither of us would be wanting the latter. Then came the cups and saucers and spoons. This was formal now, no mere mug in the hand. This meant interrogation. She sat beside me at the head of the table and said, 'Anyway, why are you lollygagging around here? I thought you had some sort of assignment in Kildare.'

'I do, but I was a bit early leaving, so I thought I'd call in.'

'And it's lovely to see you. You're sure there's no other reason?'

'Oh all right, I admit it, I had a row with Barry and I couldn't bear to be in the same house as him.'

She drew in a big breath. 'Don't you think it should have been the other way around? It is your house after all. Shouldn't he have been the one to leave?'

Still no sign of the actual tea. There wouldn't be any until the woman had satisfaction.

'You two seem to be having a lot of rows these days. Maybe it's time you had a break from one another.'

'Look, Mammy, I know you mean well, but this really is a matter for me and Barry.'

'That may be so, but you're the one who ended up on my doorstep today, which makes it a bit my business, wouldn't you say?'

'Oh for God's sake, anyone would think yourself and Daddy never had a row at all, the way you're going on.' I could have happily bitten off my tongue there and then.

'Oh, that's right,' she said, self-righteously, 'bring that up, do. The only major fight we ever had, and you have to remember it at every hand's turn.'

And it was big, that particular row.

A lot of family fights are minor in the extreme, just part and parcel of the everyday power play. If a party is involved, with everyone on show, there's often the tight command of 'family hold back', or the ultra casual, high-pitched instruction of 'whip the cream, dear', even if there's no cream in the house, dear. None of these count, they're generic to all families. My parents' 'row' happened on a day when I shouldn't even have been at home. I was off sick from school, aged eight or so. I awoke to the pleasant sound of my brothers being packed off, then drifted back to sleep. When the raised voices arrived in my head, I assumed I was dreaming. But as I came to, I realised that I was not. Whatever was going on downstairs was more than a little boisterous, and then it began to travel. And with it came the sound of crockery, plants and ornaments being thrown. A particularly ugly statue of a ballet dancer went flying to the plaintive cry of, 'Ah, me lovely dancer, now look what you've done,' from my mother, in spite of the fact that she was, as it later emerged, the throwee.

When an uneasy calm had settled, I chanced out of my sick-bed. My condition was not life-threatening, even though events unfolding around me probably were. I made my way to my parents' room, where I was greeted by the sight of my mother halfway into a flesh-coloured Eighteen-Hour Girdle. As I sobbed and staggered towards her, she sobbed and staggered towards me, with the tight, skin-toned garment clamped firmly around her knees. It was awesome.

She took off to her parents' later in the day, with a suitcase and the full intention of 'moving home'. Her father, Nobby, made her a cup of tea, then put her on a bus back to Clontarf, with words to the gist of, 'You've made your bed, now you can lie on it.'

All of this happened on a 14 February, and is still known in the family as The Saint Valentine's Day Massacre. The little ballerina didn't make it, she never danced again. And to this day, my parents have never said what the row was about.

So, if Street history was anything to go by, I was on to a loser here. I should drink my tea and leave. I planned to, if my mother ever parted with the brew, which had to be tar by now. I didn't care. I had come for tea and I wasn't about to leave without it. Or the lecture that my mother was now bound to give me.

'There's no need to go biting my head off, young lady. All I can say is that it doesn't suit some people to drink, if this is what happens to them the following day.'

She reached for the teapot; suddenly there was hope.

'And I know I'm only your mother, and that it's none of my business and I'm not supposed to interfere. But for now I'll make it my business. And all I'll say is that you're very pale, you're obviously not eating, and you're obviously not happy, and if that's the case then it's time to make some tough decisions.'

She actually began to pour.

'Barry's not the worst, don't get me wrong. But I do honestly think that you could do better.'

I wasn't sure if this was the end of the lecture, but

I grabbed the tea anyhow, poured in the milk and drank it gratefully.

'I'm sorry to be such a misery guts,' I said. 'I shouldn't be taking things out on you. And I'll bear the advice in mind.'

'Oh sure, I know you'll go your own way no matter what,' she said, playing up the maternal despair. 'You're impossible.' She sniffed while she thought about this, then added, 'A bit like meself, I suppose.'

We were both smiling as the others started to arrive home. But as Anne, Lucy and my dad made themselves comfortable, I made my excuses. This would shape nicely into one of my mother's 'what do *you* think Leo should do?' discussions, and I was guaranteed to be a blithering idiot by the end of it. I love my family, especially when they are in another place, along with their advice.

I wasn't sorry that I had visited. I was grateful for the love and attention that I had been given, I just couldn't cope with any more of it. And I could rest easy in the knowledge that I would be their chosen subject over the next hour, if they weren't busy sorting out world peace, that is. It might even make Lucy vaguely happy that myself and Barry were having problems. I said my goodbyes, and hit the road with my ears burning.

# *SIX*

Motorways suit me, I like driving forwards. Besides, the bit of my brain in charge of going backwards, particularly around corners, doesn't always work. As a fairly direct result, parking can be a bitch. I could have taken a detour to settle my nerves, but that might have involved some of the above, so I just headed straight to the Wood estate. The course would kick off at 7 p.m. with registration and a getting-to-know-you session. That left time for a relaxing drink nearby beforehand.

A large picture of a policeman holding some sort of foolish box to his face appeared to one side of the road. 'Garda speed checks in operation in this area,' it announced. What a legend, what a *tip-off*. I mean, where's the fun in trying to capture wrongdoers if you've already told them what you're up to? In fact, what are the *chances* of catching them if you've already warned them? 'Yahoo Celtic Tiger,' I said, 'we're a great little country.'

Being part of Europe has improved the roads in Ireland no end, as lots of other signs tell you along the way. And although motorways look the same all over the world, we don't worry about losing our identity as a nation. For instance, the Irish version of the motorway has the added charm of inadequate signposts, just that bit too close to the exits. It's some sort of engineer's joke.

I was determined to pull all thoughts of Barry firmly out of my mind, which meant, of course, that I couldn't think of anything or anyone else. Nancy Griffith was singing on the radio about love and its inadequacies, and that didn't help.

Nice timing Nance, remind me to return the favour some time, sister.

And I had never noticed before how downright *suggestive* road signs can be. It must be admitted that not only was I still furious with Barry, I was also in a frustrated state. I realised that one of the things I really needed and missed was a good shag (or for that matter any kind of shag, good, bad or indifferent). And so the 'hard shoulder' became overly significant, and yes I would 'beware of soft verges', and as for 'concealed entrances', well, I was educated by the nuns and knew all about them and the trouble they cause. Another sign loomed with the advice 'prepare to merge'. Of course, this mythical shag (good, bad or indifferent) would not solve the problems between myself and Barry, but at least my carnal desires would not then be getting in the way and fudging issues. A small, hand-painted sign warned 'Beware of Bull' – sound advice at last and I would take it.

I often wonder what I might have been if I hadn't become a private detective. I'm fairly unaccomplished at most other practical things. On the office front, I can't type very fast, or accurately, for that matter. And I've no real idea what shorthand means, though I believe there are two kinds, which seems needlessly complicated to me. I'm a bit squeamish about blood, so a career in nursing would be a problem, although I've seen my fair share of it in the detecting game, as luck would have it. And if I had to listen to where the rest of the world was going on holiday every day I'd go mad with envy, so that rules out hairdressing.

When I started my training with Mick Nolan, I was terrible with names. I found them nearly impossible to remember, a fatal flaw for a PI, as any child of three could tell you. I would be so busy smiling and being friendly that I'd miss the name. Paying proper attention to the details was one of my first painful lessons from Mick. And he was without mercy. Having to earn money is a great discipline, so I quickly became adept at retaining information. I got good at it because I had to; the mother of invention and all that.

The cookery school, along with a small hotel, was situated at the gateway of the 1,500-acre estate. It would have been anybody's idea of the perfect country house with stables, were it not overshadowed by a magnificent eighteenth-century mansion half a mile up the winding driveway, surrounded by the best of Kildare pasture and a world-renowned stud. This was the seat of the Wood family, and had been for generations. I swung my trusty steed into the cobbled yard and got my bearings. It looked like rain again, so I decided to take shelter in the appropriately named Stables Bar and Lounge.

The only other time I'd encountered a bar in stables was in an American detective series on television. Our hero was in 'Oireland' on a case, calling everyone 'me laddo' and 'me bucko'. At one point he needed to use the payphone in a pub. It was about eleven o'clock in the morning, and the smoky joint was heaving with singing, happy, red-faced locals. The detective asked the red-haired leprechaun of a barman, 'Why are they singing?', to which he replied, 'Because they're Oirish.' All that was missing in this awful piece of hokum was a pig running through the place. I steeled myself for the worst.

A handsome little Jack Russell terrier lay on the steps outside, enjoying his tackle. He was having a great time, and if size really does matter, he had every reason to be pleased. He jumped to his feet and barked excitedly as I opened the door. In the distance I could see another, larger dog lying by the fire, so I said, 'There's a little fellow out here wanting to come in.'

'He's barred, and he knows it,' came the reply.

'Oh, right,' I said. I turned to the dog, 'Sorry little lad, you can't come in, you heard what the man said.'

With a kind of canine shrug, he flopped back on to the steps and resumed activities.

The voice belonged to the only customer in the bar, a grey-haired, craggy-faced man in his sixties.

'Are you sure he'll be all right out there? It's quite cold and I'm sure it's going to rain again soon.'

'That dog could buy and sell you twice over. I should know, he's mine. Perhaps you'd care to join me in a drink?'

'Fast work on a first date,' I laughed. 'Actually, I'd love one, but please, allow me.'

'I wouldn't dream of it, but you can get the next one. And don't worry, there will only be one more. Johnny, the same again for myself, and whatever this young lady is having. I'm Fergus Rush,' he said, extending his hand.

'I'm Leo Street,' I said, shaking it, 'and mine's a pint of lager.'

'You have an unusual name.'

'Yeah,' I said ruefully, 'both bits of it can be troublesome. My parents were so sure I was going to be a boy, they just chose one name. And when I didn't oblige, they improvised and called me Leonora, which they promptly shortened to their original choice. As for the Street end of things, well, you can imagine what wonderful laughs that gives rise to.' I raised my glass. 'Cheers,' I said, taking a gulp. 'Yeuch, the first mouthful is nasty, isn't it?'

'Indeed, but we soldier on. *Sláinte*. My family called me Gusty most of the time. But only one other person ever really used it.'

He had a handsome profile and deep blue eyes, and I thought I could imagine him as a ladykiller in his youth; tall, blond perhaps, with the same soft, deep voice and vaguely melancholic air.

He jerked himself back to the moment. 'I do

apologise, Miss Street, at my age the mind tends to wander unexpectedly. What bad and rude company I am. Are you here for the weekend course?'

'Yes. I'm hoping the others will be as handless as I am when it comes to kitchens. I've had disasters with simple things like boiling eggs, so "Weekend Entertaining, Part One" sounds very daunting. I'm good at opening tins and bottles though.'

'All good skills and not to be mocked,' acknowledged a smiling Fergus Rush. 'I've opened a few tins and bottles myself in my time, though in general I grow whatever I'm going to eat. And I'm a vegetarian, so that makes the hunter-gatherer thing that little bit easier.'

'I'd love to be a veggie, but I just don't have the imagination. I've tried and I keep ending up with a cutlet-shaped space on the plate where the meat would have been.'

'Well, in my own case, I found that I couldn't kill an animal if I'd reared it. I can be cruel to a carrot though.' He knocked back his whiskey and I ordered us another. 'Of course, it would be a healthy lifestyle, if I wasn't so fond of this stuff. Still, it can be a long old day without it.' A wistful look crossed his face again, and again he shrugged it off. He smiled quickly. 'Nearly off on my travels there.'

I felt comfortable in his company. Not all men

actually *like* women. Of the men I would encounter over the weekend, I already knew one who probably despised most of us, and unfortunately I was working for him. And now there was this lonely, captivating man who made me feel at ease. It was a disappointment when he stood and announced that it was time for him to go.

'Do forgive me, Miss Leo, I realise that you have not quite finished your drink, but when my head alarm goes off, I do really have to leave, as Johnny will testify. Your company has been a pleasure, and I hope we will repeat the experience over your stay. I am, if nothing else, a creature of habit, and can be found in the same places at the same times each day. *Bonne chance* with your course. And remember, Mrs Wood's bark is worse than her bite. Usually. Do call in if you are in my vicinity, I'm just over the river by the footbridge. Oh, and watch out for Mr Wood, he has an eye for the ladies, and he'll certainly notice a handsome one like yourself.'

I'm sure I never blush, but I felt a little flushed at the compliment. Of course, it could just as easily have been the pints and the fire, I told myself. He opened the door and whistled to the Jack Russell. 'Home, Number Four,' he said, and off they went.

I stayed on my stool by the bar. 'So, Johnny, Mr Rush lives on the estate?'

'Yeah,' he replied. 'Mr Wood's been tryin' to buy him out for years, but he won't budge. He inherited that land and a pair of leather shoes from Padre Reilly.'

'A priest?'

'Nah, a bachelor uncle, Pio. A lovely few acres. Pio was a bit depressed one day, so he took his favourite armchair out the back, arranged a kind of pulley system with fishin' tackle, attached one end to his shotgun and the other to his big toe. Then he sat in the chair, put his foot down and blew his head off. Ruined a great patch of cabbages. A lifelong pioneer, too, never touched a drop. Mr Rush says he always had to take them shoes off before comin' in here, because they just wouldn't cross the threshold of the pub. There's temperance for ya, what?'

'And is Mr Rush married?'

'Nah. I hear he was very sweet on Mr Wood's mother for a long time. They grew up together. But she married into the money when push came to shove. Herself and the husband were killed in a car crash years back. There was only Mr Alex left then. And himself and Mr Rush don't get on at all.'

I sat over by the fire to finish my pint. I love to watch the flames and think of nothing. Today, however, my mind was agitated. I began to wonder why I sometimes feel displaced and oddly lonely, even though I'm always surrounded by people. I meet new people all the time, and of course I observe many more. Often I know them quite well, but they've never met me. I love my family and I'm close to them. I love Barry, and I think I'm close to him. Yet I feel hollow a lot of the time. It's not something I'm sad about. In fact, if anything, I'd describe my life as a happy one. I just sometimes wonder if I should feel more, or think more, or have theories and opinions about what happens in my life. Am I just too straightforward? But then, how could I be anything else?

I deal in the straightforward. People want a straight answer from me, usually to a simple question – 'Is my husband/wife/lover having an affair? Did a client cheat the company of insurance money? Where is my missing son?' They want a fact. Facts. Someone once said, 'A fact stands by itself.' Yes, I believe it does. And that's what I work with. And I don't spend lots of time pondering on great universal or philosophical questions, I'm just too busy getting on with it. And I'm sorry if all I have are small answers. That's my particular bankruptcy, and I'm happy with it. Most of the time. I also have an ability that I enjoy – I can switch off, blank my mind, disengage, then pick up where I left off, with or without the baggage of what I've just been through. But not today, obviously.

As I made my way toward the main body of the school, I collided with a tall, slim man, dressed in an immaculately crumpled linen suit topped by a full-length cashmere coat. We muttered our apologies. 'Very smooth,' I thought. As I entered the school reception area, Mrs Victoria Knowles was reapplying her lipstick. It was a very dark red which matched her long, painted fingernails. I took a mental note of the time: 18:30 p.m., in case I needed to put it in my report. He could be 'the one'. Two slanted green eyes looked up from the compact mirror and acknowledged my presence. Her fine nose wrinkled disdainfully as I told her my name. There was obviously a very bad smell in the air that only she could sense. 'Must be me,' I thought.

'Just as well you're early,' she snipped, 'you're supposed to be a man. This puts the accommodation completely out of kilter. You probably can't share with one of the other men.' She paused, and I realised that this last statement was in fact a question.

'Ah, um, no, no,' I stuttered.

'A room of your own then. Mrs Wood is going to love you,' she smirked.

Maybe I wouldn't mind shopping this one after all.

# SEVEN

My earliest memory is this: Mammy, my brother Peter and me are sitting at the kitchen table eating beans on toast. And Peter has just thrown all of his back up. But it has happened so quickly that the beans are completely intact. The table is awash with them. And they look perfect. Good enough to eat. This is the only palatable puke story that I know. And beans on toast is the only meal I cannot mess up. It's also a great favourite of mine, which is just as well.

My grandmother always treated Peter to a 'mushroom egg' when we visited her. He was convinced that a special hen laid it. My mother gave up attempting mushroom omelettes, because no one could touch my granny's mushroom eggs in his eyes. Oddly enough, when Anne was pregnant, the baby would have nothing to do with mushrooms, and made her evilly ill any time she ate them. Lucy still won't eat fungi, saying that the very name explains it all.

Standing in the reception area of The Wood Cookery School, fortified with two pints of lager and toying with some mulled wine, I had high hopes of conquering many gourmet delights, and returning to amaze my friends and family. The rose-tinted view from the alcohol bridge. Reality is all the more crushing after the false hope of a few pints. A bit like Satan and all his empty promises, I thought. Actually, I'd be fascinated to hear a few of that lad's unempty ones, they're probably great.

I had plenty of opportunity to look over Victoria's desk. It was neat, but not obsessively so. And all of the notes on folders or jotters seemed business-related. The photographs on the wall were a slightly different matter. The magazine and newspaper spreads on the opening of the school were framed and in pride of place. I recognised various society luminaries, television presenters and a few politi-cians. Most of the photos of Victoria, according to the list of names below them, also featured an Adam

Philips, the elegant man I had run into outside. He was fast becoming my main suspect. Well, actually my only suspect, so far. There was also a rather unfortunate picture of a grumpy Harry, looking very fat and very drunk, which I'm sure he can't have been pleased about. I was delighted by it; to my mind it had captured something of my client's soul.

I was gratified to see that any plug holes I might have wanted to use were full and in cluttered corners, often hidden from view. I had guessed correctly on the camera option. A heavy Sellotape holder near the telephone would suffice for my listening equipment. So far, so good.

A dozen or so students of all shapes and sizes milled about the tastefully decorated room. A murmur of anticipation and the smell of spiced wine filled the air. I actually wondered if this would be one of my more enjoyable assignments. A huge man who seemed to be six months pregnant introduced himself as Con. Then we were joined by a frazzled-looking woman in her forties called Ciara, who like myself had had a jar earlier, probably a few of them by the look of her. We found ourselves staring at a young, punky woman in her late teens, and wondering what the hell she was doing here. She was gothic, in black and purple, matching make-up and piercings, and short spikey hair. From where we stood, I could see three earrings and a stud in each ear, and one diamond nose-ring. Bangles and necklaces jangled as she moved. She marched over and said sullenly, 'Since yer gawping at me, I might as well give ye a good look up close.' She gulped back the wine and grabbed another. 'Jaysus, my parents must be really pissed off with me to send me on an oul wrinklies thing. I've a good mind to get pregnant, that'd teach them. I'm Ciara, who're ye?'

And that was how Leo, Con and the two Ciaras became the Gang.

'Ciara,' I said, and they both looked at me. 'Junior. I have to ask, do those piercings hurt?'

'Nah. The only ones that are real are the ones in my earlobes. All the rest clip on. The nose stud is just wedged in.'

'I'd hate to think what sort of noise you make going through the metal detector at the airport.'

'Loud,' she chuckled, 'very loud. Drives my dad crazy every time.'

The Ciaras decided to interview some of the other students, to suss them out. They started with a couple who were gazing lovingly into each other's eyes. The woman was pregnant, though her bump was less impressive than Con's.

'I've been growing mine longer,' he confided.

When the Ciaras were satisfied, they returned, smiling, with the low-down.

'He's a New Man,' Junior reported, 'and so is she.'

'Mmmm,' said Senior. 'The New Man is a grand lad, but he could get under your feet a bit, I reckon.'

'They're joined at the hip, so there's a lot of "we" talk,' Junior said.

'You're very cynical for one so young,' said Con.

'I'm not so much cynical as realistic and advanced,' she corrected him. 'Blame it on the education system.'

'I'd love to be there when "we" don't want an epidural, and Eleanor is in the agonising throes of childbirth,' sniggered Senior. 'God love them both then.

'Whatever happened to the Utter Bastard, who treated you mean, kept you keen, and dumped you as quick as look at you if you even got the first syllable of the word commitment out?' mused Ciara Senior.

'Don't worry,' I reassured her, 'they're still out there, in abundance.'

I neglected to mention that I see a lot of the Utter Bastard in my line of work, along with his female equivalent, the Bitch From Hell. No one ever wants me to root around in a happy marriage; I see an underbelly of the whole arrangement that would put anyone off. Not that I've had to choose between being married or single, never having had anyone pop the question. Unless I counted Andy Raynor's teasing, and I didn't.

Our guru, Esther Wood, swept in with Victoria Knowles at her side. Esther was a tiny creature with pinched features and a remarkably small mouth. I had a vision of her having to cut up her masterpieces into child-size pieces to eat. Not pieces the size of a child, obviously, but pieces a child could eat. She was steered in my direction by her aide-de-camp.

'I do wish someone had informed us,' she twittered, though not in a canary, songbird kind of a way. No, somewhere to the right of vulture.

'I'm supposed to be a man,' I explained to the others. 'I really am sorry for the mix-up, Mrs Wood. Believe me, at this moment, no one is sorrier *not* to be a man than me.'

I could see from her eyes that she knew I was being cheeky, and she logged it in on some floppy disc in her brain. We would come back to this, I felt sure, and I would regret my slightly drunken bravado.

She clapped her exquisite little hands together and brought the meeting to attention.

'Ladies and gentlemen, welcome. We like to start our courses by giving everyone the opportunity to introduce themselves. I myself would like you all to meet my staff. By now, you will probably have met my administrator, Victoria Knowles. And this is Graham, my right-hand man and factotum in the kitchen.'

Out of nowhere, a moustachioed gnome with a huge, shiny face had appeared. He was decked out in a white apron which covered his ensemble of yellow shirt, check trousers and multicoloured bowtie.

'Just call me Toto for short,' muttered Con under his breath.

Graham helped his boss into her apron, and they sprang into the action of a well-oiled partnership.

'I'd also like to show what you'll be working on first thing tomorrow morning. So, if you'll all follow me into the school kitchen, I'll demonstrate how to make delicious brown bread. And this is how we will start every day.'

It was a magic show as she waved this and that ingredient in front of our eyes. With sleight of hand she mixed them in a hat or bowl or whatever, and then, hey presto, produced a loaf of bread. We even clapped.

By the time we got to the pub I was terrified. How would I remember all of those technical cookery instructions? I couldn't even fry an egg for Christsakes. *And* I had started off on a decidedly dodgy foot with the Boss, the *Cooko di tutti Cooki*, so she was bound to take plenty of notice of me. At least Adam Philips and Victoria Knowles were together in a quiet corner. Maybe they'd do something incredibly indiscreet and public and the day would be salvaged, though I didn't fancy the bookie's odds on that one. But you learn quickly in this business that people *do* actually do stupid things, at unlikely and regular intervals, so I positioned myself at a table with a good view of their nook. 'Well, Harry,' I thought, 'while there's wife there's hope.'

Con had gone to the bar and Ciara Junior was complaining loudly about her parents. 'At least I won't have to look at them or listen to them for days. Jaysus, that house is a head-wrecker.'

'You should live with my husband,' said Ciara Senior, 'then you'd know all about it. Making a holy show of me at every hand's turn. He has me a nervous wreck so he does. What about you, Leo, are you married or what?'

'It's an "or what" I'm afraid. I live with a fella, and I could happily murder him right now.'

'Men,' said Ciara Senior. 'Can't live with them, can't kill them and get away with it.'

Con caught the end of this as he arrived back from the bar.

'Surely it can't be that bad,' he said, sympathetically.

'Well it is, actually,' said Senior. 'Do you know what the latest is, and believe me this is only one in a very long line. He has a carport business, you know, building shelters for vehicles and what have you. He took out an advertisement in the local paper recently to drum up business. And it said, "Average erection three days. No fuss, no bother". Fucking eejit!'

I honestly thought I would be sick from laughing. Even Ciara Senior eventually had a chuckle, after calling us the greatest shower of bastards she'd ever met. 'Fucking eejit,' she kept saying, 'the big fucking eejit.'

Victoria and Adam were not having quite as good a time by the look of things. She was animatedly explaining some major point to him, and he was comforting her, an arm around her shoulder. Every so often she would hold her head in her hands, and he would whisper in her ear. I noticed that her long nails were now painted a deep pink, and wondered if that was what she did all day long.

I had messed up here. I had been so caught up in the tangent of Weekend Entertaining that I hadn't brought along any listening equipment to the pub. I could clearly feel Mick Nolan's hot breath on the back of my neck, even though he was away somewhere in the ether. His ghostly voice barked, 'First rule of surveillance, Street, watch *and* listen. *First rule!*'

This probably is the first rule, it's very hard to tell. His first rule was a splendidly fluid thing, depending on the day. It could be invisibility, tact, guile, or simply good walking shoes. I was ashamed of myself, so basic a mistake, so amateur, so unnecessary.

I looked back at my quarry and wondered if she was trashing her husband. And if she was, I hoped that she wasn't holding back. I had a vision of my own Barry Agnew.

'The fucking eejit,' I said aloud, 'the big fucking eejit.'

And the Gang burst into laughter once again.

'Sweet Jesus, look what just walked in,' said Ciara Junior. At the door stood one of the most handsome men humanity had ever laid eyes on. He was tall, tanned and blond, and he ambled to the bar with the slow grace of someone who enjoyed being watched and admired. By his side was a ratty, bow-legged little man whose face was host to a permanent sneer. We later learned that the God was Alex Wood and the Rat was his stable manager, Richard Cooper.

'Christ-on-a-crucifix, he's gorgeous,' continued Ciara. 'I bet he's a fantastic shag.'

I noticed Con wincing with every syllable out of her mouth, and for a moment I wondered if he was gay. Then he said, 'Actually, maybe this is a good time to let you all know that I'm a priest, so . . .' he trailed off.

Junior sniggered and said, 'Better tone down my language then. Don't want to roast in hell any longer than I have to. I'm already booked in for a fair few decades according to the mammy.'

'Oh no, no, it's just, you know, the religious references. I don't want anyone having to watch the old p's and q's around me or anything like that. Believe me, there isn't much that I won't have heard before anyway.'

Ciara Senior stood up and tucked her bag under her arm.

'Are you off?' I asked.

'I am in my arse,' she replied. 'I'm off up to the bar to buy us all one for the road, and, more importantly, to get a good close-up of that delicious man.'

'I'll come and help you carry everything,' said Junior, leaping to her feet.

'Ladies,' I said, 'I don't want to put a damper on things, but if you look closely at that same delicious man's left hand, you'll see that he's married. And therefore technically unavailable. Amn't I right Con?'

'Oh yes, Leo, that would be my understanding of the situation also.'

'Ah yeah, yeah,' said Ciara Senior, 'but a vegetarian can still smell sausages.'

Alex Wood waved a desultory 'hello' in the direction of Victoria and Adam. She beckoned, anxiously, for him to join them, but he didn't. Then the front door burst open and a noisy gang of young, sporty types invaded the pub. They surrounded their hero and it became apparent that these were the boys and girls of the stables. The Ciaras returned, a little crestfallen.

'We only got near him for two minutes before that shower arrived,' said Senior. 'He's got this fabulous posh voice, very Anglo.'

'And he smells gorgeous,' added Junior. 'Red alert, he's coming this way.'

As he passed our table Alex Wood smirked and said, 'Hello there, students. Not the worst batch I've seen of Esther's by any means.' Then he was gone, in a waft of Armani. I stole a glance at the others and saw that each one of us, save Con, was shyly looking at the floor, content in the knowledge that he'd actually been referring to only one of us. Beautiful people have this power.

We all make associations in life. Vicks Vapour Rub reminds me of lying in bed as a child, with a piece of brown paper on my chest, reading *The Secret Garden*. Every time I turned a page, I crinkled, and was enveloped in the reassuring, medicinal aroma. A song, a taste, a smell, a word will unlock a memory. Oddly enough, when I smell Armani now, I don't think of Alex Wood, I think of Fergus Rush.

Victoria Knowles stood, put on her coat, kissed her consort goodnight and left the pub. Adam joined the noisy stable rabble. I thought there was no real point in following either of them, which was a relief as I really didn't fancy a spot of surveillance, the shattered state I was in. Being tired and a little smashed always relegated work to a low position on my list of priorities. It was a flimsy excuse, and I knew it.

I shuddered to think of Mick Nolan relentlessly picking holes in my reasoning here. For starters, it suggested an assumption that *if* Victoria Knowles was having an affair, it was with Adam Philips. Dodgy assumption. And convenient. In fact, I had no proof of this. He was someone I had seen her with and so he was certainly under suspicion. It might mean everything, something or plain old nothing. But without definitive proof I could assume neither, and shouldn't, according to the rules. Mick would be on a high horse of indignation over this one. Never presume, *prove*. I was for it, whenever he chose to strike.

'So how about you, Leo?' asked Ciara Senior.

'Sorry,' I said, 'I was a million miles away.'

'What do you do?'

'Oh, boring really, an office job.'

'Any kids?'

'Oh no. To be honest I can hardly look after myself. I have a few godchildren, mind you, though why anyone would make me the moral and spiritual guide to their child is beyond me.'

'What about yourself, Con, you got any?' asked Junior.

'Any what?' he wondered.

'Kids?'

'You cheeky rip, Ciara,' said Senior, cuffing her lightly on the arm. 'Well, do you anyway?'

'Ah, no, no,' he laughed.

'Not as yet anyway,' continued Senior. 'Well, God is good, or so they say. A friend of mine was in a café recently when a Catholic priest walked in, and some young fella stood up and waved at him and said, "Daddy, Daddy, I'm over here." No one knew whether it was true or not. But I have to admit that my friend did say that she thought she'd vomit she was laughing so hard.'

'That's not right though is it, laughing like that,' said Junior. If Con thought he was off the hook he was wrong. She couldn't resist one more joke. 'It's those priests' families that I feel sorry for. You know, their sons and daughters.'

The Ciaras cackled, and Con shifted awkwardly in his chair.

'Take no notice of them, Con,' I said, 'they're wicked women.'

'Ah sure, it's all part of the territory these days,' he said.

The Ciaras let out another peal of laughter and Con became an even deeper shade of red, so I intervened.

'Leave him alone, ye bullies, he's only a man.'

'So are you this weekend,' said Con, beaming.

Touché.

The bell sounded for 'time' and we gathered ourselves to go across the yard to our new and temporary homes. Outside the sky was clear and black, chocolate-box stars twinkled, and all was good. Ciara Senior sniffed the air and pronounced it as crisp and dry as a gin and tonic.

Because of the 'unfortunate problem' with my gender, I had been awarded my own room in the genteel hotel attached to the cookery school. It was probably the smallest one they could find, by way of punishment, but I loved it. The walls were painted a light cream, and decorated with some tasteful, original landscapes and paintings of horses. The furniture was plain, and the linen on the double bed was sparkling white. It also had its own en-suite bathroom. I was quite sure that I would be charged full whack for my extra night, that of the Spring Ball, but this was a legitimate business expense, so the pleasure was all mine.

Back in my solo room the world was still waiting for me. I checked my phone messages. Harry Knowles was ranting on about progress; I'd deal with that last. Barry's voice on the Dublin answering machine said, 'Yello. Not here. You know what to do.' I did. A bland 'settling in all right, hope all is well there, talk to you tomorrow.' I hung up, realising that I was glad I'd got the machine and not the man, it was what I'd been hoping for. No such luck with Harry.

'Well?' he barked.

'Mr Knowles, I've explained to you before that these things take time. Normally a case like this would need weeks, sometimes months. We really would be steeped in luck to get anything at all in one weekend. And that's if there *is* anything to be discovered.'

'Don't tell me you've seen nothing at all, and the money you're on.'

'For what it's worth, your wife has been in the

pub with a gentleman named Adam Philips for a good part of the evening, but that could mean anything. There was no specific action that would prove an affair.'

'Fucking bitch,' he said, and hung up. I wasn't sure if he meant me or his wife.

# EIGHT

Mornings arrive far too early, that is the rule. It's not my favourite rule, if you can have one that's a favourite, they being made to be broken and all that. And this was the morning that I would be found out. I cannot cook. I might as well stand up and declare, 'My name is Leo Street and I am an alcoholic.' And it doesn't matter how many times you tell yourself that this is just a panic attack, a *hangover*, the fear abides. Especially when you've pissed the head honcho off, or in this case the head honchette. You try all the cheap tricks. 'God, please, even though I don't believe and all that, and I know you know that I don't, could you just see your way to letting this one thing through, in the form of your choice. I know I'm in no position to ask for favours right now, and I can't afford to be picky, and I'm not, I promise, but if you do just this one thing for me, I promise I'll try to be a better person.' Who's zoomin' who? Still, it worked for the Leaving Certificate at the end of Secondary School, not counting maths.

I was here for a purpose, however, and couldn't allow for any more diversions. I placed a tiny microphone in the Sellotape holder by the telephone on Victoria Knowles' empty desk. This was voice-activated and would record the day's events here. I didn't risk leaving my bag with the video camera, in case she noticed a strange item and opened it up to look inside. I would plant it there, with her permission, later in the morning.

We gathered in the huge school kitchen. Con was all shiny and pink, and the Ciaras were quiet. Junior wore dark glasses and Senior was *very* perfectly made up. The others coughed and shifted and whispered to themselves in nervous anticipation. Diarmaid, the New Man, was shooshing his wife, Eleanor, on to a stool. One woman took a puff of a blue inhaler. A bright February morning sun streaked in through the large windows and bounced off the white and chrome presses and worktops. Ciara Junior was busy removing her jewellery.

When she was done, there was a good two pounds in weight of sparkling metal to the side of her place. We were called to order by the precise Esther Wood, who wore a red striped apron and a self-satisfied grin. Our aprons were plain white. Beside her stood a beaming Toto, and on a blackboard behind her was The Legend of Brown Bread.

'Just follow your instructions, remember my little demonstration last night, and you'll be fine,' she said. 'And bear in mind that bread-making is a bit of a knack, so don't be too worried or disappointed if you don't succeed first time. It's not a competition or an exam, so enjoy yourselves.'

Now we were all *determined* to succeed. Then, rather like an invigilator, she said, 'You may begin.'

I turned to Con. 'Should we not all just have a cup of coffee and discuss how best to tackle this?' I said. 'I mean, it's plain foolishness not to plan ahead. I know I can talk a great loaf of brown bread, and sure that's half the battle.'

'Get stuck in,' he warned. 'The Boss is coming your way.'

I flung all the dried stuff into a bowl and looked over at Ciara Senior. She was doing some sort of mixing action with her fingers, so I tried a bit of that too. It felt lovely, and I thought I looked pretty convincing. Suddenly a voice was *on* me saying, 'You'll have to put your liquid in at some stage, so stop prevaricating and get on with it.' I jumped two feet in the air and scattered flour everywhere. *Jesus*, how did she creep up on me like that? I sloshed in the water. 'Too much,' she announced and moved on.

It took me several years to get all of the dry bits wet. I decided that I would be a hand mixer, so the main problem was trying to get the liquid cement off my fingers. When I eventually persuaded the gloop off my digits and on to the floured surface, it attached itself to the sides of my hands. In fairness, there was a certain amount in my hair too, and on my face. Finally, and I was the last to achieve it, my 'loaf' was ready for the oven.

'Bravely fought,' said Con. 'There was a time there when I didn't think you'd make it.'

'It was never going to take me alive,' I said.

As we cleared up, the smell of baking bread filled the air, and everyone began to smile and chat. I even began to feel quietly confident that my first culinary experiment would turn out well.

Then my mobile phone rang.

Esther Wood whipped around and snapped, 'Whose is that?' For one mad moment I considered lying by ignoring the sound and thereby pretending it wasn't mine. But I knew she'd ferret it and me out, so I owned up. I wondered how much more she could possibly hate me, and the answer was none.

'I am *so* sorry,' I found myself saying for the second time in twelve hours. 'I didn't realise I'd left it on. I promise it won't happen again.'

'Miss Street, are you here to take my course or to conduct business? I expect full attention from my students, and you all quite rightly expect the same from me in return. Your disruption shows a complete lack of respect for all here. Please ensure that it does not happen again.'

I located the vile item, switched it off and stuffed it in my pocket. Bloody technology. Junior was delighted. 'This is feckin' brilliant,' she laughed, 'normally I'm the one in trouble.'

As we continued to clear away the detritus of the morning session, I made a note that black was not the ideal colour to wear when working with flour. I was covered in the stuff. It didn't seem to matter at all that I was wearing a protective apron à la Esther and Toto. As if by osmosis, the ingredients had managed to creep inside, as well as all around, that protection. I began to wonder why no one had yet invented a full bodysuit apron, a kind of drive-in arrangement, with in-built balaclava – a copyright opportunity, Leo, maybe the weekend would not be a waste after all.

I popped out to the reception area while there was a lull in the proceedings. 'Would you mind awfully if I left my bag here?' I asked Victoria Knowles. 'It's just getting in the way inside, and I don't seem to need anything in it. Makes you wonder why you carry around so much useless stuff, doesn't it?' She laughed, ever so slightly, and told me to put it anywhere to the side of her desk, by the coat-stand. Perfect. As I leaned down to place it pointing upwards, I pressed 'record' and left it to do the work for me.

I returned to the kitchen just as Esther wiped 'The Legend' from the blackboard and began to outline the rest of the day's endeavours. My sinking heart realised that from now on we were expected to make brown bread from memory, a cruel and unusual practice. And it was time to inspect the first loaves. They were a veritable diaspora of breads – tall, squat, pale, burnt. We were all thrilled with them. My own looked and smelled quite credible. By way of reassurance, Esther Wood said, 'If you don't want them for lunch yourselves, the stable hands are always scrounging, and they will eat anything. But well done nonetheless.' I wondered if I was included in the praise. 'Of course, you may wish to have your breads later, and I can recommend some of the splendid home produce available from our own farm shop, which you'll find near the Stables Bar and Lounge.'

Our next assignment was a visit to the herb garden. As we filed out through the hall, Victoria Knowles chatted and laughed with a stable girl, whippet-thin and probably as fast, obviously on that early lunch scrounge. Oh to have discovered her naked on her desk astride an elegant, and equally naked, Adam Philips, then I could dispatch the case and the cookery course with one mighty blow. And perhaps a little sexual voyeurism would do me some good.

The visit to the gardens held no fear for me. Gardening was somewhat hereditary in our family, along with shortsightedness, bad ears, and a propensity to being overweight. My maternal grandmother, Mary Ellen of the Mass cards, or El Dorado to my dad, had a green thumb during her more active years, though my late grandfather, Nobby, did all of the heavy-duty labour. They grew everything from cabbages to tulips, but I also remember being sent to the corner shop for lettuce and scallions on many an occasion.

'Nobby's only got rubbish out there,' she would say. To this day I don't think she knows that he was the shop's sole vegetable supplier.

The beds of plants were divided geometrically by

brick walkways and low lavender hedges. I correctly identified a half dozen herbs, much to the amusement of the class and the amazement of Esther Wood. They were very common ones and I really thought nothing of it. I grew most of them for pleasure as plants in my own little patch. But I could see her looking at me every so often, suspicious of a piss-pull. She told us not to worry if we couldn't see summer favourites at this time of year, the school had a wide selection of frozen herbs for us to use. This was where myself and the herbs parted company. In Dublin I grew them for their beauty and their smells, and the insects that loved them too. But cooking with herbs meant a packet of Paxo parsley and sage stuffing to me.

Con was mulling over the idea of setting up a herbal bed in the back garden of the parish house. It would be therapeutic for him, as well as supplying fresh herbs for his soon-to-be revamped kitchen, and it would get the older priest out of the house.

'Knowing him, though, he'll think I've put him on a hard labour detail,' he said. 'His family were very well off, and always had servants and gardeners to do all of the work. He went off to Glenstal Abbey in Limerick to be a monk, but he had to leave because he couldn't take the asceticism or the plain habits they had to wear. And he hadn't a note in his head, so he couldn't join their famous choir for diversion. He still gets his clerical suits handmade by a very well-respected tailor in Dublin.'

We rubbed our fingers on rosemary leaves and smelled. Then lavender. It was a scratch and sniff paradise. And you could eat just about everything in it too.

A volley of yelping was followed by the arrival of No. 4 and Fergus Rush. The dog scampered over the paths and back, and then jumped up and down and up and down demanding attention until Esther patted him on the head. Then, unbelievably, she gave him a little chase. As she turned to speak to Fergus, No. 4 fixed his sights on me and it was my turn to do the running.

Esther Wood was a different woman, smiling and chatting amiably to my new friend. And when he offered some pleasantries to me she didn't even flinch. She was at ease. Then it dawned on me that she was probably just as nervous as her new recruits each time she started a course, and was determined to be one step ahead of whatever smartass posse fate might throw her way. In this case it had looked like me.

As we strolled back to our culinary theatre of dreams, I explained to the Gang that in order to make amends for the mobile phone incident and for being the wrong sex, it was imperative that I succeed on the course. And the only way this was going to happen was by cheating. So they would have to help me, and cover for me. There was some muttering about currying favour. I'd begun to notice that Con was a big man for the pun, and was waiting for a further comment about 'no surrender till we see the whites of their eggs'. Instead, Ciara Junior proclaimed, 'Mission Impossible'.

Sure enough, just before lunch we were treated to a tour through sauces. I'm convinced that when I'm frightened, or very nervous, I react like a skunk and give off an unpleasant smell. (At least I think that's what skunks do, I've never actually encountered one, barring myself.) Surely everyone could smell my fear that session. Too many bain maries and whisks and drizzling. And too many methods and variations to be followed with the same lists of ingredients. Since supermarket chiller cabinets are full of self-confessed homemade mayonnaises and the like, why not crack open one of those? Why waste two people's time by not buying those and spending hours making your own? This would not be a popular thesis here, a mere snowball in hell, so I kept it to myself.

Lunch, though, made me revise my theories. It was a selection of cold cuts and vegetables, as you might serve to your guests as you Weekend Entertained, Part 1, accompanied by the most ambrosial sauces I had ever tasted. I got a little carried away as I ate, thinking that if a mortal had made these, and she had before our very eyes, surely there was some hope for me. I understood there and then how and why people would seek oral gratification of this sort to sublimate other desires – it was bloody delicious, and it didn't answer back.

'That woman certainly knows her eggs,' said Con.

'Literally,' I agreed.

'You lose points for explaining my pun.' He laughed and piled some more food into his mouth. I resisted the urge to swear at a holy man. I would have lost even more points had I then tried an explanation of the mushroom egg, and how she couldn't possibly know that one. One of life's rich opportunities missed.

'There's no way Ralph deserves anything like this,' declared Ciara Senior of her husband.

'*God*, is that his name?' shrieked Junior, choking on her food.

'I know,' said Senior, 'is it any wonder he's a complete fucking eejit, lumped with that? We can't even shorten it. Mind you, one of the creeps he plays golf with calls him Rafe, so that makes him an even sadder bastard than my lad. It's a bit of a comfort, to know there's worse out there.'

'Ye're very harsh,' Con said. 'I don't think there's anything wrong with the name Ralph. I've definitely heard worse.'

'Me too,' I agreed.

'This would go really well with a nice bottle of wine, wouldn't it?' said Senior.

We all murmured in sad agreement. We knew, without asking, that such delights were for later. Besides, we needed to keep our wits about us for the long and torturous afternoon ahead.

We compared brown breads. Mine was a dense, nutty brick, with a slightly wet aspect and a great deal of chew. It was more or less edible. In a blind tasting, Con won the Little Homemaker prize. Runner up was Junior, with myself in third and Ciara Senior trailing the field, though not by much.

I excused myself for what was left of the lunch-break to take a walk around the estate. It was a perfect opportunity to catch up on business on the disgraced mobile. As I passed the desk in the entrance hall, I smiled sweetly at Victoria Knowles. I don't think she noticed, or cared. She was still nattering away with the stable hand. The girl was long and loose-limbed, with a twist of the gawky and a slice of class. I began to feel like the shortest person ever born.

I was looking forward to my brief jaunt around, snooping into how the other half live, all the while thinking that surely a lot less than half live like this, and brooding about my brown bread. Too much liquid she'd said, well, tomorrow *is* another day.

The air was as clear and sharp as a scalpel, and a pale magnolia sun shone an unexpected brightness on the countryside. The light was merciless, leaving everything it illuminated fragile and exposed. I felt as though every spot and blemish on my face was in sharp relief, and I thanked the god of concealer as I pulled my black jacket tighter around me. Angela had recently walked Mary in her buggy to the local supermarket. Mary's nose was streaming a virulent green mucus, for which she had earned the title Snot Goblin. By the time they reached the shop the child's face was clear; the cold had sandblasted it clean. This was such a day.

The stillness carried the sound of faraway thunder through the air. The ground shook as the rumble became louder and closer and I turned to see horses and riders approaching along the track by the side of the road. Both animals and mounts were magnificently confident, and in unanimous harmony of movement as they cantered by. Trailing them on a long leash was a very small, blond boy on a tiny white pony, gleaming and shimmering in the sunshine.

They too were invincible. No. 4 raced by.

I'd never really had much to do with horses in my life. As children we took a few lessons when we went on holidays to Kerry, always with a man called Martin who would ask, in an almost impenetrable accent, 'Have oo got deh riddem?' I've been told since that horses are dangerous both ends and uncomfortable in the middle, so I give them a cowardly wide berth. Lost in my reverie, I paid little attention to my phone messages, swung absently round the corner to the stables, and into the gaze of cornflower blue eyes.

'Ah, a yuppy,' growled the voice.

I stood rooted to the spot, a rabbit in the head-lights, struggling for breath and something pithy to say.

'What's up Doc?' I spluttered, and prayed for the ground to open and swallow me.

# NINE

Alex Wood held my gaze for what seemed like hours, but was in fact all of ten seconds. I felt a thin line of sweat break out above my lip, and the spot on my chin began to throb. Without looking away, he spoke into the walkie-talkie in his hand. 'Alex to Richard, Alex to Richard. Dick, tell Amanda that she's letting Loco run away with her. I'll follow along to the gallops and watch from there. Then I'll take Reckless out. See you back at the office at 16:00 hours. Over and out.' He looked me over, shamelessly. I wished I was wearing my lovely birthday outfit, as opposed to feeling that I was in my original birthday suit.

'So which of my wife's charges are you?'

'Leo Street,' I stammered.

'Ah yes, the one who should have been a man. What a shame that would have been.'

I was now certain that I'd begun to smell, skunk-like, from my armpits. My hair hung limp against my neck, and my skin prickled and throbbed with anxious embarrassment.

'I'm Alex Wood.'

'I know.'

Again I squirmed for an eternity. Then, 'If I were you, I'd head back double-quick time for your afternoon session. My wife cannot abide sloppy time-keeping. Amongst other things. By the way, you've got some sort of dough in your fringe. I'd eat it, but I've just had an early lunch.' He turned deftly on the heels of his well-polished riding boots and was gone. I was a jelly of excitement and embarrassment. But *shit*, late for class, she'd have my guts for garters.

I stumbled awkwardly into a half run, but hadn't gone far when I heard raised voices and a dog barking excitedly. I paused to look back and saw Fergus Rush and Alex Wood in a heated argument. Angry gestures painted a picture, but the sound was indistinct. I thought I heard a 'just leave him alone' from Alex, followed by 'you're being plain pig-headed and you know it' from Fergus. I had no time to wonder, as my palpitating heart reminded me in no uncertain terms. I was breathless and uncoordinated as I rounded the corner to the school door, and again collided with the elegant Mr Philips. He was accompanied by Victoria Knowles and the hungry stable girl.

'We really must stop meeting like this,' he said, smoothing another immaculate ensemble back into place. I muttered an apology.

'You're in luck,' Victoria Knowles told me, 'she's on the phone.' Saved by the Alexander Graham Bell.

Of course, now I was stuck between a rock and a hard place. I needed to follow my principal players, and yet I really needed to get back to my class. Mick Nolan started to give me a very hard time about it being time to earn my fee, so I knuckled down. Or rather, I bent over to tie my bootlaces – not the *most* stylish move ever, but functional.

Then one of the most unfortunate things that could happen did – they noticed me.

'Are you all right there?' shouted Adam Philips. 'Did you fall?'

'Eh, no, I dropped my bag that's all. You just carry on with whatever it is you're doing.'

Oh *brilliant* Leo. 'You just carry on, don't mind

about me watching your every move.' Why not even suggest a little something? A shag on the bonnet of his sports car would be handy; there'd even be enough time to run in and get the video to record it, from the bag that you very clearly do not have with you. When your mouth is quicker than your brain, you've got a problem. That goes for most of life, and all of a private investigation.

Mercifully, they'd gone back to their business, and had stopped paying attention to me. By now Adam Philips had to be convinced that I was the clumsiest woman he had ever, literally, run into; so much for melding into the background. After some quick kisses and goodbyes, they went their various ways. I was straightening up as I heard the stereophonic 'Yoohoo' behind me. I turned to see Diarmaid and Eleanor returning.

'A working lunch,' Diarmaid announced. 'We like to take as much exercise as we can at the moment, don't we?' He kissed the tip of his wife's nose, which crinkled as she giggled.

'Yes we do,' she agreed, and giggled again.

I noticed that they had both changed their clothes, so I was in little enough doubt as to what kind of exercise had been involved. At this stage it hardly mattered, she couldn't get any more pregnant. I envied them their rude health.

I sidled back into the classroom behind them, suddenly glad that I hadn't changed my clothes for any reason. It might not look good if I appeared to be the class rebel *and* the kinky gooseberry at a pregnant couple's sex sessions. I took my place just as Esther Wood returned. Toto gave me the eye.

Con was mesmerised by Eleanor's dress. And rightly so. It was a flowing diaphanous gown, covered in tiny particles of mirror. Every time she moved she created a mirrorball effect on all of the surfaces in the kitchen, including us.

He grinned and rubbed his massive belly. 'That's my trouble,' he said, 'I don't make enough of my figure. I could carry that dress.'

This afternoon our mission was aioli, a garlic mayonnaise, and really we had no choice but to accept it. A thin veil of silence draped over the kitchen as we each perspired into our concoctions. Beside me, Con was humming 'Food, Glorious Food', whether consciously or unconsciously I didn't know. The Ciaras were a study of concentration, punctuated by soft utterances of coarse dismay. I made out three 'shites' and a 'bollox' during Junior's initial oil drizzle, underscoring Senior's gentle 'gotcha ya fecker.'

Being a detective ought to have given me a head start with cookery, at least in terms of organisation.

As a detective, you must plan your day in order to get the optimum amount of information. For good measure, a shrewd guess never goes far wrong, a little like 'salt and pepper to taste'. Then the information should be organised in a logical way. And *then* you must be prepared for the rogue element of the unexpected, people being unpredictable and all. So, for instance, I should be well able for cooking Chinese-style; the methodical preparation of all the ingredients beforehand, then the quick, calm cooking of the same. But no, I panic. It all happens too quickly. Like flash flooding, Chinese cuisine is flash cooking. I can even panic over a Chinese takeaway.

On the other side of the kitchen, a middle-aged man let out an anguished cry. 'It's curdling! I think it's curdling!' Esther and Toto rushed to his side. A curdle in a mayonnaise would be unlikely, I now know. There are plenty of other pitfalls, though. As far as the rest of it goes, I'm not sure if it's possible to reverse a sauce at the 'curdling' stage. I may have to learn that. I *can* tell you, from subsequent experience, that the oily stain from a botched hollandaise is a bitch to get out of a silk-mix blouse.

'Aioli Leoli' looked like those worthy handmade face creams in all of the health food shops: pots of Avocado and Ginger Mash (comfort food for tired faces), Strawberry Sherbet (the scintillating answer to dull and lifeless skin), Banana and Elderberry Fool (a soothing balm), or Rosemary, Honey and Hibiscus Tonic with Multivitamins and Ginseng (a zingy pick-me-up). They always sound so nutritious and delicious, it's a tough decision whether to smear them all over my body, or just scoff the lot. Worryingly, a lot of them have sell-by dates and should be stored in the fridge, so these accidents can happen.

'Oh, the old aioli is a tricky man,' said Con, glancing at my effort. 'Cross the road when you see that lad coming.'

'Belt up you,' I snarled, 'I'm beating it into submission.'

Toto and Esther had calmed The Curdle Man down. He looked around the room, nodding, to reassure us that all was well, he would survive. The group released a collective sigh of relief; no one likes to see a fellow pilgrim go under. By now we had started to recognise one another and swap names. Sadly, I hadn't needed any introduction, principally because of the mobile phone fiasco. The Curdle Man, we now knew, was Keith, a structural engineer. Next to him was a gaunt man by the name of Maolíosa. Translated from Irish, I think that means Bald Jesus. Our Maolíosa had a fine head of hair.

'I bet he's a vegetarian,' said Con.

'It's unfair to make that sort of an assumption

purely on looks,' I pointed out, 'but I think you might be right.'

'My mother always said that vegetarians had no get-up-and-go in them. She always thought it lessened a man somehow not to eat meat, or "mate" as she used to call it. Very much a "mate and two veg" woman, the mammy.'

It was hard to picture Con as a boy, or to think of him ever being smaller than he was now. Surely he was born huge. His mother must have been in a wheelchair for a month afterwards.

Esther and her familiar were gliding throughout the proceedings in a well-practised pincer-movement. They examined emulsions and cooed encouragement as they approached me as their apex. It seemed they'd been coming for me all my life. With a dull thud of the heart, I realised that I had forgotten the garlic. That's garlic, the ingredient that separates mayonnaise from *garlic* mayonnaise. Some fast thinking was required. Ironically, in all and many ways, Barry came to the rescue.

Part of the actor's obsession with life and work is made up of the parts they don't get. I have been dragged along to lots of theatre shows that Barry wasn't cast in, so that he could then bitch knowledgeably about them afterwards. One of these had a scene in which characters discussed their favourite dishes, and one favourite was an ironic venison chilli – the irony being that no chilli was involved at all. I decided to run it up the flagpole.

'An ironic aioli, you say?'

'Yes. Ironic,' I confirmed.

'Mmmm. And not simply, say, forgotten? A forgotten aioli?'

'Well . . .' I demurred.

Esther Wood turned around to make sure that she had her class's undivided attention. She had. Her eyes shone and I waited for the kill. Instead she gave an enigmatic half-smile and said, 'It's actually not a bad mayonnaise. I do, however, think that as an aioli it might benefit from some, oooh, delicious, satirical undertone.'

'Like garlic?' I suggested.

'Yes, why not, garlic might just do the trick. A nice try.'

'I think I'm going to need a little lie-down,' said Con. 'My nerves are in tatters.'

'Welcome to life on the Street,' I said. 'We're on the front line here.'

Ciara Junior was doing very well, but she didn't look too pleased about it. 'Well done. A very sophisticated aioli, actually, a delicate blend of all the flavours. Garlic is not always the easiest ingredient to control. Well done again.'

Junior looked fit to burst by now. When Esther and Toto had moved on she stomped quietly over to complain.

'Look out,' warned Con, 'here comes a tea cup looking for a storm.'

'Patronising cow. She was just really ageist there you know. It's like, if you can walk when you're two, people think you're just great. But by the time you're four, you've been doing it for years, so it's not quite so good. Never mind that you're much better at it now – it's yesterday's thing, you're burnt out.'

'There's no pleasing some people,' said Con. 'I'd happily take any praise from her, I wouldn't care where it was coming from. And I think you're wrong, by the way, I really don't think there was any undertone to what she said to you.'

'Yeah,' I agreed, 'I think you're being way too touchy. Now if it was me on the receiving end, you might have a point.'

'Great, gang up on me all of you, why don't you,' muttered Junior.

'Ah now quit, would you,' said Senior. 'I bet you're secretly delighted to be doing so well. If you're not careful you know, you'll start enjoying yourself, and where will you be then?'

'Feck off the lot of yeh, ye're all just jealous

because I'm turning out to be a genius at this. Roll on the hard stuff.'

Through the large kitchen windows I could see that the sun was setting. A huge, fluorescent red ball burned low in the sky, setting cottonwool clouds alight. It was an impressionistic canvas of colours, part blue-grey, part salmon pink, all magnificent and gaudy. Way to go, sun.

Toto flicked a switch and a kind, creamy light filled the kitchen. It made the room warm and cosy, and somehow safe. Like lying tucked up in your bed as a storm rages outside, and feeling thankful and happy that you're in the best possible place.

In the near distance, Esther Wood was finishing her examination with the asthmatic woman. All appeared to have gone quite well for the class. She commandeered our collective attention.

'Please don't worry that our subjects and demonstrations so far have not led to a coherent menu, as you might see it. We'll cover a few more basics and then progress to an actual entertaining event. What we're doing at present is giving you a versatile basis for any plans you might have for your guests. We'll move on now to pastry-making, and I'll demonstrate an en-croute, which you can try first thing tomorrow, along with your bread. An en-croute is useful because it can be served hot or cold, and if you can master this, you'll at least be able to make a superior sausage roll. While it's cooking, we'll round off the day with a little discussion as to what you all hope to leave with, just so I can be sure that you'll have some or all of the skills you'd like, if that's possible to achieve on this course. We'll do our best, of course.'

'Brilliant,' said Con. 'That's what she's famous for. She does more practical work than any of the other courses in the country.'

'Really?'

'Well, yeah. Is that not why you chose here rather than any other school?'

'Actually, this is a kind of birthday present,' I said, somewhat exaggerating Harry Knowles' association with that event.

Lying to a priest probably meant extra time in hell, a century or so, but there wasn't too much point in worrying about it now. Besides, at the back of my head was the remembered notion that once you end up in hell, you're stuck there for all eternity. If, or when, an afterlife materialised, I might try pleading mitigating circumstances with whatever super-being turned out to be in charge.

As the smell of two en-crouted salmon filled the air, we organised ourselves into a circle to discuss our hopes and dreams. Diarmaid and Eleanor were sitting so close to one another I thought they were on the same chair. Toto passed amongst us, distributing suggestions for other subjects and mixtures we might like to en-pastrycase. For the second time that day, I felt like standing up to declare that I had a substance abuse problem.

It was Con who kicked matters off by telling everyone of the demise of the role of the priest's housekeeper. Left to fend for themselves, he reckoned most of his kind were either starving to death or eating such junk that they would certainly die earlier than they should, of malnutrition.

'I had a parishioner over to dinner one night, to thank him for his work on the parish collections. After I served up the fried chops and frozen peas, I realised that I should have done some potatoes. I didn't have any fresh bread in the house, so I had to resort to giving him cream crackers. That's when I decided to take things in hand, so here I am.'

'I had to get out of the house, or kill my husband,' said Ciara Senior. 'But as well as keeping me out of jail, this should be really useful for me, because he's got mad into golf, and it's a big thing with the local club members to throw dinner parties and drinks bashes. Of course, everyone is totally competitive, and that's even before they get on to the golf course. I can drink any of them under the table, so that's one achievement, but I've no coordination, so there's little or no point in taking up the game itself. I thought I'd try the catering end of things instead. And it's costing him a fortune, because I've the decorators in while I'm away, doing up the house. He doesn't know what hit him.'

There were knowing chuckles all round from both the women and men of the company.

Diarmaid and Eleanor were doing as many things together as they could before 'we' became 'three'. They were bathed in a halo of health and goodness as they beamed at the room. 'And we just love food, don't we,' said one or other of them. Eleanor's dress shimmered affirmation.

Then the asthmatic lady spoke.

'I knew I had a problem when my husband had his boss and his wife around for dinner one night. I was going great guns on current affairs and politics, and I couldn't understand why my husband kept staring at me. Then I realised that while I was talking I'd also been cutting up his boss's meat into little pieces, like I do for the kids.'

'Well, Gladys, I don't know if we can help with the social skills end of things,' said Esther Wood, 'but at least next time you might be cutting up something very different and new.'

I looked over at Junior's disappointed face. Gladys was partnered in the class by Rita, with whom she'd arrived. They'd told us that they had been close friends for years, and Ciara had been convinced that they were, in her own inimitable words, 'complete lesbians'. She thought this very exotic. Now she shook her head sadly, while Senior smirked.

'Brilliant,' whispered Con, laughing.

'What?'

'That woman, she's Glad the Inhaler.'

I hit him.

# TEN

'Our what?' My words were louder than I'd intended.

'Your projects,' said a serene Esther Wood. Then she gave a beatific smile. 'It's a terrific chance for you to show what you've learned, in a very practical way, and it makes for a lovely farewell party. Think of it as your first self-catered "do".'

'I'm going to have to have one of your little lie-downs,' I said to Con.

I have often thought that there aren't enough hours in each, or any, day. And I've had that proved to me, fairly cruelly, on more than one occasion. But this was a whole new stratosphere of the ridiculous.

Mind you, no one else in the room was to know. After all, no one else knew that I still had a whole other day's work to catch up on. Harry Knowles' brilliant ruse of taking this course was coming back upon me threefold, or multiples of that. Suddenly the initials H.K. spelled out Hara Kiri, and not just Big Shit. We weren't talking culinary hopes and dreams any more, oh no, this was now a fully fledged nightmare. An exam.

'Please don't think of this as an exam,' continued the glowing Mrs Wood, 'because of course it's not. It's an opportunity to have a very wet run at your first entertainment idea. And in a friendly environment. Which is exactly what you're practising for, to entertain friends and family. I'm sure you'll all rise to the occasion, and I, for one, am looking forward to it. In fact, it's my own and Graham's favourite bit of every course, it's what makes it all worthwhile.'

Toto and Esther were smiling so hard by now that I was *sure* that they had sadistic intent. 'Holy, moley, guacamoley,' as Con might have said if he wasn't looking so preoccupied.

'Think theme and we'll be grand,' he said.

Sure.

'You can work in pairs or alone, whichever you wish,' explained Toto, 'but do bear in mind that you'll be sharing cooking facilities, as always.'

Oh yes, he was definitely enjoying this.

I started to get my neck thing. If I turn or stretch my neck in a certain way I can feel an even greater version of the tension that is always there. It's delicious in its own perverted way. Tonight, however, it was reminding me that all of life is a trial for which none of us is actually prepared. Delicious, and all of its evil derivatives didn't get a look in. To bring my problems home to roost, Victoria Knowles appeared. She was obviously leaving and had come in to pass on the day's pertinent business to her boss. Time to concentrate on something else and eavesdrop simultaneously. Once you've mastered this one, you can walk and talk *and* chew gum at the same time. She finished by reminding Esther of a local hospital fundraiser that they were all to attend that evening. Happily, Harry the Husband was her escort, and making the fundraising address. This meant I mightn't have to follow them, and because it was a nine o'clock start it looked like I'd have time to whizz through my tapes of the day's events.

My heart sank as we filed out. My bag with the video camera was pointing into a wall. Shit. Someone must have knocked it over at some point. Hopefully, that self-same point had been late in the day. It was a straw and I was clutching. So much for my 'back to the basics' plan.

Ciara Senior said she hadn't gone so long without a drink since sometime in her last pregnancy, a mere fifteen years ago, so the Gang decided to get her a cure. I made my excuses, explaining that I had to catch up on the day's phone calls. A drink at teatime was the last thing I had time for now. I retrieved the bag and made for my room, with the promise that I'd look in on them presently.

I had two telephone messages. The first was from Barry, asking when I'd be back. I wondered if he had only just noticed that I was gone. The second was from Annette O'Neill. Her sad voice said, 'Well, I can't say that I'm surprised, it is what I'd suspected after all. It's just a bit hard to handle when you see it all confirmed in black and white.' She stifled a sob. 'Thank you for your work, and for listening to me when I needed it. Perhaps I'll see you when you get back.'

That one simple message exhausted me. It made me realise that this particular case was by no means over. I hadn't sent Annette O'Neill the fuller, more detailed report, so she would indeed be seeing me on my return. Still, at least the first, and perhaps most difficult, hurdle had been crossed.

I had a quick shower to freshen up and clear my brain. It was time to wash off one kind of dough and earn some of a different sort. I started with the video. Victoria Knowles looked splendid in an emerald green suit. She crossed her perfect legs and began work. This consisted mostly of letters and phone calls, many of them to confirm supplies for the school and the Spring Ball. The sound quality from the video was better than I'd expected, only very slightly muffled if a person stood with their back to it. This wasn't a worry, one way or the other, as I also had the audio tape.

A variety of delivery men came and went with dockets for her to sign, and one poor eejit even tried to flirt with her. She was polite but firm, and he left with his tail between his legs.

I've seen a lot of bizarre habits in my time. One of the most uncomfortable aspects of watching people, when they're unaware that they have an audience, is that they are totally relaxed, uninhibited, and indulgent. Victoria Knowles was no different, and she had a peccadillo. From time to time she picked her nose in a distracted manner. But because her dark pink nails were so long, her finger never actually entered a nostril. I envied her, I had recently had a bit of a harvest of my own nails. There was no particular reason for this. I wasn't nervous, just bored, my fingers ended up in my mouth and then I started enjoying myself. At the best of times my hands were unremarkable, now they had the burden of ugly, torn nails. Having had a root around a nostril, Victoria would glance nonchalantly at her harvest and flick it into the rubbish bin.

As I was grinning at this 'too, too sullied' behaviour, she shocked me by starting to *rip off* the nails. I squirmed at the painful ritual. It took me a few moments to realise that the reason she wasn't screaming in agony was that the nails were false. She calmly put them in a little patterned box, and painstakingly began to apply a new set in a shade of green to match her suit. This explained how her nails had changed from dark red to pink yesterday, though at the time I had assumed it had happened in a less violent way. She checked her make-up, powdered her nose and sighed contentedly. She was obviously pleased with what she'd seen.

Shortly afterwards, the rangey stable girl arrived. She reached across the desk and kissed Victoria on the cheek, then sat on the edge of the desk swinging her legs and chatting. The swinging of the legs played havoc with the auto focus on the video camera. Each time a foot reached towards the lens, it zoomed in, then drunkenly backed off to its original picture as the foot retreated. Over and over again.

After a while, to my own and the camera's relief, she got up to hang her jacket on the coat-stand. But that was the end of my shortlived release from the visual yo-yo she had created. As she reached the stand she kicked my bag, knocking it in the direction of the wall. It calmly focused on its new vista. I fastforwarded through the rest, a dull six hours of plain yellow paint until I myself lifted it at the end of the afternoon session; then I had a short panoramic shot of her office. Great. At least the audio tape seemed to have done all that was asked of it. I rewound the tape and pressed 'play'.

Victoria Knowles had a brisk telephone manner that was just short of curt. She rarely wasted time on unnecessary pleasantries, and skilfully avoided tangents. It was hard to imagine anyone getting the better of her. She also had a reassuringly confident voice that didn't need to bully and was easy on the ear. She gave good phone.

The list of foods on order for Sunday night's Ball was staggering, as was the amount of booze. I began to make a mental tot of how much it would all cost the Wood estate, but ran out of noughts at an early stage. The floral bill alone had to stretch to thousands. But then, as the old song had it, 'give us bread but give us roses'.

The only real conversation, barring the failed

attempt at a flirt, was when the stable girl arrived.

Victoria: Well, well. I didn't expect you at this hour. Alex will tan your hide if he catches you on the mitch.

Girl: Again. He's got me up on Reckless at the moment, so that's punishment enough. I fell off the beast yesterday and hurt my arm, so my lord and master has now put me on mucking out and feeding for a few days. Funnily enough, I still have to use my sore arm, but that doesn't seem to matter, to him anyway. It's good to be away from that horse though. My arse feels like it's been split in two, and I can't even sit down in a hurry without excruciating pain, never mind anything else.

Victoria: Dear, dear. You'll have to get someone to kiss that better for you.

Laughter.

Girl: You busy at the moment?

Victoria: Oh yes, final touches for Sunday night. Speaking of which, Adam's just treated me to the most glorious suit as a late birthday present.

Girl: Brilliant. If you're not wearing your short blue number, could I have that? If I wear opaque stockings, you shouldn't see the bruises on my legs from that brute.

Victoria: Alex or the horse?

Girl: Both. It's hot in here.

She got off the desk and hung up her jacket. Goodbye video. More sundry clothes talk. Then the sound of someone arriving. Adam Philips. Greetings and kissing all round. More sundry chat and gossip, nothing remarkable. Adam wants Victoria to go to lunch with him, she's too busy and will grab a sandwich at her desk. Perhaps she'll see him later at the hospital fundraiser? No, he won't be there.

Victoria: Oh God, just my luck. A boring public evening with Harry, and no one to liven it up.

Girl: And no Joe either.

Victoria: No, but there's always tomorrow.

I wrote the name Joe on my notepad with a question mark beside it.

They moved out of doors, and I, in my perennial role of Big Bertha, collided with Adam again. The rest of that little interlude I saw. Then Victoria Knowles returned to work and had quite a boring afternoon of it. Except for one phone call, from Joe.

I wasn't actually tapping her telephone, so I only got one side of the brief conversation.

'Joe! I really didn't expect to hear from you so soon. Where are you? . . . Well, I'll treasure that image for the rest of the day . . . no, no, there's no way I'll get away from him this evening. Plus he's very, very cranky at the moment . . . No, tomorrow is a nightmare day, what with the Ball preparations and all, and of course Esther is tied up with this latest course, so it's all down to me. But we'll make a night of it on Sunday . . . (a throaty laugh) Well I'll *certainly* look forward to *that* (more laughter) . . . You too sweetheart. Bye.'

Then she hummed tunelessly for a bit, while she got on with the day's tasks. It suited me down to the ground if the two were not going to meet until Sunday night. But the watching and listening would have to continue. There is, after all, nothing more unpredictable than humankind.

I looked at my list of suspects. It had doubled in the last hour. All right it was still only made up of two names, Adam Philips and Joe, but it was a start. To be honest, I was glad it wasn't any larger than that – chasing around a strange place after two men, only one of whom you've ever laid eyes on, can be a right pain in the arse. Especially when you're officially taking the local cookery course. It occurred to me that she might, of course, be having affairs with both of them. I had come across that before. A possibility then. 'Keep an open mind' was another of Mick Nolan's rules. 'Keep an open mind until you've nailed down your proof.'

I paused for a moment as an uncomfortable

thought crossed my mind. Why, on the basis of some brief conversations and sightings, was I confining the list to just two men? Surely there was another in the locality worthy of inclusion? Even though I had not actually seen him alone with Victoria Knowles, there was ample opportunity each day for them to meet, in fact it would probably be hard for them not to. And even if the text of the conversations I had just listened to suggested that Joe was my primary suspect, infidelity often breeds infidelity, and there was nothing to say that Victoria was not having multiple affairs. Assume nothing, prove everything. And so, reluctantly, I added the name of the beautiful Alex Wood.

I got up from the dressing table, which was doubling as a desk, and gave a good stretch. Then I spotted a note which had been shoved under my door. Large, sweeping letters announced that it was for Miss Leo Street, so I opened it.

My Dear Miss Street,

I wondered if you would care to join me this evening for supper. It would be my pleasure, not only to enjoy your company, but also to introduce you to the delights of vegetarian food, and some rather splendid claret which I have been saving for a special occasion.

I enclose a small map and a telephone number, should you find yourself available to come. I do hope to hear from you.

Yours,

Fergus Rush.

His handwriting was beautifully calligraphic, and he used a fountain pen, which didn't surprise me. I weighed up my options for the evening. As far as work went I could be a bit rebellious. Victoria would, or should, be trapped with Harry all night. Adam Philips was not attending the fundraiser. And the mysterious Joe was probably not going to see her until the Spring Ball on Sunday evening. If Alex Wood were attending, so was his wife, which should focus his attention. Chances were that I could take the evening off. I could feel Mick Nolan's disapproving breath on the back of my neck again. 'Piss off, Mick,' I said, 'a girl has to have *some* fun.' He wasn't best pleased. Besides, I was ravenous.

I dialled the number.

'Ah, Miss Street, how lovely to hear from you. I hope you weren't too startled by my impertinence.'

'No, no, not at all. I'd love to come over, provided you promise to throw me out at a reasonable hour. I have an early start in the morning.'

'Consider it done.'

'Just one thing though, I'll have to call in on the others briefly first. We're planning our projects, so it's all a bit terrifying.'

He laughed. 'Esther will make something of you all yet, fear not. I'll expect you when I see you. Number Four is very excited that we're having a visitor, aren't you?' There was some yelping in the background. '*A bientôt.*'

I could hear happy chatter from the pub as I crossed the cobbled yard, and I realised that I was happy too. Content. Enjoying myself. It was the luxury of being away, the thrill of meeting new people and experiencing new things, without any of the baggage that you normally carry with you. I was meeting these people for the first time, and so they had no expectations of me, nor I of them. We were starting with a clean sheet, and it was wonderfully refreshing. No one was reminding you of some badness or slight you'd perpetrated on them back in '83. At times like this, you were who you were, right there and then in that moment in time, the person you'd grown into, and not someone who needed to be told how they came to this, and all of the imperfections involved along the way.

Both Ciaras were laughing uproariously when I got to the table.

'Con's just been regaling us with stories of his

training in Italy,' said Senior.

'Be it ever so humble, there's no place like Rome,' he nodded. 'All kinds of carrying on, it'd make your hair turn grey.'

'Everything short of chasing women,' said Junior. 'Come on though, Con, there must have been a bit of that. Did you not even wonder about it?'

'All I'll say is that some of my year won't die wondering. Other than that, I'm as silent as the confessional.'

'You mean the Con-fessional,' I pointed out.

'Indeed, indeed, Leo, you are a quick study.'

'The puns have been flying all day,' I explained. 'I think he's deliberately trying to do my head in.'

I told them about my dinner invitation.

'Jayze, you didn't take long to score, did you,' exclaimed Junior. 'Mind you, he'd be a bit old for me. I'd be afraid I'd kill him with excitement.'

'I'll watch out for that,' I assured her.

'Yeah, leave the whips and the rubber gear behind, that's my advice.'

'You are a prize minx,' I said, 'with a depraved mind. Sound advice though. Thanks.'

We had a quick drink and discussed strategy. Con's main point was that we should play to our individual strengths, and make it fun by, say, picking a theme each and working within that.

'Brilliant,' I agreed. 'But what happens when your skill is still very much hidden from the world, and yourself, as it is in my case?'

'Nonsense,' he said, 'you're getting really good at the bread.'

'Bless you for the confidence building, Con, I'll cherish it. Oh, and no pun intended.'

'It's all part of the service.'

'Don't forget to pray for her too,' sniggered Junior.

'Wagon. What do you intend doing anyhow?' I asked.

'I don't know yet, but it'll be a protest, a statement, something about my life.'

'I was thinking along those lines,' said Ciara Senior. 'It would be good practice for catering for the golfing types, you know, get back at them without them even noticing. They get yummy grub, and I have a bit of a laugh. Nothing too serious, obviously, and not mean or anything. I'll probably avoid sweet things though. My teeth dance because I need so many fillings, and I can't go to my dentist because I'm terrified of him. It's not that I'm afraid of dentists in general, it's just him. I was in my local one day when he ran in the door and said to the barman, "Vodka. Quick. Patient in chair." That spooked me a bit.'

'Time to change dentists,' advised Junior.

'He also plays lots of booming classical music, and bellows away to it. There's no way he'd hear you screaming in pain above him and the 1812 Overture, let alone anyone else who might come to your rescue.'

'I think you have to be a little alternative to be involved in medicine,' I said. 'I was at a party once when a student doctor fell unconscious under a table, he was so drunk. But the word was to leave him sleeping there until he woke up of his own accord, because he was helping deliver babies at the National Maternity Hospital the following day. He had a dead frog in a glass of formaldehyde attached to his shoulder, didn't spill a drop.'

'Delivering babies won't have done his hangover any good,' observed Senior. 'It has to be the most gory, awful thing to watch. All that gunk. Ralph fainted every time he came in to watch me having the kids. He was absolutely useless. And in the way on the floor too. I can't blame him though. Bad as it is, I'd prefer to have them rather than look at it, any day.'

'Eh, ladies, sorry to interrupt this beautiful journey through the miracle of giving birth, only I get very squeamish,' said an ashen Con.

'Sorry,' I said, 'I keep forgetting that women are much better at mucus talk than men.'

They were discussing the merits of the fan oven and eating toasted sandwiches as I left.

'Don't do anything I wouldn't do,' called Ciara Junior.

'That leaves the night wide open and full of possibilities so,' I laughed.

# ELEVEN

Even at night, in the dark, the countryside has a quiet urgency; little rustling sounds echo in the undergrowth as creatures go about their nocturnal business. But all under a cloak of seeming silence. I crunched up the gravel driveway toward the main Wood house, apologetic for my intrusion into the night's symphony.

It's not as if we city types have never experienced animal sounds or behaviour. The more the city encroaches on the countryside, the more the country-side adapts and moves in. I've met urban foxes on their nightly scrounge, and, like my mother, I only wish that I could tempt a hedgehog to live in my garden; that would give the slugs and snails a run for their money. They're around, those hedgehogs, they just don't fancy what I've got to offer. It's a real shame, because they are one of the few animals who could live with, and put manners on, the cats. A frog stands no chance.

I had been in my house in Clontarf for a month before I realised that I had never actually touched the back wall of my garden. That night, I made a mug of coffee and sat on the wall looking out over my little empire, and beyond. At the time I'd had a cat called Mutt, and he joined me. He was a big, gentle tabby, with a squirrel's tail and huge green eyes. We sat in silence and contentment, and it amazed me all over again that a member of a whole other species might want to live with me. It was such a night as this, as Shakespeare would have it. Mutt died of liver cancer when he was only five years old. I don't have much luck with the boy cats. I sat on a fence for a few moments to remember him, and to savour the night. In the stillness, an owl hooted, and some other hidden creatures moved about stealthily in a nearby copse of trees.

Fergus Rush lived in a house a quarter of a mile beyond the Wood mansion. To get to it you had to cross a little bridge over the original babbling brook. It was surrounded by trees, and had various arches along the pathway that I assumed were covered with rambling roses and honeysuckle during the summer. No. 4 had obviously heard me coming, and the welcoming committee of two was at the door to greet me. I was ushered into the main room and planted in a floppy old sofa by a roaring fire. Bliss.

'You'll be delighted to know, Miss Street, that I have held myself back today, so you won't have a roaring drunk on your hands.'

'Please call me Leo.'

'Leo, yes. I may slip into a formal "Miss Leo" from time to time. Just indulge me, it's my upbringing. Now then, a drink.'

'I'll have a glass of the claret you were promising, if that's all right.'

'A splendid choice. As I've said, I've been looking forward to it, just couldn't find the right occasion. It's definitely a wine to be shared. I think Number Four is a little jealous that he can't have some too.'

'Dogs don't handle their drink well,' I laughed.

'No,' he said, 'especially not that dog.'

When the chill from my hike had mellowed, I wandered around the room.

'I hope you don't mind,' I said to Fergus, 'but I'm hopelessly nosy, and have to poke about wherever I go.'

'You are the guest, feel free.'

The room was full of books, manuscripts and papers, piled high in every space available. But although it was cluttered, it didn't feel oppressively so. This was a lifetime's collection. A roll-top writing desk took up one corner, an armchair another, with mahogany standard lamps dotted about to give an amber glow through their pastel shades. Any spare wall space was taken up with mirrors and dusty portraits of cross-looking men and formidable women. 'The ancestors,' Fergus explained. 'They like to keep an eye on me.' The centrepiece was a baby grand piano.

'Actually, it's a little bigger, it's what's known as a boudoir grand. It belonged to my mother.'

'Do you play all of these instruments?'

'Yes, I dabble a bit. My family were all excellent musicians. But I lacked the aggression to pursue it as a profession, and they would have expected no less than excellence. We were never good at tolerating failure. So I stuck to what I was good at, things pastoral. Over the years I've returned to a gentle pleasure in playing.'

'My parents sent me to piano lessons when I was a child, but it was a disaster. I had no aptitude for it. And my teacher hated me. Well, it was mutual. I suppose those who can, do, and those who can't, don't.'

The top of the piano was covered in framed photographs. Some were of the boy Fergus, with various family members. He was a delightful little blond with a cheeky smile and a cocky turn of the head. Then Fergus during a surprisingly unspotty adolescence, often with horses. And finally, a devastatingly handsome young man in formal riding gear, as part of a team. I asked what that was.

'Ah, past glories, my dear. I was lucky enough to represent Ireland as a showjumper on a number of occasions. The body is too old to indulge in the sport now, though I did coach a bit over the years. Actually, I've taught the Woods' boy a little, though his father does not approve.' He smiled sadly. 'He has his own very strong views about that.'

I looked puzzled.

'Perhaps he feels that I will pass on some of my bad habits to the youngster. When it comes to horses,' he laughed, seeing my confused face. 'Esther sneaks me in for the odd lesson, and I must say the little chap shows great promise.'

Fergus poured two glasses of ruby wine into delicate crystal goblets. 'I opened it earlier to let it breathe, so I'm afraid you missed all of the lovely uncorking noises.'

'Not to worry. Besides, it would have been a sin not to treat this with plenty of respect, it's delicious.'

'I'm glad you approve. As I say, it's a special occasion for the inhabitants of this old house. It's not often that we have a visitor, particularly a young lady. Most others would have refused on the grounds that I'm probably mad rather than simply eccentric, and liable to do something terrible. What times we live in.'

We sat down to our meal in the adjacent dining room. It was, in part, what Fergus referred to as 'a hill of beans'. He had grown most of the vegetables himself. The pulses were all organic, and purchased along with the bulk buys of the school and hotel.

'So you're quite friendly with my teacher, Mrs Wood.'

'Esther? Oh yes. I've known her since she was a girl, really. And I've taken most of her courses. That's how I've survived as a vegetarian; she opened my eyes to food.'

Our first course was the sweetest onion soup topped with cheesy croutons. I have to confess that I'm crazy about the onion family. I love their flowers in the garden, and the taste of them in anything. I have been known to go into a decline in a supermarket if there are no spring onions on sale. Frankly, without them, an egg or a salad sandwich is not worth having. Eating organically, by the season, is a brilliant and sensible idea, but spring onions must be imported all year round for me.

'Esther has an excellent pupil in you, Fergus, this is wonderful. And your version of her brown bread is excellent too.'

'Thank you. Of all her courses, I found Cooking For One the most useful, for obvious reasons. But if I make too much of anything, I have help from Number Four. He's quite keen on vegetarian grub, as long as he gets his meat regularly.'

'I hit it off badly with Mrs Wood, I'm afraid. She thinks I'm a troublemaker, and a cheeky rip into the bargain. I'm trying hard to make it up to her now. Actually, I'm really enjoying the course and I didn't think I would.'

'She's a very good teacher in her own nervy way. And don't worry if she seems a little strict, in fact she likes nothing more than a glass of wine and a gossip. And it may surprise you to know that she does have a sense of humour, very dry and quite droll.'

'They seem an odd couple, Alex and Esther.'

'Mmm, yes. I suppose a lot of people think of her as too plain and stiff to be his wife. But in actual fact it's one of the most solid marriages I've ever come across. They both have their business empires, and they have a son, young Christopher, who is of course the apple of his parents' eyes, though he is a little wild it must be admitted. They seem to have a system worked out, a modus operandi that allows them both just enough of the freedom they need. They have their status quo, it works well as an arrangement, and I think they are very content with their lot.'

I had the weirdest sense of disappointment at hearing all of this. What did I want? To hear that it was a bitterly unhappy marriage, so that I might fantasise without guilt about the handsome and dashing Alex Wood? Cheap thrills, Leo, Penny Romance stuff.

'It's quite a set-up,' I admitted. 'A beautiful home in splendid surroundings, a thriving stables, and one of the most famous cookery schools in the country. It's the good life. What more could a person want?'

'Indeed, what more.'

Fergus produced a lemon sorbet, made from his own fruit. I was stunned. 'By way of a miracle, I can grow figs and lemons in a sort of conservatory that I built on the back of the house. I also do a mean champagne sorbet from time to time, but it seems somehow a desecration to me, as I prefer the champagne to the icicles.'

'I once read that it pisses God off if people ignore the colour purple,' I said. 'I disagree. I think the colour yellow is the important one. Excuse my language.'

'Not at all. Pissing God off, and making him angry, are two quite different things. It's good to make a distinction.'

Over a lasagne and greens we began to laugh, and No. 4 barked along. We had demolished the first bottle of claret in double-quick time, but were sipping the second in a civilised fashion. The tour de force was a bread and butter pudding for dessert, heavy on the carbohydrates, but manna all the same. The whole meal was an experience, an explosion of tastes. I had begun to realise why foodies were so devoted to their art. The only problem was trying to avoid one of the seven deadlies, gluttony.

'I don't think I'll be walking home, Fergus, just put me on my side and I'll roll there.'

On our way back to the sitting room, I admired a photograph on the wall.

'What a beautiful woman.'

'Yes, she was. Her name was Lily, but she's dead now. She was Alex Wood's mother.'

If I had wanted a love story, this was it.

'It's quite hard to explain it without sounding clichéd. But then, the older you get, the more you feel that life itself could be construed the biggest cliché of all.' He sighed and ran a hand through his hair. 'We were teenagers by the time we realised that we were in love with one another. Until then it had been a friendship, a close and special one, but this was altogether different. It made sense of everything. We were both excited and terrified by the discovery. And for a time it was perfect. But Lily had a materialistic streak, and she didn't want to be a farmer's wife. She wanted a comfortable, glamorous life and a husband with lots of money. And that's what she got. I tried to forget her, I threw myself at other women. I even became engaged to be married to a lovely girl, but I realised that she deserved someone better, not a fool on the rebound who would make her life miserable, unable, ever perhaps, to give her the entire love that she expected and was entitled to.'

He paused as No. 4 hopped up on his lap and snuggled into him.

'Are you married?' he asked.

'No, not even close. I live with an actor, but things are a bit uneasy at the moment. We're in a rut, and I'm not sure that either of us is willing, or brave enough, to do anything about that. We seem to have stopped paying attention to one another.'

'Foolish man.'

'Oh no, it's as much my fault as his. I manufacture this busyness all the time, avoiding confrontation, I suppose. We've grown distant from each other without even noticing it happen.'

'Lily and I thought we could live apart, but we couldn't. Her husband, Christopher, knew about us all along. He didn't seem to mind. It kept his young wife busy, and happy too, after a fashion. I suspect it was as much an arranged marriage for him as it was for her. He wasn't a bad sort at all really, just a bit dull. And I've discovered over the years that dull is not the worst thing in the world, by any means. When they had Alexander, they were complete. And I don't think Christopher ever cared one way or the other what we did; he had his son and heir.'

'If you'd prefer not to talk about this, about Lily, I'll understand. It must be quite painful.'

'Actually, no, quite the contrary. I very rarely get to say any of this aloud. It's a release to be able to. If I sound sad, I don't mean to, it was the best time of my life. As well as the worst. But mostly the best. To love and to be loved is a magnificent feeling, a fulfilment. Some people will never have that.'

How right he was. I thought of the Knowles' loveless marriage. I thought of Annette O'Neill's shattered life. And I wondered about my own somewhat hollow arrangement. It was humbling.

'Do you ever regret not marrying?'

'I live with plenty of regret about my life. And it's something that I wouldn't recommend to anyone. May you never feel that life has passed you by in any way, Leo. And remember that that is largely up to you yourself. You must grasp your opportunities.'

He poured some port and sat at the piano.

'What sort of music do you like?'

'Anything but jazz, really, you know, the tuneless kind. I think it's anarchy and I just don't get it. I suppose I don't like the idea that the musicians are making it up as they go along, and that they might just be having us on, chancing it and making fools of us. Do you know any fecky Baroque music? I love that, it's so jolly and up.'

'Up it is then. You're not unlike Lily, she liked lively music too.'

He began to play and No. 4 barked his approval. Then the little dog popped up on to my knee and settled down for a cuddle.

'He howls if I play anything sad, though I some-times think he's actually trying to sing along. I think he likes you, he's not often this free with his favours.'

No. 4 barked again, as if to agree. I was flattered.

'He's quite a character,' I remarked.

'Yes, it runs in the family. His father was a terrier called Rex, who belonged to Esther and Alex. Esther always bakes a huge cake for Easter. It's much like a Christmas cake, but without the icing. One Easter, she baked the cake as usual, left it on a wire rack to cool and went about her duties. When she returned, she found Rex, dead on the floor of the kitchen, in a little pool of sick. There was only a quarter of the cake left. He had eaten twice his own body weight and, I suppose, burst in the process. Apparently he looked very peaceful.'

We sipped our wine thoughtfully, remembering an absent friend. Then we looked at one another and laughed. Poor old Rex.

Fergus played a glissando on the keys. That must be the flexing of muscles for a pianist.

'Lily played piano like a dream. I missed it when she stopped calling as much. She had Alex and was confined to base, so to speak. I missed the companionship. Then I had my wild years, and there are whole chunks of those that I cannot even remember. When Alex grew older and she needed me again, we resumed, in our own way. By then we had both lived other lives, and were approaching things with different points of reference. It had grown away from us somehow, and yet we persisted. It had become an intense friendship, but a friendship now, more than anything else.' He looked into that middle distance of his. 'I still miss her, and I think about her every day. After she died, I often wondered what the point of continuing was, down through the years. But, as far as I'm concerned, I'm so, so close to the end now that

I don't need to worry about that any more. I see beauty all around me, and I abide. I abide. And sometimes I even make a new friend.' He smiled warmly at me, and I felt really special.

'You leave on Sunday?' he asked.

'No, in fact. I've been invited to the Spring Ball, so I'll stay around for that.'

'Excellent. It promises to be a good night. Alex and Esther always throw an excellent party, with the best of food and wine thrown in, as you can imagine. If you like, I could accompany you, unless you already have a partner lined up.'

'No, no I don't, and yes, I would love that. I don't think I'll know too many people there, and I hate arriving alone to a do.'

'I must warn you that you'll find me a bit of a Cinderella. I tend to leave early, but I'm yours for as long as you'd like within that time frame.'

He excused himself for a few moments, and returned with a velvet box.

'I'm not sure what your outfit for the evening is, Miss Leo, but if this were to suit at all, I would be delighted if you would wear it.'

Inside was a pearl choker. It looked ancient, very real, and very, very expensive.

'Please do me the honour of having it, it's not really my style after all.'

'I couldn't possibly, Fergus, it's far too precious. I'd be terrified that something would happen to it.'

'Do humour an old man, and wear it for the evening. It's time it got an airing. What's the point of having such a beautiful thing if you can't let others admire it? Actually, I won't take no for an answer.'

I laughed. 'Well then, I'd best not sour this lovely evening with a refusal. And much as I don't want to say this, it really is time that I went. I have a lot of ground to make up with Mrs Wood, so I'll need to be sharp in myself. Thank you so much for a wonderfully relaxing and nutritious evening.'

He beamed. 'A pleasure, I can assure you. Now, let me get my coat and I'll see you home.'

'Oh no, now it's my turn to put my foot down. I'm only a stroll down the road, and I feel perfectly safe, so there is absolutely no need for you to come along. Besides, I've got to get a plan of action together for my project and a whole lot else besides, so a quiet walk with just myself and my thoughts is exactly what I need right now.'

He eventually acquiesced, and saw me to the door.

'Celebrate yourself, Miss Leo,' he said, as I turned to go, 'you have every reason to.'

'Thank you, Fergus,' I said, guiltily, 'but really, I'm not all that I seem.'

'We none of us are, Leo. We none of us are.'

# TWELVE

A pale moon loitered in the sky, and a slight breeze rustled through the trees. The air smelled fresh and grassy, and the little river gurgled happily. I yawned and stretched, clearing my head for the walk back to my room. For some reason the song 'Everyone's Gone To The Moon' came into my head and I began to giggle, because clearly that was an unlikely scenario. If not an impossibility.

In Dublin, my office is across the road from a recording studio with rehearsal rooms, and I'm regularly treated to young bands trying out immortal song lines like 'sometimes I often wonder'. On one occasion I'm sure I heard 'I'm an uncontrollable fire, and I'm walking on a wire'. Again unlikely. I mean, when was the last time you saw a fire of *any* sort walking, let alone balancing on a wire as well. I think it was a love song.

I made a mental list of things to do the following day. Annette O'Neill was preying on my mind, so I would telephone her in the morning to make sure that she was coping somehow with her situation. By now, she would certainly have faced her husband with the evidence of his infidelity, and it would be a tough time for all concerned.

There was also the problem of 'the project'. Maybe Con was right, maybe a simple theme would be the answer. And if Esther Wood did indeed have the sense of humour that Fergus assured me of, then it just might work. She had handled the ironic aioli well, so maybe there was hope for me after all. And if there was a light at the end of the tunnel, it was important for me not to add more tunnel.

I became aware of violin music being played in the distance. It seemed to be further on in the direction I was headed. As I turned towards the Wood house I saw the source of the music, a figure of a man in a field, surrounded by attentive horses. The ghostly scene was bathed in a frosty moonlight, all silver and white and grey. The horses' breath steamed from their nostrils and billowed into an impressionistic fog. The musician swayed to his haunting music. I stood transfixed, afraid to move in case he noticed me and stopped. It was Alex Wood.

A horse whinnied and looked over at me. So did Alex.

'I'm sorry to disturb you, please don't stop, it's beautiful.'

'Thank you, I'm glad you think so.' Then he lifted the violin and played again. It was a haunting lament, and all assembled company was lost in it. When he finished he turned and said to me, 'I see your name on my guest list for Sunday night. Who did you have to fuck to get that?'

The languorous way he said 'fuck' made me feel naked, excited and horny as hell. My cheeks heated up, and I prayed that I wasn't steaming like the horses.

'Eh, my dad knows Harry Knowles, and he fixed it up for me to go.'

'Being a friend of Harry's doesn't exactly recommend your father to me.'

'No,' I admitted.

'But then I suppose the farmer and the cowboy really should be friends, and I do see an awful lot of that particular cowboy.'

'He's some mover all right.'

He was unafraid of silence or of holding a gaze. Of course. He had nothing to hide, no blemish. The violin and bow hung effortlessly by his side, a part of him now. The instrument's sensuous curves glowed in the ice-white moonlight. It looked as happy to be stroked by him as I would have been. As any living thing would have been.

He was physically beautiful, lean and athletic, but it was his face that let you in. The sardonic upper twist of his lip revealed a dimple in his cheek, and his eyes creased and twinkled just enough to soften any arrogance that you might try to find. His self-confidence was powerful and lethally attractive. I couldn't believe that I was alone with him again. Apart from the horses, I had him all to myself. It felt like Wonderland.

'Nights like this make you glad to be alive, don't they,' he smiled.

'Yes, it's a very special time.'

'Do you know much about horses?'

'Sadly, no. As children we used to do a bit of riding when we were on holidays, that's all. I think they're beautiful and mysterious. If anything, I'm in awe of them.'

'They are my life,' he said quietly, 'and I can't believe that I'm lucky enough to have them. And all of this.' He gestured to the land.

'Well you're obviously a good curator, so you deserve it.'

He was standing very close to me now. I wanted to reach out and touch him, just to convince myself that he was real, that this meeting was actually taking place. I hardly dared breathe in case I spoiled the moment. Finally, I said, 'Please play some more, it really is heavenly.'

This time he picked a lighter, happier tune. Even the horses seemed to smile. Before he finished I stole away. It was perfect, and I wanted it to stay that way.

As I passed the house a voice suddenly spoke from the shadows. I let out an involuntary yelp. Richard Cooper, the stable manager, slunk out of the darkness. His tiny eyes glittered.

'You're very lucky he let you stay. He doesn't like being spied on.'

'And what exactly do you call what you're doing?' I asked.

The Rat withered me with a look.

He walked with the bad back and bandy legs of a man who'd spent his life with horses. Gratifyingly, I was a few inches taller than him. I straightened up further in an effort to look down on him properly. His sneer seemed immovable, and even if he did smile occasionally I'm sure it emerged as a leer, with very little possibility of improving his face. I had the notion that he was probably sizing me up in exactly the same way, and deciding that I was sarky and plain. Life is all about perspectives.

'I see you were at Fergus Rush's place tonight. Like to tell me what that was all about?'

'I'm afraid not, it's private, Dick.'

Suddenly the night felt creepy rather than magical. I quickened my step and made for home. Something about the way Richard Cooper had tried to look through me made me feel hollow and a sham. I thought of the many lies and half lies I had told in the last few days. So much of my work is bound up with that, weaving a fabric of light, white lies around myself. At the very least, it's a withholding of information. Just now I had even besmirched my poor father's name with the very suggestion that he knew Harry Knowles. And the Gang thought I worked in an office job. Fergus had not asked me what I did for a living, but if he had, would I have lied to him too? The uncomfortable, and uncomforting, answer was 'probably'. I wasn't feeling too proud of myself. I didn't even try the lame argument that I wasn't hurting anyone.

The journey home always seems quicker than the outward leg, thank goodness. I really had had enough of myself and my thoughts by now, and I was looking forward to going to bed, to sleep, and hopefully *not* to dream. I had enough going on in my brain without that. But the night wasn't finished with me yet. Sitting in his red BMW in the yard of the school was a stony-faced Harry Knowles.

This was a potential nightmare for me. I couldn't see his wife anywhere, which might mean she'd given him the slip. If so, I should have been following her, not having a pleasant dinner in another part of the forest. Harry could be waiting to give me the third degree. There was one lifeline – the lights were on in the school reception, and that's where he was staring; perhaps she was in there. I was going to have to brazen this out. After all, if a detective is good at tailing subjects, the subjects should never notice they're being followed. I popped some chewing gum into my mouth; it disguised the smell of the evening's libations, and I felt it made me look tough. Then I approached the car.

Harry rolled down the window.

'Fundraisers have to be the most boring event ever invented,' I said.

He looked suspicious, but grunted in agreement.

'You on your way home now?' I asked. 'Only it's been a long day, and I'd be glad to know that you were all tucked up in the appropriate beds so that I could get some sleep too.'

He looked back at the school and drummed his fingers on the steering wheel. 'Now that you're here, you may as well go in and root my wife out of her lair. She forgot something, according to herself. I don't know if I'd believe the phone book out of her mouth any more. You're not the only one that wants to get to bed,' he said crossly. I got the impression that he didn't intend going there alone.

'Back in a mo,' I said, heading for the school.

I heard quiet sniffles as I approached the door. I knocked lightly, so as not to frighten her, and called, 'Anyone there?' She was blowing her nose as I entered. Her eyes were red and slightly swollen from crying. She was wearing a cream trouser-suit, with matching frosted nails.

'Are you all right?'

'Yes, yes,' she said brusquely, 'I've just got a bit of a cold, and I'm feeling miserable and sorry for myself, that's all.'

'Is there anything I can get you?'

'No thank you. I just want to be left alone, if you wouldn't mind.'

'Of course. I was talking to your husband outside, and he was a little worried that you were taking so long.'

'Not worried enough to get out of his car and come in though,' she muttered.

Then, without warning, she began to cry again. I think she even surprised herself. She quickly brought herself under control, giving herself hiccups in the process. She held her breath for a moment to stem them, then said, 'Please, please, don't tell anyone you saw me like this. It really is too, too embarrassing.' She blew her nose again. It was now as red as her eyes, and she was not looking quite as regal as usual.

'Don't worry, I won't,' I assured her. 'We all have to let off steam sometimes. Are you sure there's nothing I can do for you?'

'Short of killing the man I'm married to, I'm afraid not,' she said, trying to force a smile. 'If you're passing him on your way out, could you tell him that I won't be much longer.' Then she gave herself a full body shrug and reached into her handbag for some make-up. There was a certain dignity in the fact that she would never let him see her at a disadvantage. She probably knew from years of experience that tears wouldn't wash with Harry Knowles; he would see them as a sign of weakness.

As I passed by the other students' quarters, I saw that Father Con's light was on and the curtains open. I could see him kneeling by his bed, deep in prayer. I hoped he was mentioning his new friends – every little helps. I stole past quietly and headed for my room in the hotel.

Annette O'Neill had called. She was crying. 'It's

terrible now,' she sobbed, 'just about as bad as it can be. I really don't know if I can cope. Could you call me, please, if you get a chance? Please?' It was a phone call I wished I had actually taken. But it was too late to call her back now, I would do it in the morning. As I cleaned my face and teeth a weariness came over me. I began to feel that not only was I now chasing time, but paradoxically I had also hit the wall, like a marathon runner. I had a job to finish here, I had a project to prepare and present, and I needed to make sure that Annette would be okay. I felt very lonely all of a sudden, so I phoned Barry. 'Yello. Not here. You know what to do.' And even though I did, I didn't. Instead I hung up and climbed into bed.

I hate knowing that I'm not going to get enough sleep, and the insufferable awareness of time moving on as I lie there thinking, 'If I fall asleep now I'll get six hours'; then it goes to five and a half hours, five hours, four, and so on, till within an hour of getting up I fall into a deep sleep and can't wake up properly when the alarm goes. I really hoped it was not going to be one of those nights. It was so late now that I couldn't even deal with tomorrow. Instead I had to settle for an inferior 'later is another day'.

Alex Wood came to my door at 2 a.m. He knocked lightly and let himself in. I had been expecting him. There was no need to speak, we both knew why he was there. I closed my eyes in delicious anticipation as he pulled away the bed-clothes. I lay on my back, with my arms outstretched, waiting for him. His eyes looked me up and down in the moonlight. Then he lay on the bed beside me and I felt his firm body pressing along the length of mine. He kissed my mouth slowly, then moved his lips to just behind my ear, and along my neck to my breastbone, leaving a hot scorch of desire on my flesh. I was melting in the dark. I didn't dare move, even though every part of me was longing to writhe with pleasure. I could hardly breathe. I must do nothing to spoil this – I would get the cake in later. (Who'd left it out there anyway?) When he reached my nipples, I could no longer remain still. My whole body began to shake with delight and longing. I felt an agonising, aching throb between my legs. I'll never have that recipe again (but surely one of the others will?). As I reached down to guide him, I looked into his radiantly blue eyes and smiled. This was a dream come true. What a dream. A dream. It *is* a dream. A *dream*. I bolted upright in the bed. A dream. *Shit*. The radio was blaring about cakes left out in the rain, and if I didn't hurry I was going to be late for school.

# THIRTEEN

It is fatal to hear the wrong song first thing in the morning. Then it's yours for the day, like it or not. It needn't be a bad song, just the wrong song.

Instead of programming the alarm to buzz, which can be a frightening and unnecessary sound, I'd set it to be the radio when it came on. On this occasion, the radio was playing 'MacArthur Park', a frightening and unnecessary sound. And it was mine for the day.

I hummed, as tunelessly as the Richard Harris version, as I crossed over to the Ciaras' temporary home.

His final quivering 'note' always sounds like it's

really hurting him; the memory of it was certainly damaging me. I didn't want to live with those crazed lyrics all day, not unless I could be on whatever it was that had inspired the writer to come up with them in the first place. Would it not do that all involved had screwed up my dreams?

Con's hair was still wet and slicked back from the shower. It gave him a frightening edge, or so he thought.

'Come in,' he said, à la Count Dracula, 'we have been expecting you. Breakfast?'

'Oh, just a cup of blood and a virgin,' I replied.

'Looks like you had a late one, Leo,' said Senior.

'Yeah, and then I couldn't sleep, thinking about how little sleep I was going to get. Bloody vicious circle. Do I really look that bad?'

'I've seen worse. This morning, for instance, Junior wins the prize for letting herself go.'

Young Ciara came through the kitchen door. Her short hair was combed into a tiny, but relatively sober, ponytail, and her jewels were missing.

'Ah, I couldn't be bothered making an effort for you lot. And there's no talent on this course, so I'm not going to waste my time getting into the full war gear, it takes ages. Did you get the ride? Sorry Con, tell your soul to look away, it's a woman's thing, or just anyone but Catholic priests I suppose.'

'Only if they're devout,' Ciara Senior pointed out.

'Well let's consider that I am,' said Con, 'and just get on with it. Did you?'

I shifted uneasily, remembering my dream. 'Eh, no.'

'You don't sound too sure,' said Junior.

'Oh no, I'm sure all right. No.'

'No feckin' news so.' She plonked some dishes on the table. 'Breakfast is served.'

As we tucked into free range eggs and toast, I asked Junior just how she'd ended up here.

'I'm taking a year out before I go to college. That's *if* I go to college; it's more my parents' idea than mine, at the moment. I had planned to spend the year travelling, maybe in Europe or America, but I couldn't raise the money.' She filled her mouth with toast and tea, and munched happily. 'Now I spend my time annoying my mother around the house, and she spends *her* time thinking up things for me to do. This has been her best so far. I really will have to get myself something soon though, the novelty of driving them mad is beginning to wear thin. I gotta blow outta there. Besides, I'm broke.'

'Did any of you hear the commotion late last night?' asked Con.

My ears pricked up. 'Was this by any chance between Victoria Knowles and a man in a red BMW?'

'Yeah. I read my bible last thing before I go to bed every night, and last night I heard some noise outside. When I looked, I saw them both sitting in front seats of the car, really going for it, though I couldn't make out what they were saying. Then she got out, slammed the door and went in to the school. I heard the car drive off about twenty minutes later.'

'I'd love to know what all that was about,' I said, though I could probably have ventured a fairly good guess.

We shuffled across to the school, meeting other pupils on the way. An enforced jollification filled the air, a bit like being in Butlins (but hopefully with less far-reaching consequences). Today was a big day of consolidation for everyone: Our Last Before Project Day.

I could see no sign of Victoria Knowles as we filed into the hallowed hall, but I quickly set up my equipment, as yesterday, this time making sure I placed my bag where it was unlikely to be kicked over. Then I wrote a quick note to tell her that it was there, and that I hoped she didn't mind. I thought better of saying that I hoped it wouldn't be in her way, that would only put the thought into her head. As bad as sending a stamped-addressed envelope with something that you really don't want back; the temptation is too great. I also neglected to mention that it would record her every move, in the desk area at least.

Toto greeted me enthusiastically at the door. I searched for irony or malice in his eyes, but there was none. He seemed genuinely glad to see me. Today he was bedecked in bright blue slacks, a matching blue and white striped shirt with a plain white collar, and a violent yellow bowtie. He was making a positive fashion statement. It was startling nonetheless.

'Graham,' I acknowledged politely, thrilled that I hadn't let his nickname out by accident – try explaining to your teacher that you think with him it's always Oz, there could be a misunderstanding. Particularly when he had part of the Yellow Brick Road attached to his neck.

'Leo, I wonder if I might have a private word with you later?' he asked, stopping just short of putting his arm around me. I obviously looked shocked because he quickly added, 'Nothing to worry about at all, it's unrelated to the course.'

Now I was intrigued, but still a little scared.

We went through our brown bread paces. Although this was only our second attempt at it, the whole process seemed quite routine now. Esther wandered at random throughout the class, stopping to look at Con for a while. When she moved on I said, 'You were really cool there, not a flicker of nerves.'

'I've had lots of practice,' he said. Seeing my confusion, he extrapolated. 'Put it this way, you can't raise a chalice in a packed church and have a shake in your hand, no matter what the reason. If people lose confidence in you then you've lost them. So that's one of the first things you have to sort out.'

'Makes sense when you put it like that.'

We moved on to the en-croutes we'd been shown the day before, and put them into the ovens to cook alongside our bread. Then we cleared up. It was a busy little start to the day.

Esther demonstrated cheesy savoury scones, and we had a short coffee break during which I excused myself to telephone Annette O'Neill. Victoria Knowles was now at her post, looking weary but unbowed. She gave me a watery smile, and stifled a yawn with last night's frosted nails. Today's ensemble was blue, so I made an educated guess as to an outcome for the frosties. If she couldn't be bothered, I felt sure that Toto could take them off her hands, so to speak.

The phone rang three times and a little girl with the voice of an old crone answered.

'Is that Gillian?' I asked.

'Yes, my name is Gillian. Who are you?'

'I'm called Leo, could I speak to Mummy?'

'No.'

'Please? . . . Pretty please?'

'No. Mummy took tablets and now she's in the hospital.'

White noise filled my head, and my breakfast felt dangerously close to the world again. I tried to take in what she had just said, but I was totally removed from the telephone, from this conversation; she couldn't have said what she'd just said, I didn't want that. In fact it was the very last thing I wanted to hear.

'Hello. Hello,' said her little old crone's voice, very far away. 'Are you still there? Hello?'

My knees were tingling and weak. I didn't think they were going to hold my legs straight for very much longer. I pulled myself together, momentarily.

'Gillian, can I speak to someone else? Is Daddy there?'

'No, Daddy's gone to work,' she assured me. 'Aunty Margaret is here.'

'Please put Aunty Margaret on the phone, Gillian.'

In the background I could hear an adult voice. 'Gillian, what are you up to? Is that for me?'

'It's for Mummy *and* it's for you,' said the small girl.

Aunty Margaret came to the phone. In a way, I didn't want her to. In a way, if she didn't come, I didn't have to hear the bad news about Annette from an adult, a supposedly reliable source. She came to the phone.

'Margaret here, who is this?'

'My name is Leo Street and I know Annette. Is she all right? What happened?'

'Yes, she's fine, she's going to be fine. She's very groggy, but she's alive and she's going to be fine.'

She sounded calm, but then there are many different ways of dealing with shock.

'Your name is underlined here on the phone pad; she seemed to want to contact you. I've given her my mobile, so you can call her on that. I think she'd like people to talk to, actually. She may be asleep now, but do try her later if she is. I think it's important that she has lots of callers right now. She needs us all.'

'I feel so responsible,' I said, and could have bitten my tongue off for sounding so pathetic and self-regarding.

'Don't,' was the answer. 'This was coming for longer than any of us knew. And if Annette had been a bit more selfish and taken better care of herself, it might never have happened. So don't blame yourself.'

'Isn't that a bit harsh?'

'It is and it isn't. Believe me, she's my sister and I love her, I really, really do. It's just that maybe now, after all that's happened, maybe now she'll give *herself* a chance, think of *herself* from time to time. That would do her no harm at all.'

I took the mobile number and hung up.

Con came to the door carrying my coffee. 'This is going cold, and so is Esther.'

'Con, I've just had some very bad news about someone I know. I need you to explain that to the Boss, and I'd like you to say a prayer for my friend.'

He handed me the lukewarm brew. 'Sorry it's not stronger. I'll look after everything in here. You do what you have to do. God bless.'

I'm not a religious person, but I was glad he was on my side.

I dialled the number. A soft spoken, corporate recording said, 'The customer you have dialled may be out of range, or may have switched their unit off. Please try again later.' I couldn't even leave a message. This was anguish. I would try again later, but I would have liked to have left proof of contact now. I began to panic. What if the same thing happened later, and yet again I couldn't talk to Annette? I felt that there was only one thing I could do now. Reluctantly, I rang my sister-in-law.

'Anne, it's Leo. Look, this may be a bolt from the blue, but I was wondering if you'd been in contact with Annette O'Neill today?'

'No. But as a matter of fact I was just talking to someone about her.' She paused, confused. 'Did you know that she's in the hospital?'

'Yes, I just heard. But I can't raise her by phone and I'm really worried.'

'I didn't know you two were that friendly . . . Oh God no, don't tell me you had something to do with all of this. Were you doing work for Annette, Leo? How *could* you?'

'Please, Anne, don't make me feel any worse about this than I already do.'

'Annette can't afford the sort of money you'd be asking.'

'I know, I know. But no money ever changed hands, Anne, and it won't.'

This was no way to run a business. Here I was giving up valuable paid time, and desperately hoping that my conscience would be appeased and that my family wouldn't hate me. What a mess.

'Look, Anne, I know you're probably mad and disappointed with me, but what we really need to do right now is find out how Annette is, and to make sure that she's being properly looked after. I'm away and I can't do that in person, so will you try?'

'All right, I'll go to the hospital to see her. I would have anyway. But we'll be having a very frank talk, you and me, when you get back to Dublin.'

I was not looking forward to that prospect.

I slumped back into the class, exhausted. I must have looked ashen; Victoria smiled sympathetically, Esther held fire and the Ciaras came over to give me a hug.

'It's fine,' I said, for all to hear. 'She's going to be all right.'

I hoped I was telling the truth.

Esther was explaining the many uses and versatilities of bread for the purpose of Weekend Entertaining. I paid attention, but it didn't seem an important issue right now. I did, however, recognise the importance of keeping busy. Vaguely, croutons, toasties, scones and sandwiches lodged in my psyche, maybe a lot more. I could only dredge up the obvious if asked; no new technical terms were penetrating at any tangible level.

I was in a moral dead zone and I needed help.

# FOURTEEN

All I ever wanted to do was put the bad guys away. I wanted to be on the side of the law. I enjoyed Westerns as much as my brothers, and was usually on the side of the Sheriff, as long as he wasn't chasing Indians willy-nilly, that never seemed fair. He had to be after the real bad guys, unless he was a bad guy himself. Peter and Stephen noticed a lot more than me when it came to details and narrative structure. If there was a prominent woman character, they would groan and declare, 'Oh no, not women. Now there'll be kissing and all.' They were usually right. Once, when I started to blub about a hero dying, they scoffed at me, 'Don't be stupid Leo, he can't die till he's made his last speech.'

I hoped I wanted justice as well. Where was the justice in what I did now? I hadn't made it into the police force, so I was on the fringe, using my powers of deduction and leg-work, but to what end? How could I say that I did any good in the world? I confirmed suspicions, paranoias, grubby details. It was hard for me to find a positive for myself in that right now. Right now, a client was dangerously ill in hospital, her life shattered by what I had revealed to her.

Mick Nolan was in my head again. 'Quit feeling sorry for yourself. What are you trying to convince yourself of here? Do you seriously think that if you'd been an inch taller, you would have changed the world and sent all of the baddies to jail? Pull yourself together. You did your job and no one's dead, not yet anyway. So let's have less self-pity and a bit more action. Now get up off your arse and earn some money.'

These conversations with my ex-boss could be very annoying and one-sided. He only initiated them when it suited him. And if I had any decent argument against him, he ignored me. Right now I was fed up to my back teeth with him. It's so easy to be smug when you're dead and can pretend that you have all the answers.

Esther had left it to Toto to demonstrate a soup. He was in his element, flourishing his knife over onions and assorted vegetables.

'Tight set,' said Con in a low voice.

'The soup looks good too,' I said wryly.

'Is it my imagination, or does he look over at us more than any of the others?'

'It's not your imagination,' I confirmed. 'I think he fancies one of us.'

'Oh dear, that's a bit disconcerting. Don't take this the wrong way, Leo, but I really hope it's you.'

'God almighty, that's all I need.'

Our practical version of hearty vegetable broth was nothing short of murder. Toto took a special interest in our little group of two. The Ciaras found this highly entertaining, and began to torture Graham by calling him away with 'technical' queries. It became clear from his hands-on approach to helping that I was the target. What sort of magnet that made me I don't know. And I still had his 'private word' to look forward to. This day promised many more fresh hells. Oh goody.

Lunch looked delicious, but I had little appetite. I needed to contact Annette. I took myself outside and dialled her sister's mobile. This time my call was answered by a sleepy voice that I recognised.

'Annette, I'm so glad to hear your voice. It's Leo

here. How are you feeling?'

'Oh, you know, dopey and foolish. It's good to hear from you.'

'I feel so sorry about what's happened.'

'Oh don't be, it was coming like a jail-on-wheels. At least now we know that it'll never happen again.'

'I didn't intend that my work would have such a negative effect, Annette. I'm so, so sorry.'

'What?' she asked, genuinely surprised.

'Well, if I hadn't proved what I did, you would probably not have taken the tablets, and none of this would have happened. I should at least have explained it to you in person, I know that now.'

'Leo, I think you might have the wrong end of the stick here. I did take some tablets, but I don't think it was in the way that you think. It turns out that I'm diabetic. I have been for a while, but I ignored the signs, just thinking that it was thirst, and fatigue, and stress and what have you. Apparently my key tones, or ketones or something, went mad, and my whole system went down. That's why I passed out and ended up here. So none of it is your fault, honestly.'

My knees finally gave in and I sat down on the steps of the school.

'But Gillian said you took tablets and that's why you were taken to the hospital.'

'God, children miss nothing, do they? I took some aspirin for a headache but that was just coincidence. I should have noticed the diabetes thing months ago. I thought the water-drinking was healthy, and I was delighted to be losing weight. Like an eejit, I thought it might help make me attractive in Tom's eyes.'

'Oh God, Annette, I was so sure that it was my report that had tipped you over the edge. I am so relieved. It can't have been easy handling that as well, though.'

I heard her sigh on the other end.

'No, that's been hell,' she admitted. 'But you know, I think it's going to be OK. I cried my eyes out when I read your report and saw the photographs, but when I thought it through, I realised that I was more scared of being alone than anything else. It's not so much losing Tom any more, it's more having to find me.'

'Annette, I can't believe you're so calm and collected about all of this. It's brilliant.'

'To be honest, I'm not really. It's just that when I thought rationally about it, which was hard to do, let me assure you, I realised that this was all about me now, not me and Tom. I was crying my eyes out in the kitchen when it came to me that I didn't care about the situation as much as I'd thought I would. I was angry more than upset. And just plain afraid of being alone. It was a kind of Road to Damascus experience, in a way. I look back on the marriage and I think, "All right, it's not as if I've had one kid a year for ten years and come out of the maternity hospital at the end of it a different person." But I *am* different now, and I don't think he is. And I don't think that he's noticed that I'm different.'

She sighed again and cleared her throat. 'And I've been wondering a lot about this – just why do I want to hang on to him, you know? I'm still fond of him all right, but I'm not sure if I like him that much any more. Especially after what he's put me through. And the kids too; they're not stupid, they know there's something wrong. So why hang on to him? I don't really need the sex any more. I feel as if I've had enough of that for the time being, from him anyway. Sure, I get a bit lonely in the house sometimes, and I want to talk to a grown-up, just one-to-one, not with a whole load of others. And if that's all he's there for really, then what's the point? Maybe I could find someone better to talk to.'

'Annette, you're an inspiration,' I said, genuinely.

'Ah now, let's not be too hasty, I'm not exactly out of the woodwork yet.'

The tremor had returned to her voice, and she sounded very young and fragile. 'You should see me right now, all trussed up and hooked up. I'm a fright. The kids say I'm like an alien.' She cleared her throat again. 'No, it's you that I've found inspirational,' she replied. 'I think that young women like you have it figured out. There you are, with your own business and your independence. You've got yourself sorted before you need ever look for a partner. That's a great position to be in.'

I began to get that hollow, sham feeling again. But now was not the time to tell her about my, at best, lazy relationship with Barry, or that my job wasn't the wonderful and inspiring force that I'd hoped it would be. She needed the positive now, and if she saw that in me then we would leave it at that for the time being. I was back to the old withholding of information habit. I said goodbye and promised to see her on my return.

'Leo,' she said, 'don't worry about me, I'll cope. It won't be easy, but I will. Something good will come of this.' Then she half-laughed and whispered, 'It bloody well better.'

I needed to clear my head, so I set off on a walk by the gallops. Alex Wood sat on the bonnet of a Range Rover. A brown hound slobbered out of the passenger seat window. Alex looked through some binoculars, then reached into the cab of the vehicle and tooted the horn three times. He looked through the binoculars again, then barked into a walkie-talkie.

'Richard, tell that bitch Jackie that that was for her, she's letting Reckless go far too fast. Tell her to rein him in, or I'll have her sorry ass.'

He turned his gaze to me, and I remembered my dream. My face reddened and my nipples hardened. He *must* know about the dream. It had to be written all over my face.

Barry once told me about a time when he had the leading role in a Restoration comedy play, a 'snot rag' he called it, because there was so much handkerchief waving. Part of his costume was a pair of thigh-high leather boots, which he'd worn all through rehearsals so that he could become accustomed to them. They had caused quite a stir. One morning, his leading lady blushingly said, 'I suppose you know exactly what I dreamt about you last night.' 'You can remind me later,' he'd said, and she did, both in word and action. As it turned out, each of the women in the cast had similar dreams, and in turn, over the weeks of the run, they showed him. That production is Barry's personal favourite of his career to date.

I jolted back to the present, and a situation that I would have preferred not to have been in. I struggled for breath, again. I felt that dull ache between my legs, again.

'The student escapee. My wife will start to think it's personal if you keep running away from her class.'

'Lunchbreak,' I explained, 'and I needed to get out for some air. I've been having the nightmare day from hell so far. But I think things are beginning to look up now.'

'That's a racy compliment to pay to a married man.'

I almost choked in shock at the misunderstanding. Of course then I had to make it worse by trying to explain.

'Oh no, no, I wasn't trying to . . . I mean I . . . it's to do with something else entirely.'

'Relax,' he laughed, 'I won't tell anyone, it'll be our little secret.'

He was revelling in my discomfort. The better part of valour was to give up and walk away with an attempt at dignity. I had got a few hundred yards from him, with my head held very high, when I stepped in a rut and landed on my arse in a ditch at the side of the road. This really was intolerable. He ran over to help me, pulling me gently to my feet. His face was only inches from mine as he asked if I was hurt.

'No,' I whispered.

'That's good to hear,' he said. 'We wouldn't want anything to happen to you, now would we?'

I was dizzy with his closeness, and gasping a little for breath. I was sure he was perfectly aware of the effect he was having. He held me there for a few moments, as if to steady me. His eyes were daring me to kiss him, and for one crazy moment I thought I might. Then sense prevailed and I broke away and brushed down my jeans.

'I'm fine now, thank you very much. I'd better get back to my class, or Mrs Wood will not be best pleased.'

'Stick to the road on your way back,' he said, teasing, 'it's safer than the ditches around here. You never know what sort of dangerous type you might meet in one of those.'

I gave him a little wave. 'Life's a ditch,' I said. 'Goodbye.'

# FIFTEEN

'You're looking a bit mucky,' said Con, as he leaned against the cookery school door.

'I went a few rounds with nature. It won.' My bottom had begun to throb, and not in a pleasant way. I could look forward to some big buttock bruises by sundown.

'Your number one fan has been asking after you.'

'You mean Toto?'

He nodded, barely stifling a laugh.

'You know, it's funny,' I said, 'but I would have bet money that he'd be more of a man's man, if you know what I mean.'

'Oh indeed I do, Leo, I think we would all have lost money on that.'

'Unless, of course, we've all got the wrong end of the stick. Perhaps he knows that something deadly is about to befall me, and he's toying with me before pulling off my wings.'

'Mmm, conspiracy theory, my favourite.' He glanced at his watch. 'Come on, we'd better make our presence felt or the search party will be sent out. Did you speak with your friend?'

'Yes, and she's doing well, much better than expected. Thanks for asking, and thanks for what you did earlier on.'

'As I've told you before, it's all part of the service.'

Victoria Knowles had turned into a gigantic bouquet of fragrant, white lilies in my absence. They sprouted from her waist up. She twirled around to reveal the real Mrs Knowles and placed them neatly on her desk. They were wrapped in cellophane, so as to have their own in-built vase and water. She fluffed them with her hands and inhaled deeply, and with some considerable pleasure. And whaddaya know, her nails were now blue. Hard luck Toto.

'Someone's got an admirer,' I said, in passing.

'Yes, you could say that,' she beamed, reaching for the attached message. As we left the reception area, I heard her mutter 'bastard', not the usual comment, or response, for this sort of situation. I made a mental note to get my hands on that card later.

Toto was standing sentinel at the door to the kitchen.

'Just in time,' he announced, ushering us to our places, before joining Esther at the top of the class.

'Some of you may want to entertain in formal dinner party style,' she said, 'so I'll quickly go through a traditional roast and accompaniments. These can be a lot trickier than people imagine. But if you're organised, and keep it simple and classic, there is no finer way to spend an evening.'

The finest way of spending an evening, it seemed to me at that moment, would have been to go to bed with a bottle of wine. No thoughts, no problems, no company. Just a bottle of plonk, a few imaginative sexual scenarios and a lot of sleep. I realised that I was ravenous as well as exhausted. I found it difficult to focus on roasting a dead animal for a dozen people. In fact, I didn't even much like the imaginary dozen people I was imagining cooking a dead animal for.

A bespectacled flame-haired man piped up.

'I'm a vegetarian, where does that leave me?'

It was a question that had been waiting to be asked for some time. I remembered that Fergus had taken most of Esther's courses, so I had no doubt that she had an answer. She did.

'Ah, Jeffrey. Please don't worry, I haven't forgotten you. The very next thing I'll demonstrate is a delicious vegetarian risotto.' She looked around the room and smiled. 'I don't know about the rest of you, but I always feel sorry for vegetarians, they get the slim end of the wedge.'

All eyes turned to Jeff to see if he was taking offence. His jury was out. She continued.

'When I go to a party or to a barbecue, or whatever, every meat-eater there stuffs themselves with meat, certainly, but also has a go at the vegetarian food as well.'

I looked around the classroom at a sea of nodding heads.

'Of course, it's not a reciprocal situation. Obviously, when the vegetarian food runs out, a vegetarian cannot exactly sink his, or her, teeth into a pork chop or a fillet steak. So they often go hungry. In a way, I think it's a lack of respect for a whole kind of eating, an ethos, a way of life, this assumption that it's "only vegetables", which are merely treated as an accompaniment to meat by carnivores. It is an insult to underestimate a good, and particularly organically-grown, vegetable.' She laughed lightly in self-deprecation. 'End of lecture,' she said. 'But I do feel strongly about this. And may I just clarify that I am a meat-eater, though I don't indulge myself every day, and I am very careful about my sources.'

I wanted to be this woman. She could cook. She had views I agreed with. She had a thriving business, built on one of the great basics of life – food. She was passionate about it. She was progressive. And she had one of the most desirable husbands in the country. I wanted to be this woman.

I am not that woman. I never will be. I am Leo Street, Private Investigator. Purveyor of Grubby Secrets. Without a Royal Licence. But like The Urban Peasant, I use what I've got.

The vegetable risotto smelled glorious. We all, guiltily, wanted to try it, but were mindful of being gluttonous carnivores.

'You will notice,' said a smiling Esther, 'that I am making a giant version of this dish. I can see a lot of uneasy, hungry eyes. You would do well to remember to increase the amounts of all your vegetarian offerings in the expectation of locusting meat-eaters going mad. As I've said, show some respect.'

'Just as well,' said Con, 'I'd hate to see Jeff cut up savage on us if we stole his grub.'

I laughed gently at the idea. Jeff was a tall, stick insect, who didn't look like he'd give off much wind-resistance.

'We seem to have been wrong about Maolíosa being a veggie,' I pointed out. 'He didn't exactly leap up and join forces with old Jeff there.'

'No,' admitted Con. 'I wonder if he *is* one though, and because no one here knows that, he's decided to feast on meat for the weekend and start being a vegetarian again on Monday?'

'Another conspiracy theory?'

'Well that or he's got worms, or hollow legs. I've never seen a man eat so much. He's constantly chewing on something, and yet he's as thin as a rake.'

'Yeah, sick-making.'

I'd begun to feel lightheaded from lack of food. This was too much irony, seeing as I was surrounded by the stuff. I was glad when Toto announced that he would take us quickly through some dessert ideas while the rest of the food cooked. Then, and this was the best news, we would eat it all. We could also sit down for the demonstration, although this was ever so slightly uncomfortable for me since my spill into the ditch. I eased myself gently on to my high stool, and sighed with fatigue.

Everything seemed so relentless now. There was the course to finish, and I did want to finish it. I had enjoyed the newness of the experience, in spite of the terror and frustration it sometimes brought. And it was something that I would probably never have done for myself. Imagine having Harry Knowles to thank for something, I thought. I was quite sure that if he knew I had been enjoying any aspect of this weekend he would have put a stop to it immediately; it wasn't part of his remit to bring pleasure to anyone but himself. I also truly hoped that I could nail down some proof for Harry. There was professional pride involved, and it was a case that I wanted to wrap up quickly. I couldn't even let myself contemplate a scenario where I might have to continue beyond Sunday night. Failure was not an option.

Ciara Senior was looking very pleased. Toto was talking us through a white chocolate mousse in a brandy snap.

'A drop of Cointreau in that and it would be heaven,' she confided.

'Of course, you could add orange liqueur, or whatever tickles your fancy,' said Toto.

She beamed. 'I say it here, it comes out there.'

'Perhaps one of you would like to taste this,' he suggested, looking directly at me. 'Leo, come up here and give it a try.'

Both Ciaras were choking for breath, in an effort to stifle their delight. They looked at the floor and rocked with laughter. Con cleared his throat and whispered, 'Dead man walking.'

The journey to the top of the class was one of the longest of my life. I bumped into every corner of every work-bench as I tried to look nonplussed. By the time I got to him, Graham had loaded a spoon lovingly with his concoction and was stretching it toward me. I assumed it was some form of elaborate, culinary foreplay. His roundy face smiled happily, and I expected his bowtie to do a twirl. Just as the spoon reached my mouth I began to laugh, and almost choked on the mousse as I tried to swallow. He looked concerned.

'Ib's belicious,' I assured him, spitting a little. 'Ababooly belicious.'

I ran back to my place with mousse running down my chin, and tears of laughter threatening to run down my cheeks.

'Well held,' said Con, clearing his throat a few more times.

I looked quickly around the class and saw that everyone was now looking at the floor and shaking silently.

Graham looked delighted with himself, and carried on in triumph. The event had obviously been a great success in his eyes. He now talked a mean ice-cream, lingering over the details of making your own organic version. Junior winked and gave me a thumbs up.

'You've scored,' she whispered, 'you lucky, lucky woman. How we've all longed for that man to take notice of us.'

Senior snorted beside her.

'Stop it you two,' I warned, pathetically. 'And for your information, this may not be what it seems. Besides, it's not fair to make fun of either him or me.' I was really feeling the truth of my last statement, and I hoped that they would give up on the teasing.

Graham continued on his chosen theme, in his chosen style. He explained how to tart up available brands of ice-cream if you couldn't, or wouldn't, make your own. His passion for his subject was quite heart-warming, and I didn't want him to be hurt by our childish sniggers. Besides, he knew his stuff, and the long and short of it was that we didn't. We were there to learn, and he was the one with the knowledge. I was just a bit weary to be fielding romantic advances, if that's what they were. And *if* they were, why were they directed at me? Why had I suddenly, it seemed, taken his eye? In the words of yet another winning Irish entry in the Eurovision Song Contest, 'Why Me?'

Romance has to be in the final running for the oddest of all larks. It's a difficult one to carry off. Here I was, with a perfect opportunity to be wooed, and, even if I were to ignore the Barry factor, surely I should have been flattered enough to be a little receptive? No. Because here's where romance falls down – nature just doesn't always allow for you not fancying the other party. Even swans have this problem. Of course, a lot of other creatures don't, they just rut and move on. But even on my most animal of days, I would find it difficult to rut with Toto and move on. Not the moving on, the other. I guess this makes me fickle in some people's eyes, but that's the way love goes. I'm just one of those girls.

It was a relief when Esther took over for World Cheeses, and Toto went about checking the cooking dinner. I was also quietly grateful that he was back to being Toto in my mind, rather than having become Graham for any amorphous moral reason.

Packing the entire contents of the globe's cheese section into twenty minutes might have daunted a lesser woman, but Esther Wood didn't falter once. Nor did she call a halt there, but quickly ran through some drinks suggestions as well. There comes a point when so much effortless skill and learning has you looking for signs of a superior smugness, and hoping for a chance to smack the perpetrator for it. I was too weak to lift a hand if I did spot it. At this stage each item of information was melding into the next for me. All I could hear clearly was my tummy grumbling that it hadn't been fed, and all I could feel was the slight nausea of starvation, and a dull ache in my buttocks from my lunchtime encounter with the ditch.

Victoria came in with a list for Esther to scan. I took the opportunity to leave for the loo, and to have a look for the mysterious card which had arrived with the bouquet of flowers. They were now placed, impersonally, by the front door, as if they were part of the corporate image of the school. Victoria had not been pleased with the message, so the litter bin was the logical place to search. Under a crumpled sheet of typing paper lay a little hand-written note with a floral border. It read: 'I'm on to you, H.' Harry Knowles strikes again. I'd say that Harry could keep up this sort of annoyance indefinitely. He's got the money, he's got the attitude, the century is his oyster. The man wouldn't even need to be alive to continue this kind of carry-on. I jotted down the details of delivery time, flower variety, and the message. I intended to put these details in my report, because I wanted him to know that I was on to him too.

I made my way to the bathroom and splashed some cold water on my face to freshen up. This led to a mascara melt that left me looking like a panda, though not as cute. I did my best to repair the damage but the result fell somewhere short of success. I don't think that I ever want to meet anyone who works in the cosmetics industry, because I'm sure I'll bore them to death with complaints. Even though I buy make-up that has not been tested on animals, and which professes to be kind to human skin, I have situations like this, where liquid cement is attached to my face and I can only hope that time will be the great healer we all hear about. Surely if a product is *so* good for your skin it should be easy to get rid of. A little water, in a crisis, could be expected to get you out of a pickle such as this. I pulled and tugged at my skin (yes, even that delicate eye area), and all I seemed to do was spread the unction. You could say that this succeeded in rendering it all a match, but I was now a little too piebald for my liking.

I paused for a few deep breaths. I was feeling jittery and nervous, of what I couldn't tell. I convinced myself that all I needed was to eat something. With my blood sugar levels up, all would be well. It's easy to look back now and say that I was having some sort of portent of doom, which of course I was not. I'm not in any way psychic, I'm glad to say. But that's what I mean about *having* to retain your perspective as a detective – reading false meanings into a situation is of no help to anyone, even long after the event. And even if the ultimate outcome matches your theorising. Stick with the facts, and resist that attractive devil, hindsight. We never do, of course. We're all human, more or less. And we all like to bend a fact.

I returned to find that dinner was being served. One of the great by-products of a cookery course is that you get very well fed, at least after the demonstration. Your own first attempt at any dish might not always be the success you'd like. I've had a few disasters trying out some of the course's recipes, and my overwhelming feeling was of pure amazement. How could it go so wrong when I'm perfectly confident that I did exactly what I saw?

Of course we all baled into the mushroom risotto, with little or no respect for the vegetarians amongst us, in spite of the earlier lecture. And we were all agreed that it was the perfect accompaniment to the roast, apart from the vegetarians, that is. Victoria Knowles even stayed to tuck into a plate of grub. When she had eaten a dainty morsel, she came over to me.

'I couldn't help noticing that you had a bit of a crisis earlier on. I hope your friend is all right.'

'Thank you, yes, I think she'll be fine. I just got a bit of a shock, that's all. And thank you again for asking.'

She smiled and said, 'Well, thank you for looking out for me last night. No need to put too much store by anything I might have said. I got myself into a bit of a state. Too much rot-gut wine at a fundraiser, and then, of course, everything takes on a false importance. Marriage is a rollercoaster at the best of times, let alone when you're overworked and a little squiffy.'

'I can imagine.'

'I'd best get back to work. Perhaps I'll see you later, it's traditional for us to take the class for a drink the night before their project demonstrations.'

'Yes, I'll look forward to that.'

As she sashayed back to her desk, I wondered how she kept her legs so smooth. I bet she's one of those lucky people who aren't very hairy to begin with, and even then it's all quite fair hair. The hair on my legs is very *un*fair, in all senses.

# SIXTEEN

A Project. A Report. They're always waiting for us. Sometimes out in the open, bold as brass. Sometimes it's an ambush. But it's that undesirable that you think you can avoid, the older you get. Dream on. What was I going to do about The Project? The Report? Great, the hard questions first.

What were the options?

Where was Mick Nolan when I needed him?

Right then. In the absence of any *real* help, I'm just going to have to do this myself. Right then. Right.

OK, any moment now it'll kick into action. I'm not prepared to say *what*, because at this stage that would be foolish, not actually *knowing* the 'what' yet. But any moment now.

Any moment now . . .

'You look like you could do with a bit of help.'

'Con, I've never bought into organised religion, but if you're what they've got to offer, then I'm sold.'

He looked both pleased and puzzled.

'Ah feck it Con, I'm in trouble. What the *fuck* am I doing here, and I'm sorry for the language. Ah *God*, what the *hell*.'

'You're *really* mixing your metaphors now, and I *really* will have to call a halt to that. If you don't mind me saying so, Leo, I've never known someone to go so over the top about so little. If this project thing *is* what this is all about?'

This could be a now or never time. I could tell Con all about my real purpose for being here this weekend. But what would he think of me then? And would that just be a handy off-loading of a burden, the trouble shared being halved?

I half-chickened it. 'Don't mind me, Con; I'm having a rotten day, and you're right, it's not all to do with the course. I *am* trying to fit something else in while I'm here, and basically there aren't enough hours in the day.'

'Sounds fascinating.'

'Believe me, it's a lot grubbier than that.'

'You know, as a Catholic priest, I'm trained to keep secrets. As it happens, in this case, I'm also intensely curious.'

'It's not exactly the location of the Holy Grail, it'll hold till tomorrow.'

'Mysteriouser and mysteriouser.'

'You're going to be very disappointed when you find out what it is.'

'Stop! You're just making it all the more attractive. Ah, this is terrible, I won't be able to concentrate on anything now.'

'A mysterious secret, how marvellous,' said a man behind me. It was Toto, and he was invading my personal space. I stepped back and became wedged between him and the worktop.

'Really, it's nothing to write home about,' I said, 'just work stuff.'

'And what do you do?'

'Oh, insurance, that sort of thing, you know, boring.'

'Not at all,' he assured me. 'As it happens, I have a few things you might be able to help me with in that line. We'll be bringing the class for a little celebratory drink in The Stables. We can chat then.'

Now I felt wedged between Toto and my life.

'Is it just me, or have things gone into freefall in that particular situation?'

'Although this drink will involve the class,' said Con, 'which makes it a group activity, strictly speaking, I think you've just been asked out. Oh, bees to the honey.'

'Flies to the shite,' I muttered.

I needed a bit of Esther to calm me down, and that's what we all got. She was back in charge and I felt safe again. Toto was in a pinny doing the washing-up. He was wearing orange rubber gloves. They suited him.

'Traditionally, we use this evening to answer queries you may have about your plans for tomorrow. Sorry to be a bit of a cracked record about this, but I am always keen to stress that planning is half the battle, so use your time wisely. Also, some of you may even want to do a little dry run for your presentation, and the kitchen is entirely at your disposal for that. And remember, have fun, that's what this is all about. We want you to be entertained too, not only your guests. Later, as you'll no doubt have heard by now, we'll be bringing you all for a restorative tipple at The Stables Bar.'

'A bottle of arsenic in my case,' I whispered to Con.

'Now, now, Cinderella,' he chided.

I looked at my lovely new friend. He was absent-mindedly scratching his chubby cheek as he began to formulate his thoughts on his project.

'Con, how did you end up in your job?'

'Have you got three years?' he laughed. 'I didn't always know that I would become a priest. I mean, I wasn't excessively religious when I was young, or anything like that. I went to college to study Philosophy and Theology, and I guess that's when the realisation dawned. It was funny really, as a philosophy student I could reason an argument against religion, but as a theology student I could support it fully. When I finally took my vows, I spent a few years in Rome. That's where the paunch started, actually, too much food and wine. We'd spend long hours arguing theology, sitting down, mostly. I loved it, and I did well. But even though I adored the thinking and the debate, I found the rest very political. The whole system, the infrastructure of the Vatican is very hierarchical. And I really believe in a relevant Church, one that's in everyday lives. I was worried that I might disappear into a cloud of argument, and lose sight of the main objectives of my ministry. I was a bit homesick too after a few years of the clerical high life. But when you come back, you have to start on the bottom rung again, because here it's bureaucracy.'

'You can't have one without the other.'

'You've got it. And in the end, it is a job, on top of

everything else. So here I am.'

'Tummy and all.'

'Yes, strange to say, that never disappeared.'

'At least it means you'll always have a little bit of Italy in you.'

'Well, actually a very large bit.'

'I'd better leave you alone, or you'll get no planning done. And it's no good for me to be distracting myself either,' I said, heaving myself away.

I took up position by the door, to keep an eye on a typing Victoria Knowles, and sat looking at a blank piece of paper, waiting for some inspirational planning to arrive. We had two hours before the drinks treat, but I felt I would be able to cram any of my great thoughts and deeds into twenty minutes. Even at that, I was probably being overgenerous with time. What had I learned? What could I do?

The large room was a hive of happy industry. Ciara Junior appeared to be doing something lewd with an aubergine and some courgettes. Her eyes sparkled wickedly as she said, 'This will be my most cunning stunt yet.' Senior was looking into the middle distance. Every so often she would give a little laugh and write something down. She did not look in the least bit worried. Con was also scribbling and giggling.

I felt like my mother leaving her parents' home

after being married. As the car pulled away she had asked, 'How long do you cook potatoes for?' The badly done potato would have wrecked that marriage, and I might never have been born. Come to think of it, I'd never asked to be born, so it was obviously their fault that I was in this mess.

Con had said to concentrate on our strengths and possibly to think theme, for both fun and structure. The Urban Peasant would tell me to use what I'd got. Still my sheet of paper was virginal. Then it hit me – bread. That was what I had attempted most often on this course, and the results hadn't been too disastrous. I would do lots of different breads and buy some spreads, cold cuts and those global cheeses from the farm shop to go with them. Entertainment with a capital 'E'.

There was a partial problem in as much as we'd only ever trotted through brown bread and cheesy scones, so a little adaptation would be required. I turned to the school 'library' which was housed on some book shelves by the door. I would research some ideas from the experts. Things were looking up.

I began to make a list of things that I liked. I would have cheese and chive scones. I would do a very nutty version of brown bread with a seed crust. What about a tomato bread, using purée? Or a garlic one? A cheese with cardamom pods? I was going to have to go into yeast territory for some of the breads I wanted to try. This was daunting, but what must be must be. It also meant starting very early in the morning so that those loaves could rise before baking. I felt excited, and almost capable of carrying this off. I organised the tasks, copied some recipes and did a shopping list. I threw my pen down with a confident 'hah' and beamed at the Gang.

'Eureka?' asked a tentative Con.

'Oh yes. At least, I hope so.'

'But I'll still mention you in my prayers tonight?'

'Oh yes.'

There was a palpable excitement in the kitchen. Notes were guarded jealously in case of culinary espionage. Wary questions about oven times and facility sharing were thinly veiled strategies. But above the competitive edge was the feeling that we were all contributing to a special party, *our* party; we would be the first to be Entertained.

Victoria Knowles stood at the door with Esther and Toto, observing our progress and smiling. They must have seen it all before, I thought, but they still seemed to enjoy it. They were the parents and we were the children on Christmas Eve, excited and unable to sleep. I hoped that all of our little faces would be happy when Christmas Day came.

I needed to stick close to Victoria because I wasn't

sure what her movements would be later that evening. It meant that I wouldn't be able to drink more than a glass of wine in the pub, as I might have to follow her in my car. A handy by-product of this would be a sharp mind in the morning. I would need it.

The Stables was having a busy Saturday night, but a corner had been reserved for the class. It had not been cordoned off, thank goodness. I've spent far too many nights posing with Barry 'King Club' Agnew in 'secluded' areas of Dublin nightspots, with punters staring and wondering should they know who you are. Barry loves all that, so the sooner he gets a part in one of the television soaps the better. And he can buy the drinks then.

The stable hands were out in force and having a rare old time. In their midst, I recognised the female whippet who'd been on the scrounge the day before, and a casually dressed Adam Philips. He nodded cordially in my direction, no doubt relieved that I was at a distance, and unlikely to sweep him off his feet in my usual way. I wondered which one was Jackie, who had been beeped at by Alex Wood for letting one of the horses go too fast. Richard Cooper leered over and raised his glass to me. I leered back and raised mine.

'How do you know him?' asked Senior.

'I don't really, I just ran into him on my way home last night. He frightened the life out of me. I think that's his speciality.'

Victoria and Toto were mingling amongst us with glasses of wine. I nursed a white. Maolíosa and Keith were involved in some sort of brinkmanship about the use of their oven. Toto stepped in to mediate. Esther was in a circle of Gladys, Ruth, Jeff and his cooking partner, whom I realised I hadn't actually met.

'His name is Donald,' explained Con, 'but he prefers Donny.'

'Tragic, isn't it,' said Junior.

'If you'd been an Osmonds fan, you wouldn't think so,' I pointed out.

'Who were the Osmonds?'

I let it go.

'Con, are we going to have a fight over our oven?' I asked.

'Not unless you want one,' he replied, warily.

'Well, you know how I feel *sort of* confident about doing bread. So, I thought I'd concentrate my display around various kinds of . . . bread. And I'll need the oven for that.'

'It's not a problem with me, Leo, I'll be concentrating on the hob area. What a team we make, eh?'

'Care to let me in on what you're up to?'

'Like your own special secret, it'll wait until tomorrow,' he said, smugly.

Victoria waved and blew a kiss towards the stable gang. They waved and blew kisses back; she laughed and pretended to be knocked back by the breeze. As she was close enough to talk to, I asked, 'Do you cook?'

She laughed again. 'No, I can't even boil an egg. Cereal and toast in the morning are about as much as I can manage. I'm not at home a lot anyway, the cookery school and my husband's social engagements see to that.' She finished her wine and poured another. 'I'm sure it can't have escaped your attention, but our Graham has been showing an interest in you all day. We couldn't help but notice that your name is on the guest list for the Ball, and I think he's looking for someone to bring.'

So *that's* what it was all about. He needed a partner for the Spring Ball. Hopefully, it also meant that he had no actual romantic interest in me, and just needed someone to go in the door with. He was about to be disappointed though, I already had a date.

'Does Mrs Wood do all of the cooking for the Ball herself?' I asked.

'Oh good Lord no. She'll supervise and put the finishing touches to a few things. No, she has an army of ex-pupils on hand, mostly from her longer residential course. It would be an impossible amount of work for one person. That's not to say that she hasn't attempted to do it all in the past. In leaner times she had to, but she nearly ended up in hospital because of it. Now she delegates, and has a jolly good time.'

Victoria Knowles was drinking a lot of wine. I hoped that she didn't intend to drive home. But then, maybe she wasn't going home. Maybe she was being collected. Maybe this would be a break-through for me. She was getting along famously with Ciara Junior, who had admired her blue nails. I could have told Ciara a thing or two about those nails. Now they were discussing body piercings, about which I knew less. My only theory was that my fillings would dance if I encountered one with my mouth.

A man approached and Victoria's eyes lit up.

'Joseph Lindsay, where did you spring from? I didn't expect to see you until the Ball.'

I couldn't believe my ears. Joseph, Joe. Bingo.

They threw their arms around each other and laughed. She introduced us all, saying that this was a dear, dear friend of hers, who was as elusive as he was good-looking. While they drank some wine and chatted, I surreptitiously rooted through my purse for a microphone to plant on them as they left.

Then I could listen as well as video, from wherever we ended up. I began to feel excited about doing some surveillance. I was back to the cut and thrust of my job. So I was surprised, and disconcerted, to see Harry Knowles appear. I moved closer to Victoria as he made his way over and heard her say to Joe, 'Well, that's the end of my night out. Here comes my lift home.'

Joe turned to see who was coming. 'Ah, your lord and master.'

'He's being very vigilant at the moment. He drives me in to work, then collects me later on. He even sent me flowers today, with an agenda, mind you. It's all very tiresome.'

'He won't be very pleased to see me,' said Joe.

'Harry's never pleased to see anyone, except himself in the mirror, and the present Party leader, who like himself was a builder once. They probably have a great time discussing scaffolding and RSJs.'

'What's an RSJ?'

'Ask my husband.'

'Or the Party leader.'

What the hell did Harry think he was up to? I glared at him as he went past. How was I ever going to get him the evidence he wanted if he wouldn't let his wife out of his sight? He was deliberately making this more difficult for me. I will never understand men.

The energy of that thought must have beckoned Toto to me. He offered some white wine from the bottle he was carrying. Why not? It now looked likely that Victoria would be captive in her own home this evening, in the charming and inimitable company of her wedded husband. And it might help me deal with Toto. The Gang hovered on the periphery of our little group of two.

'Have you enjoyed the course?' he asked, earnestly.

'Yes, very much. I haven't done much cooking before. I'm not very good at it.'

'Well, I hope that you'll be bringing some new skills away with you.'

'Oh, I'm sure I will.'

'Leo, there's something I've been meaning to ask you all day.'

'Actually, Graham, there's something I've been meaning to ask you too.' I had to get him off this tack. 'Yeast. I need to know about yeast for tomorrow.'

And off he went on my chosen subject. It was as easy as winding up a clockwork toy and watching it go, except that Toto was more colourful. I hoped that even half of what he was telling me was filtering into my subconscious. My attention was elsewhere. Harry and Victoria were leaving, and Joe

SOMETHING FOR THE WEEKEND

had gone to talk to the stable lads and lasses. Then Alex Wood arrived and he and Joe had an extended bout of back-slapping. They drank a quick short and left together. Adam Philips stayed put.

I was secretly delighted that Alex and Victoria had missed one another. I really did not want him in that particular infidelity mix. Ridiculously, I felt that I, almost, had him to myself if he was not carrying on with Victoria. I have no idea how I thought this made any sort of sense.

'So you'll need to start very early if you want it all to be ready in time.'

'Sorry?'

'With the rising time involved, you'll need to start that bit earlier, to get everything done in time.'

'Of course.'

'I'll be in early, so I'll let you in. Maybe you'd like some breakfast?' I obviously looked startled, because he quickly added, 'I'll be making some for myself anyway.'

'Thank you Graham, you really are too kind.'

'Not at all. Besides, there is something that you might be able to do for me.'

If I had moved suddenly at that point, Con and the Ciaras would have fallen over. They were all leaning on one another, and then on me, in an effort to catch every word. It was very, *very* tempting.

'I noticed your name on the guest list for tomorrow night, without a "plus one", and I wondered if you'd like to accompany me?'

He looked lonely and vulnerable, and I hesitated before giving my answer.

'Actually, I'm meeting up with Fergus Rush beforehand, and we're planning to go together. But you'd be very welcome to join us, it's an informal arrangement.'

'Em, no, no. No, I'll find someone else, don't worry. But thank you for the offer.'

'Thank *you* for yours.'

He walked away without refilling my glass. The three angels on my shoulder cackled.

'I wouldn't expect breakfast in the morning,' said Senior.

Apparently, there is less shame in drinking your face off and getting all wobbly in public, than in doing this in the privacy of your own home, where there are, usually, fewer people to insult and to disgrace yourself in front of. And where you only need to crawl a short distance to your bed or your sofa to pass out. Go figure. Here in the heart of Kildare, we were in the dangerous position of being able to combine both. None of us was staying more than five hundred yards away, after all. That's why we took an executive and plenary decision to leave early, with our wits about us.

I still had sleep to make up from the night before; if that can ever be done, I'm not sure. But I also had tapes to watch and to listen to. Two hours later, it was obvious to me that Victoria Knowles had had a busy but rather humdrum day. Apart from the annoyance of Harry's floral tribute and a phone call from Joe.

She went through the routine of changing her nails, which still had the power to make me squirm. I think it was because of the aggressive way she went at it. It looked like it had to be painful, even if she showed no discomfort.

She was obviously delighted when the flowers arrived. I was shocked at how *flat* my voice sounded as I spoke to her; it doesn't sound like that in my head at all – in my head it's deeper, for one thing. When she read the card, she muttered 'bastard' a few times, as I had heard, and threw it in the bin, where I found it later. Then she dumped the flowers by the door, where we all admired them, and returned to her desk to do some work. She was sitting there for about three minutes before she got up and kicked the bin lightly a few times. She was so pleased with this that she aimed an extra-specially hard kick, missed, and walloped her foot off the wall. Now she was much less pleased, and limping.

She rang Adam Philips to complain, saying that Harry was 'up to his tricks again', and using the phrase 'mental cruelty' a lot. I think he must have told her to leave Harry, because she replied, 'Oh I know I should, but I'm not sorted yet. Besides, if his land rezoning deal comes to anyone's attention, I probably won't need to leave, *he'll* be going, preferably to jail and for a very long time. Some journalist type has been sniffing around and he's getting very antsy.' Now, now, Harry, what have you been up to, I wondered? No doubt I would read all about it in a newspaper soon. I hoped so.

Her conversation with Joe involved a lot more giggling. Now that I had seen and heard him, I could imagine his voice suggesting various situations to his lover. From her reaction it was obvious that he was treating her to some racy scenarios. She didn't say much, just the odd, 'Is that so?' or 'You'll have to show me that in detail.' This woman was in for a ball, or two, at the Ball. If anyone had passed by they would never have known the exact nature of the conversation; she could have been discussing building specifications. I was glad that they didn't indulge in full phone sex, it's something I never enjoy transcribing. Perhaps that's a throwback to my convent school education; a smidgen of Catholic guilt? Maybe it's just envy.

It seemed logical to call Barry. I didn't hold out any hope of telephone sex with him. I was too worn out anyway. Amazingly, he was in.

'I have a few friends round,' he explained. He named a few ne'er-do-wells that he pals around with. He was welcome to them. He had no news other than that he was on a shortlist for the impro- vised play he'd auditioned for. I was delighted; he was scathing.

'They either want me or they don't. I hate all of this powerplay stuff. Shortlist, my arse.'

This was bravado, I'd seen it all before. For all his cockiness, Barry was deeply hurt each time he missed a part. He took it personally, and would go into a crisis of self-confidence.

'Do you know who you're up against?'

'The usual suspects, I suppose. It'll probably come down to what colour eyes we've got, or something just as trivial.'

'Well, if that's the case, I'm sure you'll win hands down,' I said, reassuringly.

'As long as it's not my acting,' he said sarcastically, ticking me off.

A girl can't win.

'Barry, you know I think you're a really good actor, and I'm not going to indulge you on this now, because I'm wrecked and I badly need a decent night's sleep. So, goodnight, and good luck with the play. If they have any sense at all, they'll choose you.'

'Goodnight. I miss you.'

He was a master at pulling the rug out from under me. It was only later that I remembered that I was supposed to be livid with him.

I had one message, from Anne, to say that she had visited Annette O'Neill, and that she *sort of* understood my situation a little better now. That meant I wasn't quite off the hook. Mercifully, she added that she hadn't mentioned any of this to the rest of the family. It was bad enough that they would be discussing my love life, or lack of it, ad nauseam, without adding my job to the debate too.

It was a delight to prepare for bed. I cleansed, toned and moisturised, often one or all of these was left out. I scrubbed my teeth, and would have flossed them but for the lack of dental floss, or any other sort for that matter. If I'd had longer, better hair, I might have given it a hundred strokes of a bristle brush, again supposing that I would be able to lay hands on a bristle brush at that time of night. Instead, I climbed into bed, and stretched contentedly.

Everybody should have a double bed, even if they have no one to share it with. It is the ultimate essential, with all the trappings of a luxury. The first item bought for No. 11, The Villas was a double bed, which immediately put my mother on Red Alert. I pointed out that I had gone on to buy an electric kettle and a lot of cat food, but she remained convinced that my moral fibre was under threat. Every time she visited, she made some excuse to go upstairs to check on the bed, desperately looking for signs of defilement. She remained disappointed for a long time, as did her only daughter.

There would probably be no harm in letting her loose on the bedroom facilities now. Barry and I have a time share in the bed. He watches television late into the night, while I'm out at work or getting some sleep for an early start. She needn't worry that I'm sinning out of wedlock. Sin would be a fine thing.

I was a virgin until I was nineteen. I think I lasted this long because Andy Raynor had gone to college in Galway, one hundred and thirty-five miles away, and I saw very little of him for four years. When I did, he always assured me that the Dublin ladies' loss was the Galway lassies' gain. I didn't doubt him. When I finally did have sex, it was in the back of a very small car with another shy virgin. I didn't repeat the experience for quite a while. I couldn't see what all the fuss was about. It certainly wasn't in the same league as my encounter with Andy Raynor at the youth club.

From time to time I would receive suggestive cards with a Galway postmark. They were usually quite funny. Then, one Christmas, he sent me a pair of lacy black knickers. I wasn't expecting a present of any sort in the *post*, so I innocently opened the package in front of my father at the breakfast table. I was holding the underwear up before I realised what it was. A card fell out, bearing the message: 'Wear these always, spot checks will be made, love, Santa.' I recognised Andy's handwriting. My father waited patiently for an explanation. 'It's an in-joke,' I said, feebly. 'They're from one of the girls.' He was unconvinced, I'm sure, but he also did not particularly want to know the truth. We left it at that.

The other shy virgin from the back of the car went on to have the first Irish computer firm to be floated for over ten million pounds. He married a model, and they live with their four children in a mansion in the Wicklow hills. They are very happy.

I was drifting off when I realised that the radio-alarm was still set to give me another 'MacArthur Park' if I wasn't careful. I couldn't take that chance. I reached over and set it to 'alarm'. Even if it was a detestable digital noise, it was still preferable to this morning's offering.

As I lay back, I thought about the black knickers. They were actually very comfortable, as well as sexy. I was sorry when they wore out. By the time Andy tried for a 'spot check' they'd been consigned to the knicker bin.

I closed my eyes and wondered idly if Alex would join me again tonight.

He did not.

# SEVENTEEN

'Too many cooks,' said Con.

'It doesn't exactly contravene the laws of assembly,' I pointed out.

We both laughed, nervously.

Everyone had been in early that morning, trying to steal the march. Diarmaid and Eleanor made it first to the top of the queue. Probably because 'we' didn't have a hangover. 'We' were dressed in matching purple shell suits. I wondered if 'we' would change at lunchtime after a little exercise.

It was a big day for all of us, our first catered event. Toto had not flickered an eyelid when he saw the queue at the door. He let us in and busied himself with making coffee and croissants. He was the perfect breakfast host.

We had spontaneously burst into applause when he came into view. He didn't quite know why, and he didn't care, he was happy with the adulation. Today's outfit was a canary yellow suit, with deep red brothel creepers and a red and white polka-dot shirt, open at the neck.

'*Definitely* not Kansas any more,' said Con.

'He's outdone himself this time,' I agreed.

'He's even got the ruby slippers, if he needs to get out of here in a hurry,' said Ciara Senior. 'Just a couple of clicks and he's away.'

'Stylish *and* practical,' nodded Con.

'Wake up and smell the coffee, you lot,' said Junior, 'we're approaching kick-off.'

It was time to haul ass and make a proper start. Toto, true to his word, had given me the crash course on yeast earlier. This amounted to reassuring me about using it, and urging me to read the instructions on the packet carefully. I opted for dried rather than fresh, as I hoped it might have less attitude, but just as much character. A bit like Ciara Junior, when she's quiet.

The stuff terrified me; it seemed to live and breathe of its own accord. I hoped that it was going to be reasonable and agree to help me. I had to start all of my mixtures before everyone else because of the raising time involved. This gave me an hour and a half, generally, to organise the accompaniments to my presentation, and to make any soda bread mixtures. Then, when my yeasty doughs were risen, knocked back and kneaded, I could pop them in the oven and have the bath or the sherry that Delia Smith recommended. Or perhaps both.

Bread may be the staff of life, but it's also a tricky bugger. So many things can, and do, go wrong. It's hard to judge the exact amount of water required, because that depends on the type of flour being used. And if you're mixing those flours in a jazz free-form expression (i.e. not quite grasping a recipe), you may be headed for disaster.

Why does the word 'fall' follow me everywhere?

Too much salt might kill the yeast, which sounds like murder, and too little is just as bad. The kneading is very satisfactory, but if you don't leave enough rising time, you're doomed. And that's before you've even *approached* an oven. Each cooker is different from the next, they practically have personalities, and the ones in the school were no different. I couldn't say that I knew mine very well, or even if it liked me, so I was relying on a lot of Sabbath goodwill.

Beside me, Con was wrestling with bite-size pieces

of animal, mineral and vegetable. This was going to get a lot worse before it got better, I thought. But then, if anyone was going to do well on a Sunday, surely it would be a priest. On the other side, the Ciaras were cackling evilly, hatching their demonic plans. The air was a-hum with anticipation.

I decided to try to make things that I thought I'd like. On the yeast end, I had a cheese and chive mixture, tomato and chilli, and a heady concoction of garlic and onion. These could be dipped in the flavoured olive oils that Esther had so many gallons of. I would also try a fried potato bread, to be served with a garlic purée, a slightly sweetened version of the mighty brown bread, accompanied by an orange and honey syrup, and a white soda with caraway seeds. I was salivating at the whole idea of the spread. If all else failed, I could certainly *talk* a good bread platter.

As my yeasts rose, I calmly left the school, nodding to Victoria Knowles on my way to the farm shop to purchase some cheese and delicious farm-house butter. Then I returned, nodding again to Mrs K., to start my sodas and boil my spuds. Enid Blyton would have been proud of my slap-up feed, at least on paper. Sadly, there didn't seem to be a place for lashings and lashings of ginger beer. And I just did *not* have the time to make or source any.

Keith, the Curdle Man, was panicking again. I hated to think what he'd be like if a bridge he'd designed went wrong. Then again, he'd probably be masterful in that situation, just can't handle the domestics. He was executing a lively dance in front of the stove, dodging to the right and left and shouting, 'Make it stop, make it stop.' At that moment, Esther Wood appeared, calmly walked over to him and turned down the hob.

'Good morning class,' she said. 'I see that everything is going well.'

My fingers ached from the kneading. Ordinarily, these little muscles would have no more to do than hold a pen or type into a computer. My forearms were also threatening seizure. I put my breads into their tins and on to their trays, and put them in the oven along with some heads of garlic wrapped in tinfoil. There was nothing more to do but pray. I looked to the holy man.

Con had obviously been watching chefs on the television. They're hard to avoid, along with fly-on-the-wall documentaries, gardening and animal rescue programmes. He was arranging food on plates, and then throwing garnishes after it, in the manner of a concert pianist tapping a note and then quickly lifting the hand to exaggerate and intensify the movement.

'Very professional,' I commented.

'Thank you,' he said. 'It's all about Entertainment after all, no matter what day of the week, but especially for the weekend, and now that we're highly trained . . .'

'Thank you Father Walter Mitty.'

He laughed, 'Nah, he's in the next parish along.'

'What do you think those two are up to?' I asked.

'We'll see when the time comes,' said Con, sagely. 'And if we can't guess, there'll always be the signs to help us.'

It had been agreed that we would give a title to our presentations. Con had suggested it because he thought he'd win, being King of the Puns. It started as an internal competition between the Gang, and then word leaked out; now it seemed the whole class was in on it.

'Just that little extra spice,' grinned Con.

I arranged my butters, oils and cheeses on the trestle table at the top of the class. This must be what a village fair is like, I thought. Then I placed wire racks on the worktop and put on a pair of oven gloves for the crucial act of retrieving the breads from the oven. This was make or break time, the money shot. Coward that I was, I removed the roast garlic first; it was still in its tinfoil cocoon, and looked and smelled impressive. Then came the brown bread and the white soda, both of which were very presentable. The tomato and chilli looked a bit crisp, but had survived. The onion and garlic loaf was completely flat. I caught Con spying, and fired a shot across his bow.

'Before you say anything, Punmeister, this is not "a mere drop in the oven", it's meant to be flat. It's a kind of focaccia.' I bit my tongue and hoped that I had pronounced it properly; diction is everything with a word like that.

While my breads were cooling, I made my sign. When I had finished shading all of the letters, I looked up to find Esther, Toto and Victoria smiling at the busy room. They seemed proud of us; or were they observing, like humans watch the animals at a zoo? I placed my offerings in their designated place, and heaved a sigh of relief. Around the kitchen the congratulations flowed. Keith was being hugged by Maolíosa, Diarmaid kissed Eleanor, Gladys inhaled, Ruth looked worried, Jeff and Donny smiled weakly, and the Ciaras were giving one another high fives. It was time for the tasting.

The last thing anyone wants to be is a disappointment. A school friend once told me that her new boyfriend had asked what I looked like, after hearing story after story about me. She proudly answered, 'Oh, it's not her looks, it's her personality.' Bless. I felt ugly for years after that one. All around the room anxious faces pointed to the trio of judges. Esther smiled and said, 'I think it's time to break out the wine, don't you, Graham?' He did, and he did. As we sipped our drinks nervously, Esther and her assistants moved about with knives and forks. Soon it would be our turn.

'This is just like Jamborora,' I told the others.

Naturally enough, this was a new concept to them, it being a flight of my father's imagination, and a completely made-up word.

My dad only ever cooks one meal in the week, at teatime on Sunday evenings. This has been tradition for as long as I can remember. He would pass for what's known as 'a plain cook', because all he can do is sausages. One way. He fries a mountain of these and places them all on one big plate in the middle of the table, alongside a mound of buttered bread. Then the assembled company are given forks and told to dig in. No fuss, no washing up. This is Jamborora, and the shy go hungry.

Con's presentation was a range of tapas and finger-food. He had battered and deep fried meat, fish, poultry, vegetables – and himself, by the look of things. These were to be dipped in sauces of all temperatures and nationalities.

'Now that the world is a global village,' he

explained. The experience was called 'Habemus Tapas'. The judges approved and praised him. He lifted his glass to heaven and said, 'Thank you.' Then he drained his glass and beamed at the room in triumph, encouragement and relief.

Ciara Senior stood proudly by 'The Lost Weekend'. I knew now why she had cackled so much. Esther forked through a few morsels and started to furrow her brow. Then she tasted some more and giggled. She shook her tiny exquisite hands in the direction of the spread and said, 'I should probably stop now, or face absolute drunkenness without ever having had a drink.'

Senior had laced *everything* with alcohol. Her chicken dish had been marinated in sherry and ginger, the vegetable accompaniments had a dash of vodka, and her dessert involved a creamy liqueur. To freshen the palate between courses, diners were treated to an orange and Cointreau sorbet.

'Obviously, I would offer an Irish coffee afterwards, just to be patriotic.'

'Always warn your guests to leave their cars at home,' advised Esther.

'Oh yes,' said a saintly Ciara, an impish lilt in her voice. Esther Wood was aghast. When Senior saw this she said, 'No, don't worry, really, of course I'll tell them that. I don't *actually* want to kill any of them, I just want to see them a bit wobbly. And if I'm in any fit state myself, I might even notice and feel a bit superior. Or remember it all a few days later. Who knows?'

'That house is going to have some drinks bill,' I said.

Ciara Junior needed a revolutionary beret. She had given us 'Stuff This'. It was, as the name suggested, a range of stuffed items. She had hollowed out courgettes, aubergines, large mushrooms, potatoes and turnips, and refilled them with delicious mixtures.

'My work is political,' she said, grandly, then fell about in helpless laughter.

'It's also very good,' said Esther. Toto and Victoria nodded in agreement.

'And I don't mean that in any ageist way,' she went on, emphasising the word 'ageist'.

The rest of the Gang stifled sniggers. Ciara reddened. Esther Wood seemed to have the power of second sight, that or super-human hearing if she'd really overheard Junior's pronouncements on the previous occasion of her apparent 'ageism'.

If she was indeed an extraordinary listening device, perhaps I should recruit her for my agency? Then I would have help *and* a top notch caterer, all rolled into one. Of course, I'd also have to actually set up an agency for that, and I'd probably put on lots of weight. It would be that price to pay that my grandmother is so fond of invoking, and I was roundy enough as it stood. I shook my head to clear it of these genetically enhanced thoughts. Time enough to become my mother and/or grandmother a few decades from now. It was shocking to know that the process had already started.

My time had come. I wiped two sweaty palms against my trousers and stood beside 'Our Daily Bread', waiting for the judges' verdict and sentence.

'Mmmm, I'm getting chilli here,' said Toto, 'nice.'

'Yes, and the tomato is rich and flavoursome alongside it,' nodded Esther.

They moved on to the cheese and chive scones and murmured approval, then came to my flattened garlic and onion disaster. My heart was in my mouth, which was also full of white wine that I had forgotten to swallow due to nerves. Esther chewed on the tough mixture and ruminated, then she began to laugh.

'That particular experiment needs to be perfected, but at least you have not gone down your ironic road on us again, and this time I can clearly taste the garlic.'

The woman had total recall. I gulped the wine and started to choke. Con thumped my back soundly, and I eventually recovered. It would be some time before my chest stopped reverberating from Con's hefty lashes, however. At least I hadn't sprayed the wine forth in surprise.

'Mmmm,' continued Esther, 'soda with caraway was quite traditional in Ireland, but sadly you don't get it too often any more. It's very nice indeed.'

'And I very much like the potato bread with garlic purée,' purred Toto. 'Well done, Leo,' he said, injecting what I can only imagine was allure into my name. It seemed I had been forgiven for arranging to go to the Ball with someone else. In a way, I'd have preferred it if he'd still been a little angry with me, at least then he would have kept his distance. However, it was undeniably good to have him in my corner just now.

'And you've been inventive with our brown bread,' cooed Esther. 'All round, Leo, I think you've got a way with bread. Congratulations.'

I felt like I had won an Olympic gold. I was bursting with pride, and smiling madly through the tears that were misting my eyes. I wanted to kiss everyone and phone my family to tell them about my unbelievable culinary feat. Best of all was the relief, which was immense.

Of the rest, Keith, hero of the curdles, presented 'On Horseback', in honour of the part of the country we found ourselves in that weekend. It consisted of lots of food wrapped in bacon, and assembled into a series of bridge-like shapes.

'In honour of a jockey's breakfast more like,' said Junior. 'The ride and the rasher.'

Jeffrey and Donny treated us to 'The Egg Venture Eggsperience', which was pronounced utterly delicious by the judging panel.

'Just as we eggspected,' chuckled Con.

And, surprisingly, Maolíosa opted for 'Veg Out', which we all looked at lasciviously. 'Nuff respect! Perhaps he was a vegetarian after all, as Con had suspected.

Mr and Mrs had divvied up a collaborative effort. They called it 'An Octopussy's Garden'.

'We're mad about seafood,' Eleanor confessed.

'But we're avoiding shellfish at the moment,' added Diarmaid.

When we had all offered ourselves up, Esther made a short speech. I was dreading this, because it meant that our time together was drawing to an end, for now. She clapped her slim hands to call us to attention, as she had on our first evening.

'Each course brings new experiences to all of us. It is always an adventure, dictated not just by the ground covered by Graham and myself, but also by the group of students brought together by fate to be with us. You have been a pleasure, and also the liveliest bunch we've had in some time. I hope that you have enjoyed yourselves as much as we have, and that you leave with what you came here to find.'

I'll drink to that, I thought, looking at Victoria Knowles.

'And I can think of no finer way for us to celebrate this weekend than to eat all of your wonderful creations. Congratulations to you all.'

We raised our glasses in a toast, then dived hungrily upon the food.

'It must be unusual for you to have today off,' I said to Con.

'Yes, Sunday is a busy one for me. But I have no doubt that Father John will have more than enough fiendish ways for me to make up the lost work. He's quite ingenious when it comes to that. And he's coming to collect me in the parish car, so I owe him big now.'

Ciara Junior was hoovering up Con's tapas, and speaking with her mouth full. She had moved on from her own work, she said; there could be no looking back, she would get stuffed on other people's gear now.

'Speaking of work,' Con said to me, 'you were shifty about yours yesterday.'

I busied myself with a stuffed courgette, pretending not to hear him. He was not deterred.

'Leo,' he persisted, 'let's be having the big secret.'

'If you don't,' said Senior, 'none of us will give you our phone numbers and you'll die sad and lonely, never having seen or heard from us again.'

'There's something bad about that notion?' I teased. They were not having any of my excuses, so I waded in.

'It's really not that major,' I said, accidentally exaggerating the mystery. I looked around the room, cagily. I didn't want this going any further. I lowered my voice, which of course made an even bigger deal of the revelation. 'All right,' I whispered, 'but it's hardly the Third Secret of Fatima. I'm a private investigator. That's all, that's it. And please, could we keep that to ourselves?'

'That is so cool,' whistled Junior.

'And exciting,' added Senior.

'It has its moments,' I admitted, 'but most of the time it involves long, boring hours and lots of tedium.' I looked into Con's lovely, honest, open face. 'And, unfortunately, sneaking around where you're not wanted, and lying to people,' I added. I wondered what penance he would have given me if I had been at a formal confession. Lots and lots of decades of the rosary. Lots.

Junior seemed enchanted. 'What are you doing at the moment? Are you on a job here, now? I mean, a *case*.'

I skirted the truth. 'I'll be seeing someone this evening about one.' This was true, but open to interpretation.

'If you ever need help, will you give me a call?' she asked.

'Well, yeah, sure,' I said. 'But I really do mean it, Ciara, when I say that it can be very boring. But yeah, sure, why not? You'd have to dress a bit duller,' I warned.

'You'll have to talk to my agent about that,' she laughed.

Diarmaid and Eleanor arrived. 'We're getting everyone's addresses so that we can let you know when Baby arrives,' they said. We duly gave the info. 'We love the name Leo,' they said, 'but we must be a bit traditional because we have it on the boys' list. Who'd have thought we'd be so square?'

Who indeed?

'Great bread, by the way.'

I was ridiculously pleased. About the bread. If I'd had feathers I would have preened them. Sometimes it's plain *plain* to be human.

'We were wondering if we might trouble you for the soda and caraway recipe?'

It was the start of a torrent of requests; we all wanted a piece of another's action. It would have been more truthful of me to photocopy pages of the school's library and distribute them, but as I jotted ingredients and methods down, I also added notes of my own, thereby justifying my plagiarism. And I withheld the recipe for my fake focaccia, or perhaps it's more correct to say that no one asked for that. I ate it all myself, just so it wouldn't feel bad about itself. And I hoped that *I* wouldn't feel bad about it either, as it lay rock-like in my stomach. I was looking forward to gravity claiming that one.

We were all very aware of the march of time. The other students would soon be collected from school, and for this class there was no tomorrow.

Ciara Junior was giving Con a hard time about celibacy. Or at least she was trying to. He was unshakable. I often think that the amount of time a person spends talking about sex is a direct ratio to how much they're getting. That is to say that the *more* they talk about it, the *less* it's happening in their life. I wondered if Junior was still a virgin. The corollary of that, however, if my theory was correct, was that Con was having a shagfest, because he never mentioned sex. I decided that he was the exception that proved the rule. It was Junior's utter bad luck to find a Catholic priest who didn't have a sordid past. I interjected with some lay information.

'I don't mean to burst your bubble, Ciara, but I do have to tell you that you can share a bed with someone and still be celibate. I've done it. Correction, I'm doing it. Sadly.'

'I'll go with Leo on this one,' said Senior. 'Celibacy can arrive in the most unexpected places, and at the most unexpected times.'

'Even if it's not wanted,' I added.

'Remind me never to grow old,' said Junior, 'it sounds shite.'

'Speaking of being ancient and celibate reminds me that it is Sunday,' said Con, 'and I've got to get into my gear.' He excused himself and went off to change.

One by one our hearts sank; it was nearly time for them to go home.

We looked at each other in dread anticipation of the engine sounds of the cars. And when the first was heard, it was Toto who went to look out the window.

'Red Fiesta, Galway plates,' he announced.

'That's me,' sighed Gladys.

She did a round of hugs, then panicked because she hadn't said goodbye to Con. She reached for her blue inhaler.

'I'm sure you'll be allowed to stay until he comes back,' I reassured her.

She looked almost tearful. Then her nascent tears turned to a warm smile as she saw him appear in the doorway.

'Good God Almighty,' I exclaimed, surprised at his formality.

We were all used to the casual Con, haphazardly put together. Now he was in full clerical mode and would need the title 'Father'. This was not our friend, and yet, of course it was. This was part of the baggage of coming back down to earth, all necessary for us to realise how wonderful our time together had been, how special it would be in remembrance, and how relentlessly time and life goes on.

I realised what I had just said to a man of the cloth and apologised.

'Sorry, that was probably blasphemous.'

He smiled magnanimously. 'Like casual cruelty, it's what I've come to expect,' he said, simply. 'People just don't think.'

He didn't mean this as an admonishment, it was simply a fact, but I was mortified.

'Feckin' great uniform,' said Junior, relieving my agony. And it was. Black is a sturdy and authoritative colour, and it's powerful too – I'm surprised that more football teams don't wear it to terrify their opponents before a ball is even kicked. I could hear Mick Nolan mutter that black is a contrast and not a colour, but I ignored him; no one had asked for his opinion.

'Navy Honda Civic, Dublin registration,' said Toto.

'Feck, that's me,' said Junior. 'Stall whichever of them it is, I'm not done up yet. I don't want them to get the wrong idea.'

She ran off to the loo to put on her make-up and reinsert her piercings. A haunted woman appeared at the door. Her eyes darted around the room in search of her problem daughter.

'I'm looking for Ciara Gillespie,' she said tentatively. 'I hope she's behaved herself,' she added, nervously.

Esther took her by the arm, and steered her towards the remains of our work. 'She has been a joy.'

Junior's mum searched her face for irony and/or sarcasm. There was none. She breathed a sigh of relief and straightened up.

'Actually, she is a talented cook,' said Esther, 'and extremely confident.'

'Confidence is not something she's ever had a problem with,' Mum acknowledged. 'Unfortunately.'

They were sampling Ciara's stuffings when she reappeared at the door, restored to her original Gothic splendour; she had really gone to town on the pale foundation and black eye kohl. Her mother gave her a tentative and watery smile.

'I've discovered crack-cocaine, Mammy, and it's very expensive,' she said. Mammy gave an anguished cry, and even Ciara was touched by her horror, as she quickly added, 'Don't be a complete eejit, I'm only taking a rise out of you.'

She turned to me. 'I've written out my address and phone number in case you need me. And I really, really want a call. It sounds like a right laugh altogether.'

Junior and Senior embraced for a long time, but said nothing. Then she turned to Con and said, 'Goodbye Big Man, say the odd prayer for me, or whatever you think is appropriate.'

She linked arms with her mother and led her to the door. There, with a jangle of metal, she turned and said, 'Stay in touch, oldsters, you know you want to.' Then she was gone. Senior dabbed a runny eye.

I hate goodbyes. I rarely do them. This was torture.

By now, a convoy of cars was lined up outside. Toto announced them all and we moved out of doors. Top of the heap was a dark green people-carrier whose bonnet was decorated by a man in a golfing jersey.

'No prizes for guessing that he's mine,' said Ciara Senior.

Ralph, for it was he, was a pleasant man with a

271

kindly face. I had been expecting some sort of human toadstool.

'I suppose she's been bad-mouthing me for the whole weekend,' he said, affably.

We all laughed guiltily, including his wife. He threw his eyes to heaven. 'I knew it, she just can't resist it. You can't, can you?' He kissed her on the cheek. Ralph was obviously besotted, and so, I'm happy to say, was she.

My mother maintains that it's better to marry someone who's madder about you than you are about them. She thinks she's done that herself, but I think it's an equal measures arrangement in my parents' marriage. The same could be said of Ciara and Ralph's. She was just as glad to see him as he was to see her.

'I suppose the house has gone to rack and ruin since I saw it last,' she said.

'Oh yes,' he said, 'you saw to that when you hired those builders.'

They stared into each other's eyes at length, before bursting into laughter.

They had a system, a shorthand. I thought of the disastrous flock wallpaper incident in my parents' house; the system worked.

'If I'd shot her when I met her,' Ralph told us, 'I'd be out of prison now.'

A brooding man with a fine, patrician face got out of the sports car behind. To be more accurate, he *alighted*. I doubted he'd displace much water getting into a bath. He was regal in his beautifully cut black suit and head-of-Guinness collar, and had probably enjoyed a spot of flagellation earlier, to go with the hair-shirt he was undoubtedly wearing beneath his robes.

'I'm here to collect Father Cornelius Considine,' he told us, grandly but needlessly. We'd all guessed the collectee. Con was puce with embarrassment, principally because we now knew that Con was short for Cornelius and not Considine. No wonder he'd thought the Ciaras had been cruel about the name Ralph. It seemed like a hundred years since that first night of conversation in The Stables Bar.

'Don't worry,' I said. 'It could have been worse, your name might have been shortened to Neely.'

'Tell me about it,' he said, 'and tell my Aunty Carmel while you're at it. That's her pet name for me.'

'Well, I hope *her* nickname is Cacky, to her nearest and dearest.'

'Do you know, it just might be from now on, Leo. Thank you.'

As he started his leavetaking, he began, casually, to talk about people and their perceptions of themselves and what they do.

'For instance,' he said, 'if you were reading one of those surveys about yourself in a glossy magazine, and we all do, and say you were faced with the "describe yourself in seven words or less" scenario, what would you put? Truthfully.'

I thought for a moment.

'I dunno really. I suppose I might try "clumsy private investigator with a conscience".'

'Well then, that's not so bad is it? And only six words. You'd still have room for "nice", or some-such, at the start.'

'Yeah, "somesuch" sounds good,' I said. 'You are a kind man, Father Con Considine. Thank *you*.'

'You're very welcome, Leo Street. God bless.'

The finely sculpted Father John was barely stifling a yawn.

'Time to go,' Con acknowledged. 'See you all soon.' Just before he left he whispered, 'God forgive me for saying this, but in the tinned fruit cocktail of life, that man really believes he's the cherry and I'm the tasteless piece of pear. I can tell you, here and now, he's only the grape.' He grinned and threw his eyes to heaven. The Men In Black loaded up and hit the road, in a cloud of dust and a screech of wheels. The cherry believed in burning rubber.

'If that's the parish car,' said Senior, 'I'd love to see the parish.'

They were all pulling away now, and as everyone drove off, I felt a tug of apprehension. My safety net was gone and I was alone, the one not chosen for the volleyball team at school. Truth be told, I was always chosen for a team, if only for fun value. But this was how I imagined it would have felt to have been left out. I felt like this regularly, as I started into the unknown time and again. It would be so easy to stay at home, out of harm's way. To stay away from the unknown. To be safe. But wasn't that exactly what was wrong at home? The safety. The laziness. The laziness of not splitting with Barry, the fear of the unknown, the being alone, and the starting all over again.

Eventually, a little group of Esther, Toto, Victoria and myself, was left on the school doorstep. We all had preparations to make for the Spring Ball, and so, in turn, we too peeled away, leaving only the merest, ethereal impression on time of the week-end course that had just been. Is this how ghosts happen?

I needed some validation and a little gee-up. I thought I might try Barry, the man supposed to be my nearest, dearest, most special friend. This was warped logic, given my situation with him at the current time. Even so, I duly tried my number in Dublin, but the recording of his voice told me what to do. I was not about to come clean to an answering machine. I dialled Maeve, and, amazingly, she was in. I couldn't hide my delight.

'I cannot believe that I actually got one of our leading stars of stage and screen *in* on her day off,' I squealed.

'Oh, not only that,' said Maeve's kind voice, 'I'm still in bed.'

I squealed again. 'Oh God, Maeve, I'm so sorry to disturb you. Apologise to Michael for me as well, will you?'

'Don't be daft, Leo, I'm on my own. And damn glad of it too. It's Sunday, so he's weaving his magic for some five-year-old in Sutton. I've spent a blissful day in bed, just me, my two hands and a little imagination. I've had a great time. *And* some quality sleep, alone, in my lovely double bed.'

Maeve agrees with me about a double bed being just the right size for a single person.

'How is your case going?' she asked.

'Oh, nothing much to show for it yet,' I confessed, 'and I've a long night ahead. I was just feeling a bit sorry for myself, so I phoned. I'm pathetic.'

'No you're not, and you know it. Just go for it and do your thing. Chin up, old girl.'

'I will,' I promised. 'And thanks for putting up with my whingeing.'

'De nada,' she laughed. 'You're worth it. I think.'

We rang off and I pulled myself together. I headed for my room-stroke-laboratory, to create my monster for the evening. It would soon be showtime.

# EIGHTEEN

As hot water gushed into a bubbling bath, I laid my formal black dress out on the crisp white bed-linen. There was clear evidence of previous cat activity, which suggested that one, or perhaps all three, of the mogs had been brushing in and out of the wardrobe, and maybe sleeping adjacent to my one formal gown. Wretches. Side by side was my underwear, a black lace bra and almost-matching knickers. I smirked at my mother's phrase, 'a man on a galloping horse wouldn't notice', which now had added meaning. I thought longingly of my special Christmas present from Andy Raynor, and the years of faithful and comfortable service I'd had from those panties, which was more than could be said for their sender. I examined the tights that I had thrust into my bag at the last moment. They more or less passed muster, with only a few snags around the knee area. I have to admit that there is no more unattractive a sight than sheer tights over a pair of knickers, but as I wasn't expecting any viewers for my underwear that evening, I thought I could live with the ugliness.

In the cold light of a hotel room, my shoes looked in a worse state than I'd remembered. The suede on the insides of the heels was very bald indeed, and various flat areas had gone shiny. The only available, and vaguely suitable brush in my possession for raising the surface was my toothbrush, but after some deliberation I rejected it as an option. This would be a short-term solution, with long-term problems. One of the pleasures of a morning-after-the-night-before is a thorough scrub of the teeth, washing away all of the unsavoury nonsense that might be lurking in your mouth. Being left with black teeth after this joyous experience would undermine the whole process. I rubbed both shoes together in the hope that a nap would be raised.

This was a fresh start to the latter half of the day, and I had work to do. I padded into the steamy bathroom and switched off the taps. Then I piled my

SOMETHING FOR THE WEEKEND

hair into a scrunchie and cleansed the make-up
from my face until it was squeaky. A calming lavender aroma filled the tiled room. I inhaled deeply and
stepped into the bath. Then I stepped out again,
sharpish; too hot. When an acceptable temperature
had been reached, I climbed in and lay down.
Tension flowed from my body, and I sank down a
little further. Time to take a relaxed stock of what
needed to be done later.

Notwithstanding the fact that Harry Knowles
would not let his wife out of his sight for any
reasonable length of time, thereby scuppering her
opportunities to meet a lover, and mine to catch
them, I did have two 'suspects', Adam Philips and
Joe. Correction, three. I might not like it, but Alex
Wood, by sheer dint of gorgeousness and accessibil-
ity, had to join the other two. And there was also the
fact that Victoria Knowles was a very attractive and
desirable woman, and there was no particular reason
to suppose that Alex would be immune to her
charms. But of these, clearly Joe was the favourite
and front runner.

Tonight was going to be a difficult one to handle.
For a start, a large crowd was expected, and would
be dispersed over a large area, at least a large-ish
one for one person to patrol. In my favour, I did
know that Victoria planned to hook up with Joe,

281

and with Adam and Alex also in attendance who could say what might occur? I had loaded my video camera and fresh tape into my clutch bag; for this job, it was far preferable to a stills camera. All that remained was for me to get ready and 'go to the Ball'.

I reached out a foot and pulled the plug on my bath. As it gurgled noisily away, I wrapped myself in a towel and splashed my face with cold water. I wiped the steam from the mirror above the sink and checked out the spot situation on my face. I'd had a bit of a go at the whopper on my chin; it was still an angry red, but slightly smaller than it had been. Any other blotchiness was probably a result of the hot bath and cold splash. I had seen worse. But I couldn't leave it at that, oh no. I had to go and do the full-length mirror examination.

At what point in your life does gravity start to succeed in pulling your sweet bits southwards? I was thirty now, and looking critically at the body in front of me, I thought that the sagging process was probably a few years in. I've had a fairly big chest since I was in my late teens, and even though my mother always insisted that I wore 'a good support', I thought my tits were now definitely on the downward journey. It has never helped my side elevation that I have hefty upper arms (hereditary), and these, married with the big bust, rule out sleeveless garments. So no little scanties for the upper body.

I would love to blame my bulging tummy on the generations of women who have gone before me, on both sides of the family, but I'll grudgingly admit that an unhealthy lifestyle, with too many saturated fats and a modicum of beer, is probably responsible. Being on surveillance doesn't help either. You oscillate between comfort eating when you're bored, and starvation when you're busy. Both are equally detrimental to the figure: piling in the comfort calories piles on the weight, whereas starvation puts the body into famine mode and it hangs on to the fat for the emergency it thinks it's in.

My thighs were looking decidedly spongey at the back, matching the lunar landscape of my lower buttocks. My body was still getting away with fitting into a standard size twelve, but there was no doubt that it would benefit from a bit of toning. I'm not a great one for physical suffering, and exercise suggests discomfort, if not pain, to me. And pain hurts. No wonder everyone wants a miracle diet aid, and is willing to believe it has finally happened each time something new is invented. No one wants to suffer.

My bikini line was a roving ambassador for body hair. I had once made the mistake of having it waxed before going on a sunshine holiday. Halfway through the ordeal, the beautician asked me if I wanted her to stop. I looked at the progress she'd made and decided that it was too lopsided to live with. She agreed to continue if I would stop screaming and frightening the other customers, who were only a curtain away. I chewed on my tongue until she completed the job. And it was complete. A complete mess. Large globules of blood marked the spots where each hair had been rudely dragged from its home, and triumphant in the middle of the devastation was a ridiculous Hitler-type moustache. I vowed, there and then, never to go through that agony again. I was also barred from the beauty salon.

My mother is convinced that I stand with my legs planted like two trees in the ground. I don't think that this is necessarily a compliment, but I'm sure that, again, it's hereditary. The arms and legs of the women on my maternal line are identical, as if they've come on a roll, like wallpaper. It also means that my mother has the same afflictions, but I don't think she sees it like that. The family's legs are not a bad shape at all, and my own are certainly passable. But they bruise and mark easily, and take ages to heal. A flea epidemic amongst the cats of No. 11, The Villas, resulted in me being savaged by the hellish hoppers. The cats were unscathed, but I've been left with telltale purple scars around my ankles that I'm convinced will never fade.

And then there were my feet. When I worked for Miss Doyle, the chiropodist, we saw some gruesome examples of what goes on at the bottom of a leg. Lots of people, for instance, will have broken a little toe at some point in their lives and not realised it. It's the classic 'stubbing your toe on the edge of a door' routine. And the poor little toes can look very odd indeed in later life. I'm not sure if my own have met with this fate at some stage. They do sport their fair share of bumps and callouses, hailing from my days as a fashion-conscious teenager, when you would squash your feet into any impossibly small shoe as long as it met with the approval of your peers.

At my secondary school in Clontarf, big feet were unacceptable. The social pressure to squeeze your feet into a receptacle at least a size too small for them was irresistible. A neat size five was judged the norm, and so I stayed geisha-like at a five for years, only latterly releasing my lumpy toes into a five and a half when I thought it wouldn't be noticed, and lying through my teeth about it to back up my fashion villainy. I rubbed some cream into a few hardened areas around the heels and toes, and it was swallowed up gratefully.

Other than that I was looking great.

I carefully applied my make-up, trying to remember all of Maeve's advice and tricks from my birthday night. I didn't do too badly, I thought. I had to have three goes at my dark red lipstick, but it was worth it in the end. My mouth looked almost kissable. Then I dragged my hair into the dramatic bun that I'd worn on Wednesday, and stood back to judge the effect. Not bad from the neck up, a little underdressed from the neck down.

I joined all of my bits up with the clothes I had prepared earlier. Happily, everything matched. The pièce de resistance was the beautiful pearl choker on loan from Fergus; it made sense of the whole ensemble. As I checked myself over in the mirror, I felt the stirrings of great excitement about the evening ahead. I tucked some face powder and lipstick into my evening bag, wrapped my red, birthday stole around my shoulders and stepped into the night. I was elegant and invincible. Pride comes before a fall.

I tottered across the cobblestones towards the welcoming light of The Stables. Just as I reached it, I stepped awkwardly on a stray piece of plastic and tumbled. I was headed for a tub filled with alpines and muck, so I veered at the last moment and hit the ground on my ditch-spilled buttocks; just as well they had a layer of fat as protection, I thought wryly. I hopped quickly up on to my feet again, and looked around to see if anyone had noticed. I was alone, my graceful reputation safe. My family nickname, Big Bertha, made such sense, unfortunately. I really was going to have to do something about all of these self-inflicted physical miseries. I checked my dress for stains; mercifully, it had been spared. I staggered up the final steps to the sanctuary of the bar and Fergus Rush.

The Stables was throbbing with strangled vowels and bonhomie. I was immediately surrounded by people who dealt in cubits, leagues and guineas. 'She's not half as cranky as she seems,' said one man to another, 'she just needs firm handling.' I wondered if they were talking about a person or a horse. The search for my partner was hampered by the fact that all of the men looked identical in their formal suits. I was staring at a familiar face, searching for a name, when a voice said, 'That is indeed the most over-exposed man on Irish television, and he doesn't even take his clothes off.' I turned to a dapper, smiling Fergus Rush.

'I thought I recognised him,' I said. 'He's a right pain in the neck, isn't he?'

'You look divine, my dear,' Fergus said. 'And as I

suspected, the pearls are perfect for you.' He kissed my cheek. 'It's a long time since I appeared in public with a beautiful young woman, I expect a lot of jealous glances this evening.'

'You are the perfect escort,' I laughed, 'flattery upon flattery – very good for a girl's confidence.'

The barman, Johnny, was dashing from pump to till. He looked hassled, but delighted to show that pressure was what he thrived on. He loved being busy; he had underlings to boss around, and a top class crowd to impress. He was in his element. We ordered our drinks at the bar, and settled to look at the fascinating parade of fashions and self-confessed minor celebrities. A barking girl with goofy teeth and too much breeding jostled by.

'I feel a bit out of place,' I confessed.

'Nonsense,' said Fergus. 'I'll bet that by the end of the night you'll be tired of seeing mutton dressed as mutton.'

We clinked our glasses and drank good health to the world.

'I think I may have miscalculated in the footwear department,' I said. 'I don't know how I'll stagger up that long driveway.'

'Fear not, dear lady, a carriage awaits. The Woods are famous for their attention to detail, and there is a splendid feeder bus to ferry revellers to and fro.

He raised his glass again, 'You shall go to the Ball.'

We were approached by a suave man flashing expensive gold cufflinks. 'I enjoyed your letter about genetic modification, Fergus,' he said. 'My people are looking in to it, and as you know we're publishing a report soon. I'll be in touch.' He exited with the air of one who wanted to leave his audience gagging for more.

'The Minister,' Fergus explained, then he started to laugh. 'A ninny. I boarded with him at St Columba's and he hasn't improved with age. He's hoping for an EC job with little or no work. He'll be very good at that.'

'Bet the report costs hundreds of thousands, and says nothing that we didn't know already,' I muttered.

'Indeed. But they do say we get who we deserve in government. We are the voters and so on.'

'Bleak, isn't it, that we could hire so many eejits.'

'I don't mean to pour salt on the wound of our collective idiocy, but I do have to tell you that he's always been fond of the opera. Now, there is nothing at all wrong with that. But he did indulge in a little performing when we were at school, and believe me, there was plenty wrong with *that*. We used to call him La Trivialata.'

We both snorted with merry laughter. I wondered,

idly, how much the tabloids would pay to hear that gem.

Fergus's face lit up. He waved to a woman on the other side of the room and she crossed over to us. It was a long journey as everyone wanted to talk to her. She was loose and elegant as a thoroughbred. As she listened to people, her finely sculpted head leaned towards them, carving her neck into a swan-like arc.

'She must be a film star,' I said to Fergus.

'She could have been,' he said, 'and she was once set to be my wife. I let her down, but she did much better in the end. She lives in Geneva now, and holidays several times a year with beautiful, interesting people who realise how special she is.'

She reached us and threw her arms around Fergus in delight.

'You old dog, you look wonderful. How the hell are you?'

'Ava, you must have a portrait hidden in your attic, I swear you look younger with each year. May I introduce my newest friend, Miss Leo Street.'

A pair of slate grey eyes turned to me. Then a husky voice of liquid velvet said, 'He has an eye for the ladies, the wretch, always did.' She smiled. 'I'm Ava Van Helderen, pleased to meet you, Leo.'

Ava Van Helderen, a heavenly, Hollywood name, I

thought, as I let it knock pleasurably around my brain. She read my mind. 'It was once plain old Ava Green, but I married well.' As she shook my hand firmly, she noticed the choker around my neck and did a little double take. 'You're obviously very much in favour, I had to beg to be allowed to wear that. It suits you, just as it always seemed made for Lily.'

'Alex Wood's mother?' I asked.

'Yes. She was a very beautiful and dear friend of ours. However, if I remember correctly, the necklace is actually a Rush family heirloom. From a grand-mother?' She turned to a nodding Fergus. 'Are you looking after yourself properly?' she asked.

'You know I am,' he laughed. 'I've always been far too good at that, to the detriment of all others in my life. I'm very well and in splendid spirits. I've made some very positive decisions over the last few weeks and I intend to act on them tomorrow.'

Ava tossed her head back in a laugh. 'It's always tomorrow,' she said.

'You may mock, evil woman,' he smiled, 'but you'll see. You'll see.'

'I wait with bated breath. I am glad to hear that you're fine, you've been on my mind a lot recently, and I began to worry about you.'

'Don't,' he said, 'I've rarely been happier, or more certain that I'm going to do the right thing. I think a lot of people will be surprised by my next move, but I hope you will all realise that I do what I do for the happiest and most positive of reasons. Not all big decisions come of despair or depression, you know. And I've been an introspective old grump for too long.'

'If you say so,' Ava chuckled. 'I don't know about you, Leo, but I'm hooked now. I can hardly wait for whatever treat he has in store. Ah, I see my lovely husband flapping in the distance. Duty calls. I'll see you both later, and Fergus, I'll be expecting a dance. He's an expert waltzer,' she told me.

'It's my only dance,' said Fergus.

We watched Ava work her magic across the crowded room and out the door. Then he offered me his arm. 'Shall we?' Like a king and queen we swept out, in a swirl of expectation about the night ahead. We were about to play the Ball Game.

# NINETEEN

Wood House was floodlit, beckoning friends and strangers from the county, the country and beyond. Helicopters buzzed overhead. The bus was sandwiched in a slow-moving line of Jaguars and Rolls Royces. I had to remind myself to breathe in the excitement. Fergus was explaining some of the building's history.

'The famous architect, Gandon, is supposed to have designed or at least supervised the planning of Wood House in the early nineteenth century. It was previously called Torbally Hall, but that was burned to the ground when an eccentric ancestor set fire to himself, and it. Apparently, he would get drunk, and light a fire to keep warm wherever he fell down. Disaster was bound to happen and it did. So this new house was built on the old site. Gandon's involvement can't be proved because the house records were destroyed in a fire in the library about a hundred years ago.' He smiled across at me. 'You'll be glad to know that our hosts are very conscious of the building's predilection for bursting into flames and have taken measures to ensure that it doesn't happen as easily again.'

'Thank you for letting me know that,' I laughed, 'I will party with confidence.'

'I read an interesting story about Gandon,' he continued. 'He lived in Lucan before his death in the 1820s. A rumour went about that King George IV was going to bestow a knighthood on him as he went through the village. Gandon was ill and feeble at the time, but he made his way in his wheelchair to the end of his driveway to greet the King. But George IV didn't stop and Gandon returned to his house a disappointed man, without any honour being conferred.'

'How sad. Poor old Gandon.'

'Yes. But what beautiful work he left behind.'

We climbed the steps arm in arm, the cream of society. A liveried doorman announced 'Mr Fergus Rush and Miss Leonora Street,' and we moved into the crowded hallway. We were standing on an enormous chessboard of black and white marble tiles, a world away from the rubberised version in my office. Far above, the ceiling boasted a magnificent chandelier surrounded by ornate plasterwork. This was echoed in the white mouldings of swags and fruit at the tops of the duck-egg blue walls. Enormous vases of white lilies added a heady scent, which mingled with cigar smoke and every imaginable perfume and cologne. It was overwhelming.

'Here they are,' said Fergus, 'the rich and the very rich living together in perfect harmony.'

Women in long gowns seized the opportunity of the magnificent staircase, slowly sweeping from top to bottom, pausing to chat and to pose. Their partners took equal advantage. It was a staircase from the movies, and at any moment Scarlett O'Hara would appear. I was dying to try it out.

We helped ourselves to two glasses of champagne from a passing waiter. Fergus followed my gaze. 'As a general rule of thumb,' he said, 'if you see someone you think is famous, it's probably them.'

'So are you telling me that's Ralph Fiennes over there?'

'Yes, he went to school with Alex in Kilkenny. Would you like to meet him?'

'Oh God no. I'd be terrified. I'd probably trot out

something pathetic like "I think you're great" or "can I have your autograph?" and then I'd start to drool. Thanks for the offer, but no.'

Ralph Fiennes waved over, Fergus waved back. I was rooted to the spot. Then a woman's voice cut through the air.

'Firgs! *Firgs!*'

We joined a party of three standing just inside the doorway of one of the rooms leading off the hallway. The woman's ample breasts were heaving with excitement.

'Tilda, how wonderful to see you,' said Fergus, kissing her on the cheek. 'What a ravishing gown.' He was an old smoothy and no mistake. The gown was an extraordinary creation of taffetta and lace. It had a low-cut bodice, from which the frisky breasts were straining to escape, short puff sleeves, and a full skirt, which was very full of Tilda. She was five foot tall, and as wide as she was high. Her jolly face lit on me.

'Tilda Fitzgerald Roe, I'd like you to meet Leonora Street.'

'Hahrjardoo.' She gripped my hand and shook it vigorously until we could all hear my arm rattle in its socket. Then she was satisfied and let go. My arm dropped limply to my side. I didn't wince once; I realised that would be a hanging offence.

'This is Maurice Cope, one of our local vets,' continued Fergus, indicating a man with a face like a melted basin. I extended my numb appendage to him, and he was considerably more gentle than Tilda. He was also very, very drunk.

Maurice's dishevelled appearance gave him the look of someone who'd been out all week at this sort of bash, wearing the same dress suit each time. As he turned to take more champagne from a passing tray, his jacket rode up and I saw that there was bird shit on the shiny seat of his pants. I marvelled at the aim some birds have, and the ability to dive-bomb without being noticed. In Maurice's case, however, he may have been too inebriated to appreciate either of these laudable achievements. And he obviously didn't care about the result, assuming that he had even noticed it.

'And last, but by no means least,' Fergus continued, 'I'd like you to meet Teddy Roe, Tilda's husband.' Teddy took my hand and kissed it lightly, whether to take the pain away or not I don't know. I smiled gratefully. He was the same height as his wife, but not quite as rotund, and he was wearing trousers, so it wouldn't be too difficult to tell them apart.

'You old devil you,' he said to Fergus. 'Where have you been keeping this lovely creature?'

'Leonora is here with us for the weekend, staying at the hotel.'

'Joo rye?' asked Tilda. At least I thought it was a question.

'I beg your pardon?'

'Joo rye?'

'Tilda is wondering if you ride,' explained Fergus. 'She's a member of the North Kildare Harriers and no doubt wants you to join them at some stage. They're always looking for fresh blood.'

'A hahd dey to honds nevah het enyone.'

I was beginning to get the hang of Tilda, and I didn't like what she was suggesting. I could do without a hard day to hounds, whether it was good for me or not, thanks very much.

'Sorry to disappoint you, but I really object to hunting. So I'm afraid I won't be joining you.'

Fergus was smirking, waiting for an interesting spat, no doubt. Teddy took up the gauntlet.

'Can't remember the last time the Harriers actually caught anything, can you Maurice?'

I felt he was setting his sights too high, hoping for an intelligible response from Maurice Cope. To my surprise, the latter squeezed out the words, 'Bloody useless.'

'Ah Alex, wonderful party, as always,' said Teddy to a spot behind me. We all turned to look.

Alex Wood would have looked good in a sack. In a dress suit, he was sublime. I couldn't believe it was an accident that he'd let a lock of his hair fall nonchalantly on to his forehead, giving him a devil-may-care schoolboy look. He let his eyes take their time appraising me. Then he leaned over and kissed my cheek. The luscious smell of Armani filled my nostrils.

'Glad you could make it,' he said, 'you look stunning. As do you, my dear Tilda. Stunning.' He kissed her, and shook hands with the men.

'Elix,' said Tilda, 'I do bleeve wehev a bleeding heart liberal emongst es.' She was well able to release her words for common understanding when she wanted to. 'This d'litefel creechah desent bleeve in hunting.'

'Ah. A very emotional and emotive subject. I will remind you all that this *is* a party, and you should all be enjoying yourselves and not standing on your soap boxes. I'll see you later.' He smiled and left. I felt rebuked. Fergus could see my discomfort.

'Actually, Alex doesn't hunt, whether for a moral reason or not, I don't know. When you live in the countryside, as we do,' he gestured to the others, 'the issues become more complicated. And he's right, we should be concentrating on having a wonderful time.' He raised his glass, 'Cheers.'

I needed to move around and locate Victoria Knowles, so I excused myself and began my travels. In the next room, a string quartet was bravely sawing away in a vain attempt to get some notice. The room's French windows were open on to a terrace. I went out, but couldn't spot Victoria amongst the chattering groups. I could hear the sound of more live music coming from around the corner. I walked over, to find a striped marquee on the lawn at the back of the house. Ahead of me and going in the same direction was a group which included a woman in trouble. She was wearing shoes with stiletto heels like spikes. She sank deep into the grass with each step, and was taking twice as long as her companions to get to the tent. Finally she gave up and abandoned her footwear, leaving the shoes as garden sculptures where they had last sunk. Inside the marquee, a band was butchering a version of 'What A Swell Party This Is'. I paused by the drinks table at the entrance and helped myself to a glass of orange-flavoured punch, while I reviewed the scene.

A baldish man in his thirties came over and asked me if I'd like to dance. He was flailing his arms wildly, more or less in time to the music. I didn't think my own arm would be up to as much energetic activity after the seeing to that Tilda Fitzgerald

Roe had given it. Before I could muster an excuse, the band launched into 'The Lion Sleeps Tonight', to the delight of my erstwhile dancing partner. He began to yodel along with the chorus, while still gyrating in front of me – 'Ooh ee ooh ee um um away'. His face was now pink from his exertions, and the few blond hairs on his head were pointed upward in fright. I sipped my punch. I didn't seem to be required to do much more than pay attention. Then he simply forgot about me, and drifted away. The rest of my dance card was empty for the moment, so I slowly circled the floor in search of either Victoria or Joe, or hopefully both. In fact, I didn't mind who I caught her with, as long as the job was finished tonight.

The lead singer of the band was now scratching away at a fiddle, and treating us to an extra long rendition of a song with very little in the way of lyrics. 'That's All Right Now Mama' was the recurring theme. It was all right, now, Mama, any way she pleased, apparently. I jostled through the crowd, I checked gloomy corners, I tapped lots of shoulders and said, 'Oh I'm sorry, I thought you were someone else,' and fifteen minutes later, as I neared my original point of entry, it was still all right, Mama. I hadn't located Victoria, or anyone else that I recognised, and I had to leave this place before I went insane, Mama.

I checked the line of Portaloos behind the marquee, waiting in line and scanning the queue and those leaving. One of the cubicles was locked and unyielding. I sat in the one next to it and listened. It was clear that it was being used as an uncomfortable love nest by a man and a woman. I discounted the presence of Victoria Knowles when I heard a heavy Cork accent say, 'I just told him to fuck off. I'm a leggy blonde, I can shag for whatever I need. Fuck 'im. The tosser.'

I retraced my steps via the stiletto sculptures, to the verandah and beyond. The string quartet looked as happy as the one that played on the *Titanic*, after the iceberg had hit. A small boy in pyjamas and slippers whizzed by, shouting, 'Make way, make way.' I did as I was told, otherwise I risked losing a leg. He was galloping along, slapping his bottom as he would a horse's flanks to make it go faster. As he wasn't quite dressed for the occasion, I guessed he was an escapee from the nursery.

I decided to try navigating the house from the other side of the entrance hall. I made my way to where I had left Fergus and the hunter-harriers, but they had disappeared, and in their place, chatting to a group of women, was my first boyfriend, Andy Raynor. I ground to a standstill. The world is too small a place.

The lovelies of the Raynor harem were impossibly slim, with golden tans, and wore strappy sheaths and fuck-me sandals. When they were blonde, they were very, very blonde, and when they were brunette, they were burnished. They laughed at his every comment, no matter how inane and bland. The tallest, blondest and thinnest of them was hanging off Andy's shoulder and pawing him at every opportunity. She was wearing a sequinned pelmet over legs that were a mile and a half long. She shook her long shiny hair and laughed a lot, probably too much. Oh yes, I was jealous and I had it bad. I was also rooted to the spot with an open mouth. Classy.

I shouldn't have been surprised to see Andy, and looking back, I don't think that I really was. This was his milieu. I will admit to being disgruntled, however, he has that effect on me.

My ex-boyfriend excused himself from his scintillating company and came over.

'This is an unexpected surprise,' he said, leaning in to kiss me. I recoiled – force of habit.

He stood back and let out a low whistle. 'You look fantastic.' I pulled a face. 'I'm disappointed to see that someone else has already given you a pearl necklace this evening,' he continued. 'Now that I know you're here, and obviously alone, I might have hoped to have seen to that myself.'

How did he know that I was alone? Did I *look* alone?

'Always the lowest common denominator with you, isn't it, Andy.' I was calm, and scathing, I hoped.

'Just breaking the ice. You don't seem overjoyed to see me.'

'I'm just a little surprised. Other than that, it makes no difference to me, whatsoever, where you are or who you're with.' Wow, I had it *really* bad.

He pounced. 'So you *are* glad to see me.'

What kind of bizarre hijack was my body doing here? I assumed that my mind was not involved, I had to give it that benefit. After all, reason and experience would rule out having anything to do with this man.

'Andy, I'm busy, I've got things to do, people to meet.'

He smirked. Andy Raynor smirked. He knew, he bloody well *knew*. I had to go, I had to get away.

'I'll catch you later,' he said, airily. 'I have a spot check to make.'

Incredibly, my buttocks clenched, and I wondered if my knickers were presentable.

'Cocky fucker.'

'You betcha.'

I could not give him the satisfaction of the last word, though afterwards I wished I had.

'Andy,' I said, self-righteously, 'please don't take this the wrong way, but I really don't want to see you again this evening. I'm working, and the last thing I need is some lush messing up my pitch.'

'Did you ever notice the way pitch rhymes with bitch, Leo?'

I had a nervous, tingling, loose feeling in my bottom. I get it whenever I have really fucked up, or am so embarrassed that I want to die.

'As it happens, it doesn't suit me that *you're* here tonight. I'm working too, and on something to do with Harry Knowles that is of far more national importance than whatever it is he's signed you up to do. So you stay out of my way, and I'll stay out of yours. Deal?'

'Deal,' I said quietly, looking at my shoes.

'Don't look so down, Leo. If you're good, I'll be very forgiving, and I might still make that spot check.'

He strode back to his fan club.

How can any one person have the constant and unerring ability to get into my mind and rattle it around so thoroughly? Apart from my mother, of course, the woman who is his number one fan. As alliances go, it's watertight. I needed to get back to work. And what work was *he* referring to? Could this be something to do with the dodgy planning deal Victoria had mentioned in one of her telephone conversations? Or worse. I could imagine Harry Knowles capable of murder. Right now, however, I needed to get Andy Raynor out of my ridiculously jealous mind. God, he looked good.

I ignored Ralph Fiennes as I crossed the chess-board hallway, and entered a library on the other side. I stopped at the door to readjust myself. I had noticed an incredible strain on the calf muscles of my legs. In an unconscious effort to be elegant, I had been walking on the balls of my feet. It can't have looked that good, and now I was in agony. I sent the command 'heel, toe' to my feet, and hoped for the best.

The library was thronged with revellers, but lacking music; the sound was of the chattering of gossip and scandal. It was oddly calming. Harry Knowles was holding court in one corner, dragging on a thick cigar. He had made the mistake of wearing a fuchsia cummerbund, which drew attention to his girth. I don't think Harry knew that it was a mistake, but I'm quite sure his wife did. The crisp white of his shirt threw the florid red of his complexion into unpleasant relief. It was also a size too small for him. He looked happy enough, and threw me a curt nod as I passed by. His wife was nowhere to be seen. I grabbed another punch from the sideboard, and continued into an adjoining room.

This was the place for eating. In medieval fashion, the tables were groaning with food. The little boy in the pyjamas was feeding potato salad, by hand, to the hound I had seen in Alex Wood's Range Rover the day before. It appeared to go one scoop for the dog, one scoop for the boy. I felt a tapping on my shoulder, and when I turned around, Toto was in my personal space. Again.

He hadn't let himself down. He shimmered in a maroon suit, with a ruffled shirt and a sparkling silver bowtie. He looked great.

'Graham, do you ever take a night off?'

'Oh, just checking, you know, we have a reputation and all that. I was having a little peck too, to line the tummy before the excesses of the evening.'

'Good thinking,' I agreed. He immediately offered to load up a plate for me. It was tempting, I was feeling hungry, but I was behind on work and had to refuse. 'I'm actually looking for Victoria, Graham, and I wondered if you'd seen her.'

'Yes, as it happens, although it was a while ago. She was headed to the marquee with Adam.'

'Well, I'll head out there then. Perhaps I'll see you later.'

'I'm sure you will,' he said. 'I'll be wanting a dance.'

Something to look forward to, Leo.

So, Victoria was on the mooch with Adam Philips. Perhaps she would indulge herself in him as well before the night was over. Perhaps I was getting overexcited. She was, after all, supposed to be hooking up with Joe. Time to start my trawl through the house and grounds again.

Guests were still arriving in a constant stream at the front door. Ralph Fiennes had disappeared from the hallway, but I found him ignoring the string quartet in the drawing room. I was sorry that Ciara Senior was not with me to discuss the finer points of how her Ralph would never get away with being called Rafe, but this particular Ralph would. Fergus was talking to more friends near the French windows. I didn't want to be rude, so I grabbed another punch and joined the company, briefly. It seemed safe enough; Tilda Fitzgerald Roe had gone. My arm ached in its socket at the memory of her. I wondered if I'd be able to predict rain now that she had opened up my body to the elements.

After about ten minutes of an argument about the place of antibiotics in modern farming, I excused myself again. Fergus took me to one side and said, 'You know by now that I tend to disappear when my time comes. It's lovely seeing my friends here, but when I've done all of my goodbyes I'll steal away. And so, in case I don't see you again, I'll say goodnight and goodbye now.'

'Oh, right. Are you sure? It is awfully early yet,' I pointed out.

'Yes, I'm very, very sure.'

'Right. Well, I'll see you in the morning anyway, I have to give the pearls back before I go.'

He paused, then said, 'Don't come over too early, if you don't mind, Leo. I have some business to attend to, and you wouldn't want to be around for that.'

'Fine,' I said. 'I'm never inclined to get up early after a good night anyway, so if that suits you, it suits me.' I kissed him on the cheek. 'Thank you for being my escort, I really appreciate it.'

'My pleasure entirely. Enjoy the rest of your evening.'

He held both of my hands in his and squeezed them lightly. It was like being loved.

# TWENTY

I stepped out on to the terrace and breathed in deeply. The night was remarkably balmy for this time of year; I wondered how Esther had managed to book that. I scanned the groups to my right and left and skipped a heartbeat when I saw Joe Lindsay. I clutched my bag closer to me, ready to press the 'record' button on the video. Then I noticed that Joe was speaking to Andy and his assorted bimbos. Andy Raynor was fast becoming a pest. And furthermore, varmint that he was, his entourage did not include Victoria Knowles.

I scuttled past, following Toto's tip about the marquee, when a familiar voice stopped me in my tracks.

'Leo Street, get back here this instant.'

'Maeve, what the hell are you doing here?'

'Of all the gin joints, eh? So this is where you've got to. And *this* is what you have the cheek to call *work*?'

I pulled her over to as quiet a spot as I could find in the middle of a packed Spring Ball. I wanted her well out of earshot of both Andy and Joseph Lindsay.

'Maeve, it may only be a rough memory at this stage, but surely I was talking to you on the phone only a few hours ago, and you were in bed, alone, and having a great time according to yourself.'

'Yes, well, that was then, this is now, as they say. I had a call from a mate who'd been let down at the last moment, and you *know* that it's *impossible* for me to turn down a good time. I'd have had my party card taken away if I'd refused an invite to this. Isn't it *tops*? And have you ever seen so many *gorgeous* men?'

'I'm not really supposed to be concentrating on them at the moment.'

'Well the *minute* you've finished whatever mysterious thing it is you're up to, you *have* to come and find me and I'll introduce you to all of the *hunks* that I've met.'

'Dare I ask about The Amazing Armand? You know, your boyfriend.'

'Leo, he may have to go. *Anyway*, I've just met a guy called Andy Raynor, who has *definite* possibilities.'

I released a strangled choke.

'Have I said something wrong?' she asked.

'No, no. It's just that I grew up with Andy, and I couldn't believe it when I ran into him here. And now you. Jesus, who's next? Barry?'

Maeve looked at me in a strange way, then obviously made up her mind about something and began to speak.

'I'm glad you mentioned Barry, Leo, because I saw him earlier this evening and I was a bit taken aback about who he was with.'

'Yes?' I said, slowly, warily. I was fairly sure that I didn't want to hear the rest of this.

'He was walking along the seafront, arm in arm with your niece, Lucy. They looked very cosy indeed.'

'What? The *bastard*. She's only fifteen. What exactly does he think he's playing at?'

'I know. Well, look, let's not overreact, it may be nothing. But it does seem a *little* convenient that *you* were out of town, and we all know that she has a *massive* crush on him. I just don't want to see either Lucy or you being taken for a ride. *God*, that was an unfortunate turn of phrase, sorry Leo.'

'Don't worry about it. I'll wring his scrawny neck

when I get him. As if he wasn't in enough trouble. Honestly, Maeve, I'm done in with men. If I never saw another one it'd be too soon.'

'What you may need, my dear, is a *change*, which we *all* know is as good as a rest. Perhaps the lovely Andy?'

'Oh, don't you start. You're singing my mother's battle cry.'

'Well I wouldn't want to tackle *her* on a matter like this. If she's picked him for *her* girl, I'll just have to have someone *else* for my supper. Right you, back to work, and I'll go shmooze. There are lots of *types* here from the arts, and it's *always* good to be seen. See you later, alligator.'

'In a while, crocodile.'

I had to take a few moments out to calm down and gather my thoughts. I had now lost all sight of what I should have been up to there and then. I was so angry with Barry for taking advantage of an impressionable teenager, and my absence. His copybook was now filthier than a porno movie. But I had to make light of it, because I was still on duty, and distractions were making this job even more intolerable than it need be. 'Men is worms,' I thought to myself, as I finally re-embarked on the lead that Toto had given me. No doubt it was now as cold as my heart.

My shoes were still pinching. Well, what did I

expect? I ignore them from one end of the year to the next, and then imagine that they'll behave in a civilised manner when they're finally released into society. I didn't have a leg to stand on, or certainly wouldn't by the end of the revels.

The marquee had become a very dangerous place since I had last visited. Not only were there more people crammed into the stripy canvas confines, a traditional Irish music group had taken the stage. I was assaulted by a sea of flailing arms and legs, with feet reaching higher and higher, and bodies falling downwards in failed flight. Partners swung each other in ever speeding circles, and it was only a matter of time before we experienced some projectile vomiting. People on the periphery of the action were clapping their hands and whooping encouragement. Progress through this crowd would be slow, bumpy and perilous.

Irish dancing was never like this when I was growing up. We learned our steps methodically and by the text-book. Then we fried our hair into ringlets, screwed on a smile and took to the stage in the mortal combat of competition. But most of all we kept our arms rigidly by our sides, and *never* bumped into another dancer.

I have a few medals to show for my time then. Not as many as Assumpta Boyle from number 24.

She had a specially-made individual costume, and won the All Ireland under-14 for the reel three years in a row. Her dad even made a display board, covered in black felt, to put her medals on, and they hung it in their front room for visitors to admire; he was a dab hand with a jig saw, appropriately enough. They also had a trophy cabinet for all of her cups. My father wouldn't even change a plug, on the grounds that it was dangerous to mess with electricity. He still won't.

But even Assumpta would have been hard-pressed to make an impression here. It was a pagan outpouring, and several million miles away from the orthodox competition style. I lost count of the number of times I got stood on or elbowed in various tender places. My shoes didn't pinch any more because my feet had temporarily lost all feeling. I dreaded the time when my body realised what had happened and started to send pain signals from the afflicted areas. At least it would keep my brain from obsessing about Barry and my problems in that department. It struck me that this would not be Victoria's scene and that I was probably wasting my time. But I was so far into the marquee and the mêlée now that it would have been as much trouble to turn back as to press on. I duly pressed on. And was pressed on.

I emerged to find Esther Wood supervising the moving of the drinks table to just outside the giant tent. She smiled when she saw me. We both looked at my shoes at the same time. They were battered and covered in miscellaneous globules of food, mostly potato salad, it seemed.

'You look like you've just had a lucky escape,' she remarked.

'Yes, it's a sneak preview of the Apocalypse in there.'

'Well, have a drink and feel glad to be alive,' she said, handing me a punch.

'This is delicious, what's in it?'

'At this stage, who knows? It's a mixture of fruit juices, sparkling water and vodka, and whatever else is to hand by the end of the night. It tends to get made up as it goes along.'

'Use what you've got.'

'Yes.' She sipped some of the brew and said, 'Seems palatable enough. Hopefully it won't kill anyone.' We both laughed. I thought I might as well go for broke.

'I was looking for Victoria and Adam, have you seen them recently by any chance?'

'Yes, actually. Adam has gone back in to the house for a bite to eat. And Victoria went in the direction of the stables about ten minutes ago. Probably needed some air.'

I was delighted. A recent sighting of Mrs Knowles, even if she had been alone. Adam was eating, and Joe had been on the terrace with Andy ten to fifteen minutes ago. Still, there was nothing to say that they couldn't have arranged a rendezvous at the stables. Any combination of the suspects would do, as long as it included Victoria. I was excited at the prospect of capturing a clandestine encounter on tape and ridding myself of the lot of them. It was my best chance so far. As usual, my subconscious, and if I'm truthful my conscious mind, doggedly refused to accommodate the spectre of Alex and Victoria together. I could understand perfectly Lucy's crush on Barry, because I had an enormous one on Alex Wood. It was the total discomfort of being a teenager all over again.

My pulse quickened as I hobbled past the terrace; Joe had gone. Unfortunately, Harry was now in place. He beckoned me with a crook of a stubby finger.

'I saw you hanging around with Fergus Rush. Drop him, he's a loser.'

I was infuriated, and quite possibly a little drunk from the mysterious punch, because I replied, 'Harry, you may have hired me, but that doesn't mean that I have to like you. My friends are none of your business. Now piss off.' I had the luxury of having my fee in my pocket, before the job began, but this was probably still unacceptable behaviour as the customer is always supposed to be right. Too late. Boo hoo.

In a freak of nature, the moon's light was suddenly eclipsed. I turned and found myself buried in a man's chest. This vastness was clad in a blue, ruffled shirt, with the top three buttons undone. I stretched my neck back until it was at a right angle to my body. A monstrous American with wild, straw blond hair bore down upon me.

'Hey there, sassy lady. I couldn't help but overhear you there. You sure told that burly guy where to get off. Y'know, I've been hoping to meet someone like you all night long.'

Dear Lord, my neck was in agony now.

'Whaddaya say, little lady, like to hook up?'

I'd like to look down!

'I could show you a real good time.'

He made a clicking noise with his tongue, and raised one bushy eyebrow. I suppose it was meant to be enticing, but I found it deeply disturbing. 'I got *whatever* you need, booze, coke . . . me.'

I was battered and bruised and the last thing I needed was Happy Hank showing me a good time. He'd probably break me. He was also flaking dandruff all over my bosom.

'Thanks, but I'm with someone.'

'Well hey, call me old-fashioned, but I don't see this someone.'

'You're old-fashioned.'

I stumbled off down the path leading to the stables, brushing his white flakes from my chest. I was furious, frustrated and muttering to myself. I really, *really* wanted to take my shoes off, but I knew that if I did, even for the briefest moment, my feet would double in size and the shoes would be impossible to wedge back on. I didn't dare chance it. Cruelly, they had to carry me around for a while yet. Suddenly a man emerged from the tall hedges, with a familiar contempt smeared across his face. I gave a yelp and stepped back.

You would think that when you'd fallen for the 'frightened to death' bit before, you would be fore-warned and prepared. No. Richard Cooper grinned, showing his small pointed teeth. He was every bit the shark. I was much taller than him now, in my heels, but it didn't seem to count; I didn't feel in any way superior.

'Looking for the lovebirds?' he sneered. 'They went thatta way.'

The Prince of Darkness had given me such a fright that I was temporarily rendered speechless. How he did not have the same effect on horses and other animals was beyond me. When I finally squeezed out a reply, it was a pathetic, 'No, no, I'm just getting some air to ward off the effects of the punch.'

He snorted and said, 'I'll leave you to it so.'

This whole night was getting on top of me, and at the back of my mind I felt like a heel about the Knowles case. That's saying something, seeing as my own heels were feeling raw and betrayed. Sensation had finally caught up with my feet, and it was all falling very short of an *acceptable* sensation. I continued on my course, because I had little enough imagination to do otherwise. What was in that punch? I was beginning to think that I had enjoyed myself, not wisely, but too well earlier.

Which puzzled me, as I hadn't really had that much to drink. Mick Nolan was on my shoulder pointing out that I shouldn't have had a drink at all. And he was right. I hate it when that happens. I was on duty, and my duty was to get the information that Harry Knowles had paid me for, up front. I had let myself get involved in all sorts of ways here. Not least that I wanted to have a good time myself, in fact I felt I deserved it with all the aggravation I'd had to put up with that evening. But that was nowhere in the charter, and I had overstepped the mark. Time to make amends.

I didn't like the idea that Richard Cooper might be spying on me now. I looked back to where he had pounced on me, but he had disappeared. He was a master of manoeuvrability, and the night was his cloak. I would have to disregard him and crack on. I could see a light in the stable tack room, so I headed for there. As I neared it, I could hear the soft moans of a woman's pleasure.

The door was slightly ajar. I carefully and noise-lessly crept up to it and lined up my camera. I stayed in the shadows, gently craned the camera around the doorframe, and pressed 'record'. I could see the lovers in the viewfinder. Victoria Knowles was sit-ting on a table with her back to me. I couldn't see her partner clearly, but I could hear Victoria softly calling the name 'Joe.' Joe was obviously kneeling in front of her attending to that most splendid of pursuits that Andy Raynor had introduced me to as a teenager. The thought of Andy made me squirm. It was also exciting. I envied Victoria. She writhed and groaned and threw her head back as she came, hissing a triumphant 'yes'.

Joe stood up and kissed her full on the mouth. It was beautiful. It was also a surprise. Joe was not the Joseph Lindsay I had been expecting. Joe was Jo, the hungry stable girl. Well now. She pulled away from the kiss and said, 'My turn,' and they swopped places. This was a voyeur's heaven, and, guiltily, I was that voyeur. I stopped recording.

Harry had as much as he needed, and I couldn't bear the thought of him using this tape as his own personal soft porn channel. I felt a little strange that I had enjoyed watching the women too. Did this leave me on the same level as Harry? Was I no better than a man that I despised? Who were the bad guys here?

I retraced my steps to the party. If I could find Harry now and give him the tape, I would be finished with the job, and abdicated from any more involvement in the Knowles' marriage. But an unstructured doubt was nagging at my brain. I shivered in the cold, unsure of how to proceed. In fact, there should have been no doubt at all in my mind, as Mick would have been keen to point out. My job was to get Harry his evidence, full stop. And I had now done this.

I was glad to reach the warm indoors again, and headed for the dining room to get something to eat before leaving for the night. I spotted Harry Knowles in the room adjacent to the hall. He was swigging on a glass of red wine and smoking his cigar. His companion, on this occasion, was a severe young woman in a stark, black dress. Her face was completely expressionless. Harry looked shifty, and without quite knowing why, I pressed 'record' on the camera and pointed it in his direction. I was glad that I had, when a few moments later he turned the woman around, keeping his hand firmly on her buttocks, and led her towards the stairs. As she turned away, he deliberately tipped his wine over the pale upholstery of an antique chair and left his lit cigar lying on an ancient occasional table. I decided to follow at a discreet distance. As I passed the table, I removed the cigar and put it into an ashtray. There was nothing that I could do for the chair.

As Harry and his escort hit the top of the stairs, I began my ascent. It led to a long corridor, with doors opening off it, which I presumed were bedrooms. I didn't know which one Harry had gone through, so I waited a couple of minutes and then began a systematic opening of each one. The first two rooms were empty. I opened the door to the third and came upon a man sitting in the middle of a bed. As the light from the hallway hit him, he cowered against the bed-head, shading his eyes. Then he began to claw the air, warding off some imaginary demon. 'I'm an orange, I'm an orange,' he shouted. 'Don't peel me. *Don't peel me.*' I didn't.

Room number four yielded an unsavoury sight. At first I couldn't figure out what exactly I was seeing, but the phrase 'what's wrong with this picture?'

kept repeating in my brain. As I worked out the geography of the furniture and grew accustomed to the dim lighting, I realised that Harry Knowles was facing away from me, on all fours, having his naked bottom spanked by the young woman he had disappeared with. His cheeks wobbled and flapped with each stinging crack, and angry, red weals appeared on his skin. He seemed to be groaning the words, 'More, you bitch, more.'

Harry was as startled to see me as I was to see him. He shuffled around on his knees, with his mouth hanging open in shock. My eyes found their way to his crotch. There, escaped from his dress trousers, a short, bulbous penis pointed angrily at me; we were finally seeing eye to eye. I felt like shouting, 'Members only!' Harry's companion turned to me and I saw that she was smiling. It gave her an eerie glow. I offered hasty and profuse apologies and scarpered. 'You've been a very naughty boy,' I thought, as I smirked my way back down the stairs. Needless to say, my video camera had recorded the event for posterity.

I stopped by a sideboard and had another punch, because I was as pleased as that. It tasted twice as strong as the last glass I'd had. I tried to work out the ingredients, but they were elusive. It was clear, however, that the ratio of vodka to fruit juice had risen considerably. This was dangerous and potent on a hungry body. But I was happy with my night's taping and feeling untouchable. I looked forward to the simple pleasures of a bite to eat, a hot bath and a splendid sleep. This was not to be.

I spotted Happy Hank coming out of one of the downstairs rooms, so I ducked behind a potted plant. When he had passed by I emerged, only to swap the frying pan for the fire; I bumped into Toto. He was looking slightly crumpled now.

'Where have you been?' he asked, almost tearfully. 'I've been searching everywhere for you. When am I getting my dance?'

'Oh yes, of course,' I stuttered. 'Actually, I'm just off to the ladies' room, so why don't I see you at the marquee later?'

He began to shake his head from side to side quickly. 'No, no, no,' he said, 'it won't do. It won't do at all. I'm a man you know. Most people think I'm gay, but I'm not. I love women. I'm a *man*,' he wailed, 'AND I HAVE NEEDS.'

Then he slumped into a chair and passed out. It was a great relief to make good my narrow escape.

I was ravenous and a little disorientated, so I headed in what I hoped was the direction of the dining room. To do so, I had to pass a huge sheep which was sitting by a table. As I came closer I

realised that it was a large, white dog. In fact, it was
a Pyrenean Mountain dog, very similar to one that
lived near the family home in Dublin. It was looking
balefully at the small boy in the pyjamas, who was
asleep in its basket. I patted the dog on the head and
said, 'Tough luck buster, there's no room at the inn.'

'Ah, there he is,' said a husky male voice. Alex
Wood had come to collect his son.

'Poor doggy,' I said, 'he's not too pleased to see
someone in his bed.'

'He is a she,' Alex smiled, 'and her name is
Ophelia.' He ruffled her fur, and reached for his
child. 'Come on, Christopher, it's long past your
bedtime.'

As he turned to go he said, 'Perhaps I'll see you
later for a nightcap.'

'I hope so,' I said, and meant it.

As they walked away, I looked at the sleepy child
draped over his father's shoulder and made a realisation. In a cinematic sequence, image fell upon
image, identical pictures overlapping in my mind,
and I saw clearly who the child was. It was the
young Fergus Rush. But it was not. This was
Christopher Wood. So Fergus had been telling me
something on the night of my dinner with him.
Was he Alex's father, and Christopher's grandfather? If so, I could feel his sadness at being

banned by Alex from seeing the child, his and Lily's grandchild. Something would have to be done. It would be wrong to let the situation fester any longer, that would just waste precious time, and Fergus had told me never to live with regret. I would discuss the matter with him when I visited in the morning to return the pearl choker.

I finally made it to the dining room, but the remains of the feast looked like the aftermath of an enormous bun fight. A discreet army of caterers and their assistants were clearing away the debris. A polite young man asked me if I would like something to eat. I could tell that he was terrified that I might say yes and perhaps start another feeding frenzy.

'I'm fine,' I lied, 'just greedy. Back for dessert.'

He was still looking worried. I grabbed a banana, a triangle of camembert and some bread and left. It didn't exactly match the gourmet delights on offer earlier, but it was fodder. It was also quite dry, so I washed it down with another glass of punch. Then I refilled my glass and headed for the terrace to have a last look around before I left. I positioned myself behind a grey, stone urn and relaxed.

The night had turned chilly, but this helped keep the alcohol from doing too much harm, I thought. I pulled my birthday stole closer around me and watched the rhythmic, light clouds of my breath. My head was still a little light and dizzy, and I had an illusion of warmth, created by the punch no doubt. None of this mattered much, because I was done. I could finally wash Harry Knowles out of my hair and go home. And even though that came with its own set of problems, I was looking forward to the relative safety of Dublin. I smiled to myself.

I thought of Victoria and Jo, and what I'd seen, and felt a frisson of excitement. I could hear Andy Raynor's voice asking, 'Did you like that?', and my own gasping reply from all those years ago. And the longing for him to do it all over again. Perhaps he was pleasuring the lithe, blonde model even now. I wanted to be desired like that. The fact that Barry did not seem to want me in that way made me sad and angry all over again.

'There you are,' said a voice behind me. I turned and faced the man of my dreams and moonlight walks. Alex Wood was back and smiling at me alone. I was enchanted. This was no fairytale dream, it was real. I could reach out and touch him. But I didn't dare. My heart was thumping against my ribs, desperate for oxygen. I gulped in some air.

'Is he in bed then?' I asked. It was an oddly intimate question.

'Yes, out like a light.' His smile was radiant. He

was right beside me now, but I couldn't look into his eyes any longer. If I did, he would see straight through to my wanton thoughts; he would see my longings. I turned my head to look across the darkened gardens.

'Leo,' he said, caressing me with my own name.

'Yes?' I turned my face to his. He was very close now. I could smell him. I wanted to touch him, taste him. I had been so neglected, and my whole body tingled with desire.

'Thank you for coming,' he said. His hands gently cupped my face. He leaned down and kissed me slowly and forever on the lips. And I was glad that I had come. And then suddenly I *was* coming, very deeply, just as I stood there. His tongue flickered hungrily in my mouth. I didn't need to breathe any more. I didn't need anything but this moment. He pulled me closer to feel my rhythmic spasms; he drank me in. He knew.

# TWENTY-ONE

The first mistake I made was to clear my nose. The second mistake occurred simultaneously; I opened my eyes. As I did, a wave of stale alcohol invaded my face, while a searing pain ripped through my head. Double whammy. Then my stomach lurched. I needed the loo and quickly. I lowered my legs over the side of the bed and sat there, willing the room to stop spinning. My tongue was stuck solid to the roof of my mouth and my teeth were furry. Every bone and fibre in my body ached. I was no longer thirty years old, now I was somewhere the wrong side of a hundred and thirty.

My stomach started to heave ominously, so I

moved my body unsteadily to the en-suite, stubbing my toe against the doorframe on the way. I knelt in front of the white bowl just as a scalding stream of vomit erupted from within. The bowl was now a multisplendoured thing, mostly orange. I lay my head on the wooden seat and dribbled. Then another heave produced a fresh, hot torrent, burning my throat and mouth as it went. The acid began to eat away at my teeth, and the enamel of the toilet bowl. I broke into a sweat – across my forehead, under my arms, behind my knees, my breasts slithering against my ribcage. I prayed for God to have mercy and take me from this world now, without delay.

There is no God.

I could feel a gag at the back of my throat, biding its time before it struck again. The awful certainty of another retch was twice as bad as the event itself. A third dryish heave suggested that my innards had little more to offer upwards, at this time. But there are other directions in the human body, and they seemed about to take over. I should have kept the loo roll in a fridge overnight, I discovered. My body was obviously poisoned. What had that punch been made of? I sat with my head between my knees, panting, and saw that my legs needed shaving. Several thick, black wires were bluntly sprouting from my pale, overwintered skin. Was it any wonder that Barry didn't want to shag me, if this was what he could expect to encounter? I didn't dare check the bikini line.

As I stood, the back of my left thigh refused to budge, and I felt a pinching sensation. I was stuck to the seat. A long thin crack had appeared in the wood and it was now full of my hungover flesh. Like quicksand, it held on tighter if I pulled. Because I was now neither standing up nor sitting down, an enormous strain was being put on my upper thigh muscles, and they started to shake. I held on to the towel rail for support, and hoped that it was very firmly attached to the wall. I looked at my straining hands as they clutched the rail and noticed that my nails had grown since I had arrived. At any other time I might have been delighted with such progress, now it was somewhat overshadowed. And it just meant that there was more area for dirt to embed itself within. Maybe I could do a Victoria Knowles, and paint them a vivid orange to match the contents of the toilet bowl.

My head had begun to rhythmically pound out the pain for extra emphasis, and my stomach was giving dry belches at all too regular intervals. I decided to try to slide my left thigh out of the wood. It was agony. It seemed like a knife was slicing open my flesh. I was afraid to yank it out in case I left part of me in the seat. Three years later, I had freed my upper leg, and a trickle of blood ran down to my ankle.

I gently closed the lid on the toilet, a habit. But it also meant that the vile contents were now captive within. I pulled on the handle, and listened as technology flushed my shame away, hopefully to a far-distant place. The roar was deafening. My over-loaded head threatened to burst. A wave of nausea passed through me and I leaned against the cool wall for comfort. I leaned too hard, too fast. My head hit the tiles with a resounding thud. I left it there. There was no point in moving it away just yet, because when I did I would feel pain and would not be able to return. I was now carrying another injury.

Strange gurgling noises emanated from my body. Each time I sniffled, a chunk of some unknown parmesan-coated particle entered my throat and had to be swallowed. The dribbling had abated, but the taste in my mouth was rank beyond words. It was also marinaded. I decided to wash my sponge-coated teeth.

The mirror over the hand basin was not being kind. It showed me a shadow of the investigator formerly known as Leo Street. Black stains, of make-up and of weariness, underlined my blood-shot eyes. Each time I blinked, two sheets of coarse sandpaper scraped my eyeballs. My lips were dry and flaky, and decorated by crusty saliva in both corners. My forehead had broken out in spots. Greasy, lank hair framed this portrait. It was a salutary lesson to all who party.

I loaded the brush with minty toothpaste. I can't bear that bi-carb stuff, it makes me want to gawk. As if I could tell the difference now. One more stomach heave produced a loud, prolonged belch. I was disgusted with myself. I began to brush. I found that if I reached in to my back teeth, I started to gag. This was the last thing I needed right now, so I stuck to the cosmetic cleaning of the front china. Everything tasted a bit better now, and presumably smelt better too. Minty is usually more acceptable than cheesy, as far as general social breath odours go.

I checked the mirror for any progress. No go. I looked haggard, and felt worse. Something would have to be done. Again, more decisions. This time a shower came out as the top suggestion. The added bonus was that if I had any sort of emissions accident in there, the water would wash it away. Unless it was very chunky.

The shower was placed over the bath, so I had to climb in. Ordinarily, this would have posed no problem at all. Today, however, we were dealing with an unbalanced, perhaps even unhinged, Leo Street. And a bathroom that wanted to be an assault course when it grew up.

I misjudged the first step in, and grazed the previously stubbed-on-the-door-toe on the rim of the bath. I did manage to get it over the rim eventually, and the whole leg plopped down in there. A problem. I had stood too far away from the bath in the first place. And so I was about to cleave my body in two. I prayed that one or other, or both, surfaces had purchase. If my legs started to move in opposite directions, I would be not only powerless to resist, but also banjaxed.

In order to make a good job of a bad lot, I held on to the bath between my hairy legs, and hauled the last leg in. In doing so, I slipped back on to my already bruised buttocks. In spite of an anti-slide mat, the landing was a heavy one. I gripped the side handles, normally used by the likes of my grandmother, and made a valiant attempt to hoist myself into a standing position. My efforts were all in vain. I lay back into the relative comfort of the porcelain tub and took a breather. In fact, I nodded off.

My saviour was Alex Wood. Of course. He knocked lightly on the door and let himself in. I had been expecting him. There was no need to speak; we both knew why he was there. He kissed me briefly on the lips, then cut to the chase. He reached for my breasts with both hands, fondled them lightly, then, grasping them, lifted me up. When I started back to consciousness, I was standing. I was also disappointed to be alone. Well, whatever gets you to where you need to go. I chanced one more clearing of the nasals, and when I had swallowed the unidentified chunk, it struck me. I reeked of Armani.

I couldn't believe it at first. Then I started to try to sniff every bit of myself. We're not as dextrous as other animals, so this was not only awkward but also impossible. Armani was everywhere on me that I could reach with my nose. What did it mean? Shit, SHIT, *SHIT*. I half remembered a clinch, but so what? Did it mean that . . .? *Could* it mean that- . . .Then sheer panic hit.

OHSHITWHATHAPPENEDWHATDIDIDOWHAT-DIDINOTDODIDWEDIDNTWE? *WHAT?*

My breathing was laborious now. It filled the little tiled bathroom, gaining a slight echo as it travelled around. Oh dear God. Wash it away. Just sluice it all away. It wasn't sophisticated, but it was a solution. I pulled the shower curtain around me. The only piece of solid advice I've found consistently useful, is to always make sure that the shower curtain is tucked into the bath. I reached for the dials, and, fumbling, found them and turned them to release the water. It came, but there was no humming sound. Instead, I had warning bells in the drum-and-bass of my pounding skull. I hadn't pulled the release cord by the door for the electrics of the shower. Just as the first drops of water fell, my body warned itself that it was in for an arctic experience. It was. I shrieked and stepped back. Not far enough.

I had to get out of this bath, and fast. The spray was indiscriminate. It needled any part of me that it could reach. I turned my back on it, it stung my buttocks. I faced it to turn it off, it got my eyes and my chest. In fact, it was really lashing the whole breast area. It occurred to me that exercises were useless if they couldn't immediately produce this kind of result – an exultant, pert breast with rosy, pointed nipple. I still had to get out of this bath.

I tugged at the curtain and pulled it back a fraction. Then I paused to get my bearings. This was wise, I was in no state to rush at anything. I went to the other end of the bath and looked out at the cord I needed to pull. It was by the opposite door jamb. I had spent so long getting into the bath, it seemed a waste to get out and back in again, so I reached out for it. My arms were too short. I reached again. Nearly there. One more time. I grabbed it and pulled, I just couldn't let go. I was stretched across half of the room, swaying from side to side. What is known in football as 'a result'.

The humming had started and the water was heating up. Then it got far too hot. I could tell because my ankles were beginning to burn, and each time I swung back over them, I could check on the deeper shades of red they were displaying. I used my left arm to stop my momentous journey, and let go of the cord. My upper torso flopped downwards, and I banged my ribs off that evil edge. I looked like that French lad who was murdered in his bath, minus the head-gear.

I righted myself and went at the dials again, while the hot water plucked out my eyes. When an acceptable temperature was reached, I stood with my hands on the tiled wall and let the water wash over me. It would be some time before I could go in search of soap and shampoo.

The warm water massaged my aching body and I began to fall asleep again. I didn't doubt for one moment that this could happen while I was still standing. If I lathered myself down now, I could pop back to bed for a little snooze, and hopefully the day would make some sense later on.

I love sleeping. It is quite definitely my favourite activity of all, if you can call it an activity. And whenever I'm feeling ill, my body likes to shut down in order to recuperate. So it was no surprise that it wanted to switch off now. I was looking forward to it.

I reached for a sweet-smelling body wash on top of the shower unit. My arm ached slightly as I did, but it was an almost pleasurable ache. The promise of lying down in a warm, comfortable bed, with no disturbances, had let all of my muscles relax. Each movement was in slow-motion. My fingers massaged the lather into my hair, releasing tension from my troubled skull. The fragrance soothed my sinuses. Every crevice, every nook and cranny of my body was cleaned, slowly and in turn. The soap cleared away the night before, leaving only today, and the promise of rest and home.

I stepped carefully out of the bath and reached for a huge fluffy towel to dry myself. I wrapped it around me and stood there for a moment, savouring the safety. I was almost human. My body and I seemed to be on the same side again, though we were both very literally washed out. I gently dried us, from the bottom up. Then I wrapped a towel in a turban around my head and put on a robe that was hanging on the back of the door. Time for that snooze.

I was now deliciously woozy. I banged lightly against the door jamb as I floated out. It didn't matter. I hardly even registered that it had happened. I was smiling with gentle delight at the prospect of my morning nap. Then I froze in horror. There was someone in my bed.

# TWENTY-TWO

The pain flooded back through my brain, and a buzzing started in my ears. I became totally disorientated, and the room began to swim before my eyes. I took some deep breaths to steady myself and slowly made my way over to the bed. I couldn't see who was under the covers, but whoever it was appeared to have their back to me. It was a sizeable bump, perhaps a man? I needed to get over to the other side of the room to see clearly. As I crept across, I stumbled against a chair and went flying into the opposite wall. My towel turban moved off-centre, dragging my head awkwardly sidewards, and my robe fell open. I jerked myself upright. I was rattled.

The body shifted and a man's head appeared.

'Good morning, Princess.'

'Andy Raynor, what the fuck are you doing in my bed?'

He smiled wickedly. 'Having a wonderful time, of course. How kind of you to ask. And it's *very* nice that you're so glad to see me,' he said, looking shamelessly at my breasts. My robe was still open and my nipples were hard and pointing at him. I hastily tied the belt, covering my traitorous body. He flashed me another smile. 'I could murder some tea.'

I needed time to think. Tea-making might be just the thing to allow me that.

'Normally, I'd suggest what you could do with yourself right now, but you're in luck, I need a cup of tea as well.'

I picked up the kettle and made for the bathroom to fill it with water. I had to put some distance between myself and Andy Raynor. As I poured the water I leaned against the mirror and groaned aloud. How many more fiendish twists could this damned hangover take? How many more twists could *I* take?

I tried to piece together the events of the night before. I was clear enough until I kissed Alex Wood, then everything was a blank. That still didn't answer whether I was party to adultery. And it didn't explain how I'd ended up in the same bed as my ex-boyfriend. Then a cold fear ran through me. I dashed back into the bedroom, looking right and left.

'Don't panic, Leo, your precious purse and all of its contents are intact and on your dressing table.'

I sank into a chair and put my head in my hands. My heart was in my mouth and I was gulping back tears. I squeezed out 'Thank you' in a very small voice.

'Don't mention it,' he said cheerily, 'I'll get you again. Any sign of that tea?'

I retrieved the overflowing kettle and plugged it in. I sat with my back to it; this was one kettle that I really did want to boil, and as soon as possible, if not before then.

Andy sat up in the bed and arranged some pillows behind himself. His face was lightly stubbled and attractively wasted. I had never noticed before how beautifully shaped his lips were, and how white and even his teeth. All the better to eat you with, my dear. The sun was streaming in through the bright, white net curtains behind his head and blinding me. White was the theme of the day, and the colour of the pain ripping through my head.

The unwatched kettle boiled and I poured the water over two teabags in the little hotel cups. I squinted across at Andy.

'I'm afraid it's not real milk, it's only the UHT shite. Weird really, seeing as Esther Wood is such a foodie, and is always banging on about excellence and fresh produce.'

'You seem very pally with her husband.'

I grunted. I really couldn't think of any other response. Best avoid that subject, at least until I could remember more about it. If there was a more. I handed Andy his tea, and he patted the bed for me to sit down beside him. I went back to the chair by the dressing table. There was an awkward silence.

Andy relished my discomfort. He allowed the silence to sit, puncturing it only occasionally with loud slurps as he drank. These were deliberately exaggerated. He was testing me, pushing my hangover. I was too weak to put up a decent retaliation. He finally finished his tea and clanked the cup back on to its saucer.

'You were very energetic in that bathroom earlier,' he remarked.

'It tried to kill me. I was fighting back.'

'You should have called me, I could have helped defend you.'

'To be honest, I didn't know you were here.'

'Ah.'

He leaned back into the pillows and sighed. 'Strange, I never thought that this would be my first dirty weekend away with Leo Street.'

'It is not a dirty weekend, Andy, and you are *never* to speak about it to anybody.'

'Can we not even discuss it between ourselves?'

'No way. Besides, there isn't anything to discuss.'

'Oh no?'

'No!' I tried to sound as certain as possible, but of course I was anything but. The night was still a blank after a certain, and memorable point. I hoped there wasn't too much more in the way of memorable to uncover.

'Don't be so touchy, Leo, we'll laugh about this in our dotage. It'll be our little secret.'

The last time I'd heard those words had been as a result of a harmless lunchtime misunderstanding with Alex Wood. Now they might be laden with meaning, I just didn't know.

'It's not a secret, nothing happened.'

'Mmm. I suppose. Strictly speaking though, we did sleep together.'

'That wasn't sleeping, Andy, I was unconscious.'

'Yes, you looked very peaceful. And damned sexy.'

'Andy, just put me out of my misery, would you?'

A simple question, old-fashioned as it may be, is still usually the most effective way of getting information. And I must have looked pathetic, because he took pity on me.

'All right, there was no sex, principally because we had no condoms. But also because when I do make love to you, I want your undivided, total and sober attention. Then you'll realise what you've been missing all these years.'

'Andy, you and I both know that you're just curious about what sex with me would be like, because I'm probably the only female of our growing-up gang that you haven't had. You'd nail me and chuck me, I wouldn't see you for dust.'

'Is that so,' he said quietly.

'You know it's so.'

He lowered his eyes. 'If you really tried, Leo, you could probably make me even more shallow in your eyes.'

I had hurt him, needlessly. 'I'm sorry, Andy, it's just that I've never been in this situation before and I'm panicking a bit.'

He stretched his arms high into the air and yawned. I felt he'd forgiven me, because he smirked and said, 'You seem to have it all fairly well thought through. Seems like you've at least considered the possibility of ending up in the sack with me. And now that you have, we're halfway there.'

'Andy, don't try me,' I warned.

'Think of how happy it'll make your mother.'

He got out of bed and casually strolled to his

clothes so that I could admire his physique. There was no denying that his body was beautifully put together, and perfectly maintained. His skin was an attractive cream, from just enough sun and outdoor activity. His muscles were firm, lean and shapely. He radiated health.

'You obviously didn't have any of that punch last night,' I commented.

'Oh no. First rule of posh parties – never touch the punch. God only knows what might be in it. You're obviously a novice, you couldn't be expected to know that.'

'Thanks for warning me.'

'Leo, you know perfectly well that if I told you to do something, you'd do the opposite. There was no point.'

'I wish you'd tried,' I said, petulantly.

'How did your work go?' he asked.

'Very well. And yours?'

'Mmm, I was observing the Knowles beast in his habitat, if you like, getting a feel for who he pals around with. He's going to be in a lot of shit soon because of some shady land deals. And it's not just money, there are missing people, the whole nine murky yards.'

'He owns a lot of quarries, doesn't he? I'd check those first.'

'Correct. He's a bad bit of skin, and I hope you won't be seeing much more of him.'

'Why are you so interested in investigating him? I don't understand that.'

'When the exposé appears in the newspapers, and is syndicated worldwide, the in-depth piece will be by none other than yours truly. Think how proud our mothers will be.'

'Good for you, Andy. And, you know . . . be careful.'

He stood before me in his formal suit, his shirt open at the neck and his bowtie loose. He was a perfect picture of irresistible, faded splendour. I had an urge to reach out and do up his shirt button for him. A little act of love. If he were just to bend down now and kiss me, I was his. And I wanted him to. I had to break this spell.

'Why *did* you stay?' I asked. 'Really.'

'Really? Well, as you know, I am still somewhat interested in being near you the odd time, although you'll no doubt be glad to hear that that feeling is fading as time goes on.' My heart skipped a beat then sank a little. 'But mostly it was because I was afraid that you'd choke on your own vomit if you were sick during the night.'

'Not very romantic, if this *had* been your first dirty weekend away with me,' I said softly.

'No.'

He turned to go, then stopped, as if reminding himself of something. He turned and said, 'By the way, you're a great kisser, and I still respect you. See you back in the Smoke.' He laughed and ran. I threw a shoe at the closing door and swore a bit.

Then I lay on the bed and hoped for oblivion to take me, even for a short time. And it did. I was alone when I awoke twenty minutes later, which was a relief. This was an altogether more refreshing start than my earlier experience of the day. I lay heavily on the pillows, wanting to abandon myself to more sleep. That was not actually an option, and so, groggily, I took stock. My head was still in tatters, but I had become accustomed to the dull thud. My stomach was sore from its earlier exertions, and every last bit of me was aching. The only positive outcome of the morning was that I felt thin.

I tried to raise my head from the pillow but it wouldn't budge. Maybe I wasn't recovering quite as well as I had supposed. In fact, my hair was still trapped in a heavy, damp towel. I could no doubt look forward to a crazy, twisted rug beneath. Hey, it was good to be alive.

My brain could not be relied on to function properly, or to remember everything that had to be done. I would make a list, I'd check it twice. And when I'd done everything on it, I could go home, leaving a cleanish sheet behind. This was a positive idea and I was cheered by it. Not *very* cheered, but it was a start. I would follow this list through, and then I could go home. That was all the reward I wanted.

I dressed in my usual black 'uniform', drank a pint of water and sat at the dressing table. Getting rid of Harry Knowles was a priority. I would copy the video on to an ordinary sized cassette using the school equipment. I would forward a typed report during the week, even though I wasn't sure that he would even bother to read it, not when he had the visuals. I felt really uncomfortable at the thought of Harry getting off on his wife's sex life, and I wasn't too sure what to do about that. I would copy the video, then have a little think about it as I visited Fergus to return Lily's pearls. And then I could go home.

I threw my clothes into a suitcase, and left it at hotel reception. Not a soul stirred. I put on my leather jacket, slung my bag over my shoulder and stepped out into the world. I immediately regretted not having my sunglasses with me. It was far too bright out here. I blinked back the pain, hoping that this would not re-ignite the savagery of my hangover. I quickly crossed to the cookery school and let myself in. To be perfectly honest, I jimmied the lock and broke in, I had neither the time nor the inclination for the niceties of tracking down a key. Security was lax enough. The school didn't even have an alarm; obviously they trusted everyone. It was eerie to be there without the bustle of class. I felt a shiver of loneliness.

I copied the tape, without editing Harry's appearance, and replaced it safely in my shoulder bag. I was still undecided as to a proper course of action. Of course, there was no real choice – Harry had employed me to prove his wife's infidelity, and I had done so. He just didn't know that yet. All that I was required to do was pass the tape on to him and walk away. QED. But he wasn't around just now, so I would take a little more time to think the thing through. How best to handle this, so that everyone got something from it? Then we could have losers and losers, and that seemed an acceptable status quo for this particular situation. I was letting a disgraceful amount of my own personal agenda in on this one, as a fuming Mick Nolan was trying to point out.

'You're wasting your breath,' I told him, 'I'm not even listening.'

I seemed to be the only human being up and about in Kildare. Perhaps the world had ended last night, and I had been too drunk, or unconscious, to notice. Perhaps I was the only one left alive. Apart from Andy Raynor. What an unexpected irony, if Andy was the only man left on the earth and I was the only woman. My mother's dream come true, even if she wasn't around to enjoy it.

My skull had tightened around my brain, and I could understand all too well why our forebears drilled holes in their heads to release pain. The ground seemed more uneven and treacherous than usual. Why can't nature be straight and flat? I twisted my ankle several times and the ditch beckoned once more. Perhaps I was still a little drunk. I was hellishly thirsty.

I decided to try a shortcut across the fields. The sooner I got to Fergus's, the sooner I got some water to slake this awful thirst. I climbed unsteadily over a wire fence, and fell into an adjacent field. It was comfortable to be lying down, so I stayed there. This was like my childhood, running wild through fields, falling down and lying there safely. According to popular literature the happy childhood is not worth the paper it's written on; wrong, wrong, all wrong. For a moment I was that happy, safe, young girl. I closed my eyes and let the sun shine on me; it felt deliciously warm and soothing. I would probably be covered in freckles as a result, something to show for my visit to the country, something for the weekend. Then it occurred to me that no one knew where I was right now. If I hurt myself, or knocked myself unconscious, I might not be found for days. My mobile phone had a flat battery, so I couldn't ring for help. It was just me and nature, and I felt comforted to know that no one could interfere with us.

My late twentieth century brain couldn't leave it alone, of course, and soon I hoisted myself to my full five foot four inches and struggled onwards. Every colour and sound was heightened in my jittering brain. A multitude of vivid greens painted the fields before me. Are there really forty shades, as the song suggests, or more, I wondered? I made a mental note to change the soundtrack of my life; I couldn't be doing with most of what I'd endured in the last few days. I tottered unsteadily on. The back of my tongue had stuck to my tonsils, causing added discomfort to my tortured body. 'I'll feel better tomorrow,' I thought. How wrong I was.

When I look back now, I want to know that I could see what was about to unfold. And also to come up with reasons for it, some justification. Is this futile? Do we really search for answers or are we just passing time, filling in, hoping that our random lives will all add up in the end? To a validation and not just a CV of achievements. Do we not all want to *matter*? And to be missed when we are gone?

# TWENTY-THREE

I'd love to say that great thoughts buzzed through my head when I heard the gunshot. They didn't. I just wondered what that unnecessarily loud noise was. Rooks flew into the air, cawing. If it had been misty, I would have expected a man in a cloak and a top hat to appear. But then there was an eerie silence, and between that and my hangover, I began to panic and suspect that something was horribly wrong.

I broke into a stumbling run towards Fergus's house. Each stride I took seemed to be hampered by a dreamlike slow motion. Try as I might, I could get no closer. My legs were leaden blocks and my lungs would not fill with air. I used my arms in a swimming motion to propel me forwards. No. 4 was barking hysterically inside. I knocked at the front door and peered in through each of the windows. I couldn't see Fergus anywhere. I went around the back of the house.

At first I could only see a windshield erected in the vegetable patch by the back porch. Then I noticed that it was protecting an armchair. I knew that I had found him. Slowly I walked around it, my breathing even more laboured now, my legs unwilling and weak. They had every reason to be. Fergus had positioned a shotgun opposite his favourite armchair, threaded fishing line through some pulleys from the trigger to his big toe, sat in the chair, jerked his foot and blown his head off. It was a mirror image of his uncle Pio's death, the man who had left him this land. A strange and upsetting homage.

We all imagine that if we are attacked we will be able to call for help or to scream loudly, like on the television. And we're all sure that we'll be able to deal with a situation like this. I could feel a scream gurgling into my throat, but by the time it got out, it was a pathetic, ineffective squeak. My knees buckled, refusing to keep my legs straight. I doubled over and threw up over my shoes.

I knew he was dead, there was no need to touch him to confirm that. The gun had blown his face away, and it was now a black and bloody mess of tissue and bone. The shield was splattered with blood. I remember thinking that he'd probably put it there to protect his crops. I needed to get help.

No. 4 was howling in the house. I let myself in to phone the police and to comfort him. He was inconsolable and ran into a corner, whimpering. The table was covered with carefully addressed letters, one of them for me, another, I noticed, for Alex Wood. That's where I would go for help. I locked No. 4 in and began to run to the Wood house.

I was in waves of panic now. I wasn't sure that I had done all of the right things. Had I established carefully enough that Fergus was dead? Had I tampered in any way with the death scene? Should I have taken No. 4 with me? If I had been earlier, could I have prevented this? I felt tears sting my eyes. I had to run, *run*, to tell someone, across the bridge, along the road. I was outside my body now, watching a weeping woman desperately trying to be anywhere else but here. Then I collapsed into Alex Wood's arms.

'Fer, Fer, Fer . . .' I gasped. Great choking sobs wracked my chest. 'Fergus . . . is . . . shot . . . he's deh, deh, dead. He's *dead*.'

I threw my head back and wailed. And over and above my tears and panic, some slut-muscle was telling me, 'You smell of vomit, and you're dribbling.'

The police had arrived by the time we got back to the house. An ambulance screeched into the driveway. Men in white overalls were cordoning off the vegetable garden and walkie-talkies crackled loudly through the air. I was amazed at the sophistication of the response. Alex read my thoughts.

'A lot of very rich people live in this neck of the woods. You'd be surprised how well we are protected by the state.'

The detective in charge was a flame-haired giant, who introduced himself as Gerard Cook. I told him what I knew, and then he drew my attention to the letters on the kitchen table.

'I saw them when I was phoning you earlier,' I said, 'but I didn't want to touch them, in case I disturbed something.'

'Thank you, that was thoughtful. There is one for you, as you'll no doubt also have noticed. Would you read it and let me know what's in there?'

My hands trembled as I opened the envelope. This was my second letter from Fergus in as many days. I'd never had a single one from Barry. His large, bold handwriting was a comfort, as was the letter.

My dear Leo,

Forgive the manner of my leaving. It is a violent one, I know, but I wanted to be sure that I would be completely successful, and this particular method worked well for an uncle, once upon a time.

I have lived my life and there is little more to say or do. I mean my death as a positive step, and it is not some lamentable cry for help. I know very well what I am doing, and I am calm and happy. Remember this and believe it, it is the truth.

My only concern now is who will look after No. 4? I believe you were sent to me as an answer to that. Will you take him? He likes you, and it is somewhat fitting that he would be a No. 4 in your household too. I hope that your feline colony will understand. And that you do.

Thank you for your kind and gentle friendship over these last days. You made everything so much easier. Please keep the pearl choker as a token of my gratitude. Enjoy your life, and celebrate yourself, Leo.

There is no need to wait for my earthly body to be dispatched, Alex and Esther will see to that.

Until we meet again, I remain

Your friend,

Fergus Rush.

P.S. I've packed a little bag of No. 4's favourite things. It is green and is by the front door.

I handed the letter to the detective. He scanned it quickly and said, 'Looks like you've got yourself a dog.'

'Yeah. Could I have the letter back when you're done with it?'

'Of course, but you can take the little fellow now.' As I turned to go, he said, 'I met Mr Rush a number of times at functions since I was posted here. He was always polite and welcoming, a real gentleman. My mother always maintained that there are two classes of people – class, and no class whatsoever. I know which one Fergus Rush was. It can be tough to settle into a new assignment, and I was always grateful to him for his interest in me and my family. From the letter I can see that he liked you, you should take comfort from that.'

'Thank you, Detective, I will. And yes, he was a gentle man.'

I left the kitchen and told Alex that Gerard Cook would see him now. No. 4 was cowering in the corner, looking as frightened and bewildered as I felt. I patted him and made some soothing noises. Then I picked him up and held him close. I could feel his heart beating solidly in his little chest. He licked my face and I started to cry.

Alex Wood was grey when he emerged.

'Are you all right?' I asked.

'Not really, I've just had a bit of a shock – Fergus Rush might have been my father.' He sat on the couch and rubbed his eyes wearily. When I did not answer, he gave me a searching look. 'Did you know?' he asked.

I walked to the piano and took up the photograph of the cheeky little blond boy. I handed it to Alex. He looked puzzled and said, 'It's Christopher.'

'No,' I said, 'it's Fergus.'

I left him with his thoughts for a few moments.

'He spoke fondly of you and Esther and Christopher. He was proud of you.'

'Damn. Why did I have to be such a bloody pig to him this last while?'

'Don't do this to yourself,' I said softly. 'We all wonder what might have been if we'd acted differently. I wonder what would have happened if I'd been here earlier this morning. Could I have prevented this? It's torture, and it doesn't help.'

'Hard to avoid though,' he pointed out.

'He must have had his reasons for not telling you. Even if they're hard to understand now.'

He smiled kindly, and ruffled No. 4's furry head. 'I believe you got the dog. Congratulations, he loved that mutt.'

There seemed nothing to keep me there any longer, so I stood to leave. The little house was just a building now, its driving force gone. All that was left were remnants, meaningless without the man.

'I'd better go, I'm expected back in Dublin, I think.'

I got No. 4's green bag from beside the front door, as instructed. I put him on a leash that I found inside.

'You're a private investigator, aren't you?'

I stopped dead in my tracks. 'Is it that obvious?'

'No, I made some enquiries. Why were you here?'

'I can't tell you that. But I wasn't following you or your family around.'

'Was it someone I know?'

'This is really unfair, you know I can't tell you.'

'We've been through quite a lot now, I think you could give me a hint at least.'

'That's emotional blackmail.'

'I live in the country, it's a cutthroat place,' he shrugged.

I sighed. 'This is against every rule of my profession, but I've got very little fight left in me, so I will say that it is someone you know.'

'It's not that business with Graham again, is it?'

'Toto? I mean, Graham? Fascinating as that sounds, Alex, I don't think I want to go there, if you don't mind.'

'Well, if it's not Graham, I'll take an educated guess that it's Victoria, and *if* it is, and I'm not asking you to tell me, then I can guess who has put up the money. And *if* I'm right, all I'll say is, do the right thing.'

'I'll try,' I said, wearily. 'I really do have to go now.'

'And do the right thing?'

'I hope so. Goodbye.'

I stood in the doorway and looked back.

'Leo,' he said, 'it is probably just as well for all concerned that we were interrupted last night. I was enjoying myself far too much. Andy Raynor is a good man.'

'He's certainly flavour of the month with everyone I know.' Tears began to fill my eyes.

'You could do worse.'

'Goodbye, Alex.'

I stepped outside and was once again blinded by the sun. I waited until my overtaxed senses adjusted. No. 4 tugged on his leash, he wanted to be away now. It was time for a fresh start. February had become March. Birds were singing in the trees again, and nature was about to burst into Spring. The river sparkled and gurgled happily. Fergus Rush had chosen a beautiful day to die.

# TWENTY-FOUR

It was a beautiful day to die, and a beautiful day to live. I let No. 4 drag me all the way back to the hotel and school. I needed to use a public phone, so I went into The Stables, just like the American TV detective who had called everyone 'me bucko'. There were no singing locals, no Oirish hokum, just Johnny pulling slow pints.

'I heard about Mr Rush. That's been a long time coming.' He looked sadly at me. 'I'll have to ask you to leave that dog outside the door.'

'I'm just using the phone, Johnny. Besides, it is a funeral, in a way, and I thought most pubs gave a kind of dispensation for those. I know my local does.

PAULINE MCLYNN

And Fergus was a good customer.'

'All right,' he said, 'just this once. But only because it's a special occasion.'

'You won't regret this,' I told him.

'I hope not,' he said, darkly.

I dialled my home number. Even though it was mid-afternoon, the voice on the other end was groggy.

'It's me,' I said. 'Another late night?'

'Yeah. I got that part that I didn't want, so I had to get drunk after I accepted it, to dull the pain. The money's good, so I couldn't very well say no. My agent would have gone ballistic if I had. It'll be shite though, mark my words.'

'I should be home in a few hours, you can tell me all about it then. While I have you here on the line, Barry, is there anything that you want to tell me? Anything that I can be digesting on the drive home?'

'Is this to do with the drunken phone message you left for me last night?' he asked.

My bottom began its panic tingle. I had played with the mobile while drunk last night. Brilliant. No wonder the battery was dead. No choice but to go on the offensive.

'If this is about you and my niece, Lucy, then yes, I would like to know what is going on. And I hope to God that you have a decent and coherent reason as to why you were walking hand in hand with her

368

early yesterday evening along the bloody seafront. Oh, and incidentally, in case you hadn't noticed, she is actually underage, and would come with a prison sentence. So to speak.'

'Leo, would you just calm down. We both know that Lucy has a bit of a thing about me. She turned up at the door, all dressed up, looking for you, because she had a birthday card for you that had come to their house from that bloke Raynor. Yeah, Andy Raynor, you know the one. She obviously wanted to plant herself for the night, and she knew you were away, so I gave her short shrift by saying that I was expected at a friend's and that I'd walk her home because it was on my way. Satisfied? Jesus, you must think nothing of me.' He sounded genuinely disgusted.

It all made sense now. My mother had been surprised to hear that Andy hadn't sent me a card, because she knew that he had. And I was so adamant that he hadn't, she doubted her own recollection. Lucy had held on to it, knowing that I would be away for the weekend, and that she could use it to visit Barry. Adolescents are a devious bunch. If I wasn't so old now, I might have remembered that. Industrious though, I had to hand her that. I would whoop her sorry ass when I got home.

'I'm sorry, Barry, I've had a tough weekend, and I suppose I overreacted.'

'Leo, why would I look at a child when I have a fine woman like you in my life?'

I watched as the carpet swept out from under my feet again. When would I ever learn? Did I even want to learn?

'I'll be home shortly,' I said. 'And I have a bit of a surprise for you.'

Now I had *more* than his full attention. I heard him choke on the other end of the line.

'Jesus, you're not pregnant, are you?'

'Don't be ridiculous, Barry, it would be the immaculate conception if I was. No, I'm not pregnant. You'll see when I get back. Just be prepared for some disruption in the house for a while.'

'Leo, I don't like the sound of this.'

'Well, it's not negotiable, so tough.' I hung up.

I checked the messages on my answering service. One was from Barry, obviously late last night when he'd come home and had been subjected to my drunken accusations about Lucy. His answer ran along the lines of, 'Go fuck yourself if you think so little of me.' The second, and last, message was even more urgent. It was my mother's voice saying, 'Leo, it's only your mother. No, now, I don't want to worry you, but Angela was taken into hospital tonight. The baby hasn't turned around and her blood pressure is a bit high, so they might do a

Caesarian. Now, it's nothing to worry about, as I've told you, but I knew you'd want to be kept up to date. Stephen is with her and the two monsters are here turning the house upside down.'

I dialled Street HQ immediately. I thought I might throw up again. My father answered.

'Leo Street, you must have read our minds. We were just going to call you. Angela and Stephen have had a beautiful baby girl. He says she has a cross face on her like her grandmother, but they haven't decided on a name yet. Here's your mother.'

I was crying by the time she got to me.

'Arrah now, Leo, it's great news, what's the problem? And you know, I was just thinking that it might not do you any harm at all to be thinking in that direction. If the right man comes along. Isn't it marvellous though? We're all getting ready to go in and see them. When will you be back?'

'Soon, Mammy, soon. I'll be back soon. And don't worry, I'm only crying because I'm so relieved, and so happy.'

'And why wouldn't you be? There can never be enough women in the world.'

'And never enough Streets.'

'No,' she laughed, 'even if people think the world is full of them!'

I hung up and blew my nose.

PAULINE MCLYNN

It was time to tackle the Knowles' paradox, while I was feeling positive and empowered. I sat at a table and wrote a note to Harry, saying that my full, written report would be typed and sent to him early next week, but that I felt everything he needed to know was on the enclosed video tape. I put them both into a large, unsealed envelope and addressed it to him c/o The Esther Wood Cookery School.

Victoria was at her desk and looking pale when I entered the reception area. She was wearing a simple, black suit, but hadn't done the goth thing on the fingernails. Ciara J. would have been disappointed.

'I believe you've had a nasty shock,' she said, sympathetically. 'Would you like a brandy to settle your nerves?'

'You know, you're the first person to offer me anything today. Except for Fergus. He gave me his dog.' I smiled sadly. 'I know I shouldn't, but I could murder a brandy with a drop of port if you've got it.'

'I'll join you in one of those, if you don't mind.' She poured the drinks and we raised our glasses. 'To absent friends,' she said.

'To absent friends,' I said. No. 4 barked in approval.

I shouldn't let personal feelings get in the way, I know that; I'm hired to do a job, and I'm paid for that, not to make moral decisions about the use of the information gathered. I'm not supposed to take sides, or have opinions about who is right and who is wrong. At that moment I just didn't care. I know that life is not a 'compare and contrast' question in an examination, but when I thought of Annette O'Neill and how her life had changed because of my involvement, and compared it with Victoria's situation, I had a blip. Sometimes we need a perspective to get by; it needn't be right or wrong, just serviceable. Something to be getting on with. Why mess this woman's life up without giving her a fighting chance? It wasn't fair. It wasn't any of my business either, but again, I just didn't care right now. I wasn't sure if I knew what 'the right thing' was any more. But I knew what I was going to do, and I felt sure that Fergus would approve.

'Your husband asked me to do a little work for him while I was here,' I said to her. She looked understandably surprised. 'I wonder if you might pass this video tape on to him from me. It's not very long, and it should be very interesting for all involved. Oh, I seem to have left the seal undone, perhaps you'd see to that for me before giving it to him. Thank you for the drink, it was just what I needed. I'll be off now.'

As I left the school I realised why her nails were *au naturel*. Long, sharp talons would do damage to a person's soft bits. Victoria Knowles had been in love mode the night before.

I loaded my bags into my battered car and took one last look around. The sky had clouded over and we could look forward to rain later. The place was empty and still, as it had been when I arrived. Maybe nothing had happened here? But I knew differently. I had No. 4 as proof. He wagged his tail and barked.

'You and me both,' I said. 'How did we do?' I looked around once more and said, 'Nearly not bad.'

I could hear Mick Nolan choke in exasperation – it was one of his favourite phrases and I was probably misapplying it. I tried reassuring him, 'It's a blood-sport, Mick, don't bother with it.'

'Onwards and upwards,' I said, climbing into the car. I started the engine and headed for the wrought iron entrance to, and exit from, the estate. I wanted to go home. I wanted to see my cats and my family and our new baby girl, and I realised, almost with surprise, that I wanted to see Barry. We needed to talk, to work things out, to stop the slide we were on. We had to pay proper attention to one another again, to recapture some of the magic and fun of our early days together. I needed safety and sanctuary. I needed a rest. Sunlight broke through the clouds, sending a shaft of light to the ground about a mile away. I thought of my brothers and the family drives in the van when we were children. 'Look lads,' I said, 'it's the resurrection.'

A line of horses and their mounts slowly walked in towards the stable. They nodded as they passed. Behind them, and last in the line, was a god on a tall black horse with a flash of white across its forehead. The rider stopped them both and touched his hat as the car passed by. It was Alex Wood Rush. I lifted one hand from the steering wheel to acknowledge his salute, and drove on, out of his life.

No. 4 stood with his back legs on the passenger seat and his front paws on the dashboard.

'You should probably be wearing a seatbelt,' I said to him. He wasn't bothered. I thought of the furore he would cause at No. 11, The Villas.

'Some day,' I said, 'you're going to have to tell me just why you were barred from that pub.'

# Suddenly Single

## Sheila O'Flanagan

What do you do when you find yourself suddenly single?

Go suddenly suicidal?

Suddenly sex-crazed?

Or simply collapse in self-pity?

Alix Callaghan, who thought she was in control of her work-packed life, feels like doing all three when her long-term boyfriend insists on settling down to a sensible existence – complete with children, proper meals and early nights – but without her.

Though motherhood is the last thing on her mind, losing Paul hurts more than Alix will ever admit – especially to herself.

Now, with the men at the office eyeing up her job, not to mention the discovery of her first grey hair, she's beginning to wonder if being single again is all it's cracked up to be . . .

'Sparkling and inspiring . . . a must for the contemporary woman' *Ireland on Sunday*

'Fabulous . . . thoroughly enjoyable' *RTÉ*

'A rattling good read' *U Magazine*

0 7472 6236 5

HEADLINE

# Simply Divine

## Wendy Holden

*Champagne looked pointedly at Jane's dress.*

*'I tried that one on,' she said sweetly. 'But it looked cheap and nasty on me.'*

*She paused. 'Suits you, though.'*

Champagne D'Vyne is a celebrity socialite with a charmed life – and a mania for men, money and fame. Jane is a journalist with an ordinary life – love stress, work stress and a spare tyre that won't go away. As their contrasting worlds become bizarrely inter-twined, Jane realises that the blonde, busty and blatantly ambitious Champagne will let nothing come between her and what she wants. Least of all Jane.

'It is rare that comic novels live up to their titles, but *Simply Divine* is just that' *The Sunday Times*

'Wickedly witty' *Esquire*

'Wonderfully high-spirited . . . a writer poised to become formidable in her field' *Sunday Telegraph*

'A comedy of modern manners . . . frothy, frivolous, and fun' *Harpers & Queen*

'Fast-paced, funny romp' *The Big Issue*

'Bitingly witty' *OK Magazine*

0 7472 6129 6

HEADLINE

Now you can buy any of these other bestselling
Headline books from your bookshop or
*direct from the publisher.*

FREE P&P AND UK DELIVERY
(Overseas and Ireland £3.50 per book)

| | | |
|---|---|---|
| Olivia's Luck | Catherine Alliott | £5.99 |
| Backpack | Emily Barr | £5.99 |
| Girlfriend 44 | Mark Barrowcliffe | £5.99 |
| Seven-Week Itch | Victoria Corby | £5.99 |
| Two Kinds of Wonderful | Isla Dewar | £6.99 |
| Fly-Fishing | Sarah Harvey | £5.99 |
| Bad Heir Day | Wendy Holden | £5.99 |
| Good at Games | Jill Mansell | £5.99 |
| Sisteria | Sue Margolis | £5.99 |
| For Better, For Worse | Carole Matthews | £5.99 |
| Something For the Weekend | | |
| | Pauline McLynn | £5.99 |
| Far From Over | Sheila O'Flanagan | £5.99 |

TO ORDER SIMPLY CALL THIS NUMBER

**01235 400 414**

or e-mail <u>orders@bookpoint.co.uk</u>

Prices and availability subject to change without notice.